JACQUI L'ANGE

The Seed Thief

UMUZI

For my father, Gerald,
who gave me the words

Published in 2015 by Umuzi
an imprint of Penguin Random House South Africa (Pty) Ltd
Company Reg No 1953/000441/07
Estuaries No 4, Oxbow Crescent, Century Avenue,
Century City, 7441, South Africa
PO Box 1144, Cape Town, 8000, South Africa
umuzi@randomstruik.co.za
www.randomstruik.co.za

First edition, first printing 2015
1 3 5 7 9 8 6 4 2

ISBN 978-1-4152-0756-7 (Print)
ISBN 978-1-4152-0648-5 (ePub)
ISBN 978-1-4152-0649-2 (PDF)

The poetry quoted on pages 5, 32, 35, 36, 95, 127, 262, 287, 297 and 305 is from *Poems* by Elizabeth Bishop, published by Chatto & Windus. Reproduced by permission of The Random House Group Limited.

The line of poetry quoted at the top of page 189 is from 'Tonight I Can Write' by Pablo Neruda, translated by W. S. Merwin, in *Twenty Love Poems and a Song of Despair*, published by Jonathan Cape. Reproduced by permission of The Random House Group Limited.

The lyrics quoted on page 208 are from 'Angel from Montgomery', words and music by John Prine © 1971 (Renewed) Walden Music, Inc. and Sour Grapes Music. All Rights Administered by WB Music Corp. All Rights Reserved. Reproduced by permission.

Cover design by publicide
Text design by Nazli Jacobs
Set in Sorts Mill Goudy
Author photograph by Odette Howell

Printed and bound in India by Replika Press Pvt. Ltd.

The art of losing isn't hard to master.

– ELIZABETH BISHOP, 'One Art'

Prologue

A girl on a boat on a river.

The river still, the boat motionless, the water no colour, or all colours, so deep it mirrors the green around it.

Trees taller than apartment blocks, denser than any city, reach up, trunks to leaves to sky. Inverted on the mirrored river they thrust down, leaves reaching out as if to scoop up the girl, the sky left behind so that she tips forward, falling, tumbling into green and flipping back out again without moving.

Reflections double everything – as above, so below. One is real, the other only an image of it. But which is which? If she were to dive into this image, she would discover something else altogether.

Space.

The spaces between molecules, pushing up to create a reflecting meniscus that fooled her eye into thinking there were trees there, and roots there, when in fact there were only fishes.

Everything rests on this illusion.

And then the colours rush in and spoil everything. Drums pull her back, out of the silence and the Amazon green, into yellow and blue and red – too much red. It swirls in front of her. The drums are deafening, and she smells the heat of bodies. The thick press makes her dizzy. Her feet seem a long way away. There are other feet next to hers, small, thin ones with red-painted toenails in leather sandals. She recalls that they were there before she tumbled into green. She longs to be back on her quiet river.

Then the slim-footed woman is on her knees, then on her side, rolling, spinning along the floor. People step aside, pull red and blue and yellow skirts out of the way, swing their strings of coloured beads, but the drums keep urging, and no one tries to stop the woman. She is a log caught in a turbulent river. Her body reaches the far end of the hall and starts back again, spinning in the other direction. Why does no one help her? The drums are frenzied and bodies are whirling, people are shouting and the colours are running into each other. Zé – where is Zé? The drums don't stop, not even when she hears a shout, and the crack of a gunshot, from outside.

Breathe – breathe!

But still the drums won't stop.

PART I
OUTGOING

In Transit

22:50 00:00	HEATHROW	BA573	CANCELLED
23:15 00:00	MUNICH	LH4698	CANCELLED
01:15 00:00	BOGOTA	XA439	DELAYED
02:20 00:00	RIO DE JANEIRO	TP796	DELAYED
03:45 00:00	SINGAPORE	SQ212	DELAYED
05:30 00:00	TOKYO	JAL342	DELAYED
06:00 00:00	MADRID	VL5069	CANCELLED

I would curse this volcano, if only I could pronounce its name.

Usually, I like transit space. There's nowhere else in the world I feel so honestly, anonymously myself. As long as I'm travelling solo. Solitary travellers have no witnesses. There's no one to confirm or contradict your version of events. No one to impose demands or expectations. No one to require anything of you at all.

But the petulant volcano has undone all that by spewing ash. All flights grounded for an indeterminable time. So now this transit lounge is crowded with people and their sweaty frustrations, all stranded, on hold. Fug-headed travellers wandering from one fast-food outlet to the next, lugging their personal time zones between terminals, looking for a quiet oasis. If they've found one with wi-fi, they crouch over tablets explaining to loved ones why they won't be home for dinner.

They're all heroes and victims in their own private narratives, but I have no interest in making friends or sharing stories.

I've brought books with me, actual paper ones. Right now I'm using them to barricade my private colony of orange scoop chairs. My daypack protects one side, on the other I've stacked *Dona Flor and Her Two Husbands*, *Poems* by Elizabeth Bishop, and Wole Soyinka's *The Seven Signposts of Existence*. Kolade gave me the last just before I left: 'For good luck and safe-keeping.' It's small enough to read in an hour, even though it promises to unlock the infinite potential of the universe. I have too much time on my hands, but not enough mind to contain all that.

I wanted to enjoy this limbo time, but nature abhors a vacuum. So along with ten tons of atmosphere pressing down on every square metre of me, I've got the looping replay of my failed relationship. I've tried unspooling ribbons of shiny brown tape from the mental videocassette of our time together, but it keeps tangling, rewinding, replaying. And if it stops for a moment, a little commercial break in my B-grade melodrama, there are plenty of other anxieties eager to rush into the space. Such as: what the hell was I doing, agreeing to this trip, this Mata Hari mission? Or, how long can I put off calling my father? Or – cue heart-strings music – how do I *really* feel about going back?

Saudades. That's what Brazilians call this affliction. Sow – daa – jeez. The stretched middle vowel hangs like a hammock, weighing down the word. A longing for something that may not exist outside of sentimental imagination. The very concept requires a sleight of mind.

I'm definitely missing *something*. I just wish I knew what it was.

Tea?

I really need a cup of tea.

But getting one means negotiating the bland bling of duty-free. And fighting crowds. All for a cup of tepid beige in polystyrene – will it be worth it? And if I get up now, I'll lose my space. And I might be tempted to make that call. And then Lucia will probably pick up the phone and then I'll have to pretend to be nice, which will spoil everything.

I could never forgive Lucia the monkey. It gave me an excuse to distance myself from the-woman-my-father-took-up-with-too-soon-after-the-death-of-my-mother.

Back then, Lucia's was the only pet store in Manaus. The city never loses its dusty frontier town feeling, even though it's in the middle of the Amazon jungle. Lucia's main trade was parrots, supplemented by the occasional sloth. She kept the macaco on a rope outside her shop. It spent its days picking at the threads of its tether, looking at me with accusing eyes. When I was a child, I only had to practise monkey-avoidance once a year, during school holidays. Once I got older, I avoided the town altogether, stayed out in the jungle with the plants. And the free animals.

It's still dark outside. Through the floor-to-ceiling plate glass, I can tell from the vague contours in the colourlessness that it's raining. Hercules, that monkey was called. What a cruel joke to play on the powerless.

With hindsight, I realise that my childhood disdain was misdirected. I know Lucia was never anything more than a soft-skinned, middle-aged dona who watched novellas in the afternoons, cooked sweet pudim to eat after dinners of chicken, rice and beans, and made few demands. Who could not, or would not, get used to the fact that I drank my tea with milk instead of lemon. 'Chá com leite?' She feigned surprise every time. Her fake incredulity would hang in the air as she hauled herself up to fetch a tin of preserved milk. I always fought the urge to comment on how far that tin had come from the cow that had produced it.

Lucia did this year after year, during every single one of my visits. When I studied botany, I assumed I would be based in that jungle and have to endure Lucia's sporadic milky surprise for the rest of my life. But then fynbos seduced me. So fine, so feisty. Such a resilient little plant kingdom. I found another almost-home in a place with a solidly entrenched British colonial-era tea tradition. And an excuse to put an ocean between my father and me.

I don't even know if Lucia has that pet store anymore.

The air here is stale and fusty. There isn't a green plant in this transit lounge. Not even a fake one. This closed climate isn't designed to sustain long-term life. Just enough recycled oxygen to get you from plane to plane, or plane to taxi. No windows that open, no doors to the outside.

On the way to claim my scoop-chair archipelago, I passed a place where smokers huddled under a huge metal umbrella designed to look like a beach bar. A giant fan sucked their smog straight up and sent it out to mingle with jet and diesel fumes. Or maybe that air was also in transit – recycled like the shared odours on a plane. I heard that airport terminal ground staff sometimes draw straws before a plane arrives. Nobody wants to be the one to attach the carrier to its arrival gate; to face the blast of concentrated body odour that gets released when the capsule pops, the depressurised stench of three hundred passengers, slow stewed for hours. All of them digesting airplane food.

Don't think about it. Think about green. The green you just came from – *that* smells heavenly.

Fynbos doesn't have the majesty of Amazon flora. But the world's tiniest plant kingdom has more diversity than any other on earth. Rare and unique and intricate and hardy enough to survive the winds and the storms and the fires on Africa's southernmost tip. You either get fynbos, or you don't. I got it so badly, I made a life collecting its seeds.

Fynbos has teas too. Buchu, rooibos, honeybush, all fragrant in their ways. But good old Ceylon is still my brew of choice. I wish I had my Five Roses tea with me right now, but it's buried along with everyone else's luggage in some stagnant loading bay.

I once took some to Manaus, long ago. When I pulled the small red box from my suitcase, my father went pale and sat down hard on the bed. *Your mother used to drink the same brand*, he said. *You looked just like her, just then.*

It was his first mention of her in years, too overdue to help either of us. Was I sending a signal, my red box a semaphore? At what age does brand recognition hook the unconscious? Nico would have a theory about that. Nico, my emotional homeland these past eight years. But no more.

I need a cup of tea. And to stop thinking about Nico. Although I might, in time, feel saudades for him.

1

Precipices

Ten days earlier, Cape Town

I was plucking my eyebrows and contemplating suicide when the phone rang. Or maybe contemplating is too strong a word. It suggests some kind of intent. What I was doing was just thinking about it. I was 'entertaining the possibility' of suicide. Which I do quite a lot. I am a gracious hostess to the thought.

I remember my exact state of mind because I was so irritated by the shrill interruption. Or by my response to it. That involuntary flutter of hope – Nico! – followed by the immediate urge to snuff out that hope, hating that the hope was there in the first place, and the dense downward spiral of dread that I might be forever chained to it ... all this in the few seconds it took me to reach the phone. So that for a moment I was even relieved to be called in to a meeting, on my first day off in weeks.

I had actual plans for the day. Killing myself was not one of them. Walking Vavi in the mountains was. We both needed it. A good dose of green, after weeks away in the semi-desert, was the only thing that would set me right. Now it would have to wait until after my meeting.

Some people like the endless aridness of deserts. I need green. The road over Constantia Nek to the Institute is a winding green tunnel, lined with old oaks, and what remains of the indigenous forests that gave Hout Bay its name. It was balm to my irritation, but I still drove way too fast.

The day was clear and warm for midwinter. Behind me the flat blue horizon receded, bisecting my rear-view mirror. I've never been a beach person – you can keep the sand, the sunburn, the bikini creep. I just need to know the ocean is there. A big blue highway to other places.

Or a place you can lose yourself, be the proverbial drop in the ocean. I think about that every time I gun over Chapman's Peak Drive, when I'm pulled by the sea churning against the cliffs far below. Do you open the windows as you plummet, or keep them closed? One of them gives you a better chance of getting out when the car starts sinking, but I can never remember which. In my mind I always look down on myself, teetering on that edge. I soar over that abyss like a bird of prey, commanding a bateleur-eye view. I can tap into an air current, let it lift me up and away. The way thoughts circle the thermals within and swoop away from any catastrophic knowing. Minds are clever like that.

Driving into the green, I felt tired. I'd been looking forward to hunkering down for a while, hibernating through the Cape Town winter. Fires, red wine, books. Solitude. 'Don't unpack,' Kirk said. Which filled me with dread. He wouldn't say more over the phone, other than an enigmatic, 'Hurry up – this could change your life.'

I pressed my foot down on the accelerator, felt the back of my jeep swing out as I nose-dived into another corner. Twisting corridors of yellowwoods opened up at the last minute to let me through. I willed the adrenaline to wake me up.

2
Planet seed

I couldn't help but be lifted by the way the sun bounced off the flank of the mountain to light up the green amphitheatre below. I parked my car and paused to pay respect, running my hand over the ticklish top fronds of a confetti bush, ruffling the hair of a favourite child. I crushed a few of the tiny lime-green tips, inhaled the fynbos scent on my fingers – not quite lemon-geranium, something entirely its own. The cleanest smell on earth.

Leaves, shoots, roots – they're all part of the miracle, but for me, the real magic is in the quantum possibilities of the seed.

The seed bank looks like an alien capsule come to land against the craggy slope. When the imperialist Cecil John Rhodes claimed this valley, he infested it with invasive northern oaks and starlings. Future generations took better care of what was originally here, and now Kirstenbosch is an indigenous botanical garden of international renown, a fynbos haven, and a satellite repository for the Millennium Seed Bank. My Institute is a pod that supplies the global biodiversity mothership at London's Kew Gardens.

The unseasonal berg wind was puffing off the mountain, too hot for my winter fleece. I pulled it off and focused on the barrel-vaulted entrance, anticipating the cool misters inside, designed to trick herbaceous borders into thinking they were in the tropics rather than Africa's temperate tip. Through the glass doors, I could see the public face of the herbarium, with its touch-screen displays for busloads of distracted children, designed to reassure donors that their money was being well spent.

My entrance was at the business end, a steel door with bargain-basement biometric security. Before I'd even reached up to the thumb pad, the intercom crackled into life. 'Request?'

'Permission to come aboard, Captain.' I pushed down yet more irritation. I wasn't in the mood to play Spock in Kirk's *Seedship Enterprise*. He must have been glued to the camera, waiting for me.

When the door clicked open, the cool hit me in a blank wave, along with the institutional perfume of Jeyes Fluid and formaldehyde.

'Warm out?' Kirk was in short sleeves, his greying ginger hair awry, the fluorescent light glinting off his steel-rimmed glasses so I couldn't see his eyes. Kirk is one of those people who always come in too close – no respect for personal space. He's so tall and lanky, he could be the model for *Where's Wally?* – in my mind's eye, I always dress him in red and white stripes. On days like this one, I like to picture losing him in an Arctic environment, even though he never seems to feel the cold. I think his ebullience is its own internal furnace.

'How was the field trip?' Kirk talked over his shoulder, loping down a passage between long tables where interns and volunteers sorted through piles of dried plant specimens. Bent like seamstresses in a factory line, they used tweezers to pluck out very tiny seeds, or sieves to separate seed from chaff. Some of the succulents I'd just collected in the Richtersveld would be worked over here. In the nursery alongside the lab, my colleagues would be planting out seed samples, testing for viability. The good seeds went north to Kew to join twenty-five thousand other plant species from around the world. We'd reached our 2010 target of banking one out of every ten plant species, but with four species lost globally every day, that wasn't nearly enough. Someone had pasted a bumper sticker on the wall: *Inaction is a weapon of mass destruction.*

I nodded greetings to some student volunteers and ducked into the next room. Kirk was waiting next to the refrigerated vault. 'Good to have you back,' he said, and hefted the steel sliding door open.

My exhalations clouded in front of me as we entered the storeroom. The temperature here was a mild 15°C, but the low humidity made it feel colder. I pulled the fleece back over my head.

Since ours is a short-term storage facility, seeds stay here three months at most before they're sent to Kew, where they're stored at temperatures of –20°C. The theory is that seeds will keep for five hundred years or more in suspended hibernation. Kirk likes to joke that ours is a job with great future prospects.

You need to wear a full Arctic suit when you go into the Kew vault. Low humidity will dehydrate you within half an hour – which is the maximum time anyone is permitted to stay inside. I've only been inside once, when I visited with Kirk last year. Disorientation set in before I'd even registered thirst. I was making mental poetry out of the Latin on the seed-jar labels when the buzzer sounded to tell us our time was up. I remember eyeing the round red emergency button and wondering whether I'd be able to get a hand to it without Kirk there to lead me out.

'You'll get used to it,' he'd said afterwards. 'Think of it as a decompression chamber.'

I wasn't there long enough to acclimatise. But I've never enjoyed a drink of water as much as the one I had straight after the Kew vault.

'Any tea on this craft today?' All the warmth had left me now, and I rubbed my hands together to try to get it back.

'Of course.' But Kirk made no move towards his office, which had a kettle, and a window out onto the sunshine. Instead, he turned to the banks of high steel shelving, crammed one against the other, and cranked the metal-armed levers to open an access aisle between them.

It always reminds me of a library, one without books. There are so many stories here, histories and geographies and family chronologies. They're not written in symbols and hieroglyphs, but in four-letter genetic code, A, G, C and T, with a syntax and a grammar that remain a mystery. Catalogued and ordered according to a system that honours taxonomy, rather than the Dewey Decimal. The volumes of information here are a fraction of what's available in the wild, and a fraction of what's already been lost or destroyed. Instead of burning books, the zealous ignoramuses go plundering habitats. Either way, the stories are lost forever.

It's high-tech work, but we still keep our seeds in ordinary wide-necked Consol jars, labelled with the kind of stickers you find on children's school books, ones with brown paper wrapping. Kirk picked one up and held it out to me. *Newbouldia mundii.*

I knew the plant. Native to West Africa. Its cousin was a common tree; this particular sub-species much less so. Endangered now, after rampant strip mining had destroyed the narrow band of coastal forest it called home. Its bark and leaves had been used by the Yoruba people since time before memory to make remedies for a variety of maladies. There had even been talk of potential cancer-fighting properties. If it hadn't been overshadowed by the interest in *Hoodia gordonii*, Namibia's miracle weight-loss herb, some pharmaceutical company would have a patent locked away by now.

It always comes down to ownership. My colleagues spent the last three years fighting to keep hoodia in the hands of the indigenous San peoples who traditionally tended it. They didn't need it to lose weight; they used the succulent's thirst-quenching power to help them survive desert droughts. But when locals were offered more money than they would earn in an ordinary year to deliver the plant to unscrupulous buyers – no questions asked – they went into a harvesting frenzy. Within months, every last plant had been stripped from the Cape's West Coast. Authorities stepped in just in time to stop the same thing happening in the Northern Cape and Namibia.

Properly protected, *hoodia* might bring in enough revenue to build schools and clinics for communities in its territories. The same can't yet be said for *Newbouldia*. The slim, tall trees, once planted before the houses of kings, were being felled at a frightening rate by people who considered an inert metal under the ground to be far more valuable than a pillar of leaves.

I tipped the jar, watched the *Newbouldia* seeds slide from one side to the other. Each one was about the size of a large peppercorn, russet-brown and spiked, like a Saint-Exupéry planet, or a virus under a microscope. There was a sack of silica gel inside the bottle. The crystals had turned a faint pink. 'Kirk – these need to be dried out . . .'

'Too late for that.' He took the jar back from me. 'We tested them last week. No go.'

You never know how seeds will respond to enforced dormancy. Some last for millennia. Botanists recently grew the Chinese sacred lotus *Nelumbo* from a seed carbon-dated back twelve hundred years. But this is new science. The uncertainties of method, the urgencies of global warming, and the limitations of human patience don't exactly favour a millennial timescale.

'Scanned too?' I needn't have asked. A digital X-ray is the first thing we do to find out whether there's a seed inside the casing, or whether it's been emptied by a worm or some other blight. Kirk nodded.

'So, someone's out in the field?'

This time he shook his head. 'Remember that big fire in Benin last year? It took out the last known stand of plants. It appears *Newbouldia mundii* is now extinct in the wild.' He shook the jar, a little too roughly. 'These were the only banked seeds in the world.' He placed the jar back on a shelf. 'That's where you come in.'

3
Transatlantic

Brazil?

The steaming mug between my hands was doing very little to warm me up. Even less so the idea that Kirk wanted to send me on a mission to infiltrate a religious sect and find some seeds.

'You grew up there.'

'Well, on and off . . .'

'And you speak the language.'

'I'm a little rusty . . .'

'And your father is there.'

There was a row of seed-filled jam jars on a shelf behind Kirk's desk, silver lids glinting. They looked as if they should be in a kitchen, not a lab. 'He's in the Amazon, Kirk. I haven't seen him for a while.'

'So combine it with a family visit.'

I could have told him that in a country as vast as Brazil, the city of Salvador was about as far from the Amazon as London from Moscow. Which would save me telling him that my father and I were currently estranged. But Kirk's mind was made up.

'What about someone from UPP?' I heard my voice take on a pleading minor key. The guys in the Useful Plants Programme were both specialists in medicinal plants. Technically, they were better qualified than I was for this particular gig.

'Ntumaleng is in Tanzania. Theo's on his way to a conference in Oz.'

I tried a different tack. 'Kirk, you know this isn't a good time for me.' Discomfort leaked across his face.

'I heard about you and Nico. I'm sorry. We kept meaning to have you two over.'

Now it was my turn to feel bad. Kirk's wife had been battling cancer for so long, it was easy to forget that each day was still a struggle. They had chased the disease around her body with chemicals and knives and radioactivity, but the cancer was a crafty shape-shifter.

'How is Gwen?'

'She's holding up. We both are.' Beneath the mask of cheer, his face was cragged with exhaustion. 'They're talking about a bone marrow transplant next. But ...' Kirk had recently sold a coastal property – the one they had planned to retire to – to cover Gwen's medical costs.

'About the timing ... I meant for tagging.' I hadn't, actually. But I wasn't going to win this battle on emotional grounds.

I guess he was surprised because I usually jump at the chance to go on a trip. Just not this one. And it really *was* the most inconvenient time for me to leave. We were experimenting with a new method of tagging bulbs while they were in flower. The tags helped us to differentiate the plants once the flowers died down; by the time the seeds were ready to harvest, you couldn't always tell the subspecies apart. Our method worked well, until the porcupines and baboons learned to read the signs. The red and yellow tags became an animal invitation to a fast-food buffet: *McBulbs over here!* So last year, we tried turquoise and blue tags and found far more intact seed. Whether the animals were colour-blind, or simply hadn't yet cracked the new code, is what we were about to find out.

'Simpiwe can tag without you.'

Of course he could. Unlike me, Simpiwe had infinite patience. But this was my project, and I wasn't about to give in easily.

'Look, I'm sure there's someone . . .'

'You're going, Maddy. I'm pulling rank on this one.'

This was a definite first. I'd always been able to have my way with Kirk, professionally speaking. He pressed the advantage before I recovered my powers of speech. 'I'd go myself, you know. If I could. But there's no one else I can trust with this.'

Flattery – the last resort of the scoundrel and the downfall of the vain. When I finally made my way out of the glorified Frigidaire into the heat-fuzzed daylight, I was glad. Glad to get away from the chamber of enforced dormancy, with its jam jars, chrome and cryogenics. Grateful to breathe in the warm mountain must. And there was something else. Beneath my knee-jerk resentment, I was starting to feel that it would be good to get away. *Really* away.

In my seven years at the Institute, I'd carved a niche for myself. Or dug a rut, depending on how you looked at it. This would be a chance to expand my scope. Even if it was a little out of my ordinary range of activities – way out, really. Securing the seeds for our little substation would be a coup. It would bring recognition, and more funding.

I sensed something else behind Kirk's urgency, though. He'd made this a personal mission. Of course the plant's potential cancer-fighting properties had special significance for him. Maybe he just needed to save *something*. Still, I was the one he was sending to 'voodooland', as he called it. Because the place that the seeds were being kept – if, in fact, there were any seeds – was one of the most fiercely guarded and deeply religious places on the planet.

I stopped to watch an iridescent green sunbird hover over an erica, its wings blurring into invisibility as it poked its beak deep into the flower tube. I was supposed to visit the gardens of a particular Candomblé terreiro, a temple for the Afro-Brazilian religion whose rites and rituals had travelled with slaves from West Africa during three centuries of human trafficking.

I knew enough about Candomblé to know there was a time when its practitioners had been persecuted. Now it was an accepted part of Brazilian culture, the pride and thrum of black Brazil. It was the spice in samba. It was the heartbeat behind the spectacle and the music and the dance that Brazil's most African city showed as its outward face. It was ancient, and it was potent. And it wasn't something I'd ever wanted to poke around in.

But I'm a scientist. I'd stick to the task. I had just over a month – a proverbial forty days – to travel to Bahia, on Brazil's north-east coast. Visit the place where *Newbouldia mundii* was rumoured to be growing. Find some seeds. Bring them back.

After that we would bank them, test them, grow them, and hopefully reintroduce them to the deforested West African tract where they first came from. *Newbouldia mundii* would be snatched from the brink of extinction. *If* I found the seeds.

If ... then. If we could establish a viable nursery, we could make the plant available for testing and research. That elusive cancer cure might be hiding in those virus-shaped seeds. No wonder Kirk was so anxious to get his hands on some.

I knew there would be reams of bureaucratic red tape. There are layers of regulations about transporting plant material across borders: international laws, national laws, and customary usage laws ... This was where my 'particular expertise' came in. Kirk was counting on the fact that I speak Portuguese and could supposedly convince the people in the terreiro that our intentions were righteous.

The thing that *isn't* my forte is paperwork. Kirk knew that too, and sweetened the deal by offering to take charge of all the bureaucratic stuff.

I warned him that getting the permits might be tricky. If there's one area where Brazilians are oversensitive, it's in the exploitation of their national and natural resources. Fair enough. I just didn't want to be caught with my hand in the cookie jar without Grandma's say-so. People had been jailed for less. I had no idea what colour Brazilian prison garb was, but I didn't want to find out.

'We'll have import and export papers by the time you actually find the seeds.' Kirk made a real effort to reassure me – unusual for Wally-man. My hatred for red tape soon won out over my hatred for loose ends. And that was my big mistake.

To be honest, what really threw me was the reminder that everyone knew Nico and I were buried neck-deep in emotional rubble. 'On its last legs' – people apply the cliché equally to flogged horses and relationships. Ours had been paralysed for the last two years, maybe more. We had almost stopped pretending there was any hope of recovery. Maybe Kirk was right. Maybe a change would do me good. Someone had to do the humane thing, and pull the trigger. It might as well be me. 'Tonight,' I told myself. 'I'll do it tonight.'

And that's where this whole thing started.

In Transit

Thanks to the new undersea telex cable, it took just four hours for news of the eruption to reach London from the South Seas. The voice is in my head before I remember where I am. Sleeping upright – never a good idea. I rub out the knob of pain at the top of my spine as the man on the monitor morphs into focus. He's talking about the Krakatoa eruption of 1883. Apparently it marked a revolution in communication and the beginning of modern times. *Just a few years earlier, news of Lincoln's assassination took fourteen days to reach Britain from America.* Nowadays, you just can't get away from the news.

Especially here. This eruption affects everywhere. Volcano 'experts' are falling over themselves to get in on the action. Airport shutdowns around the world ticker-scroll along the bottom of the screen. It's been thirty-two hours since I last lay down flat. It feels even longer. How long was I out? Quick check – possessions all accounted for. Times like this I'm glad I keep the essentials safely wrapped around me when I travel. I've had this money belt for years. It's made of old, faded denim – hardly a high-fashion item, but it's comforting.

Everyone around me is hunkered down, wrapped in resignation. Most of them are plugged into iPods. Device distraction is the only way to get away from the incessant volcano commentary. It's on every screen, and screens are suspended all over the transit lounge. I could plug in, tune out. But my charger is in my suitcase, and who knows where that is. I'm saving the battery life for when I might really need it.

I can't use my phone to go online, either. South African and Brazilian mobile systems are incompatible, so I didn't bother activating international roaming before I left. I had no idea I would be spending so much time in limbo, without a working SIM card. Now if I want to connect, I'll have to find a wi-fi hotspot and use my laptop.

The sunsets were spectacular in 1883. Even European skies were affected by Krakatoa's donation to the atmosphere. Edvard Munch's *The Scream* is on the monitor now. A Norwegian-inflected voice-over reads an excerpt from the artist's diary. *The sun was setting – suddenly the sky turned blood red – there was blöod and tongues of fire above the blue-black fjord and the city – I stood there trembling with anxiety – and I sensed an infinite scream passing through nature ...*

If they don't get me out of here soon I might start running around with my hands over my ears, screaming. This limbo space is turning into a pressure cooker. I need to do something. Find a hotspot and email Em. The Munch volcano connection is the kind of factoid she loves to collect. With luck, I'll find a place that serves tea.

But who will mind my space? No one around me is paying attention to the screen. They're all podcastaways, adrift on syncretic atolls, connected to their portable MP3 tribes. Instead of Munch-kin hands, little white earplugs block out their anxiety. Look at grunge-boy lying down across four scoop chairs, bucking the ear-wear trend with a bulbous set of old-fashioned headphones. Or *Economist*-man in his pressed chinos, which have miraculously maintained their crease. Japanese-san in the velvety pink leisure suit has her eyes closed in on whatever she's listening to. Rastaman, his mountain of dreadlocks tied at the end with fluorescent bands like some acid-flecked Medusa, has the most open face. His paperback is folded back so I can't see the cover. I imagine him dip-jiving to a reggae beat – Stereotypes-R-Us – but he keeps perfectly still.

All that I push away with doubt and travel, todays and yesterdays alike, like bodies. I discovered Auden in one of Em's scattered books. I don't know why those lines come to me now. Along with the thought that it doesn't matter how many bodies you bury yourself in. Emotions catch up with you.

I should have told Nico *that*.

I haven't told Em about Nico. She'll just worry. She liked the fact that I seemed to be 'settling down'. Who knew she harboured such conservative values? Maybe it comes with age.

'The Witches of Eastcoast.' That's what they called themselves, the three aunts who tried to raise me, each in their uniquely ineffectual way. Em was the one who came up with that. But then, she was the only one with any real witchiness about her. The only one I really related to. Eventually. Because she's my mother's sister. Or because she was the one I came to as a last resort. After Pittsburgh and Baltimore, after my father's sisters, Bella and Dot, both threw up their hands in defeat. I guess I should be grateful they didn't try harder.

Em never misses a deadline, never lets a participle dangle or an infinitive split. You always know exactly where you stand with Em. She often quotes Anaïs Nin: 'I spell god with a small "g" because I do not believe in him, but I love to swear by him.'

Em is a no-nonsense bohemian. As an editor and expert navigator of the New York art world, she made sure I read Eliot's *Old Possum* before I saw *Cats* the musical. She steered me away from the suicide poets – Jonker, Plath and Parker – towards Auden and Bishop, with her exquisitely lonely sensibility. She knew I would get that. She became my 'Aunt exemplary and slim'. There were no unfunny uncles.

Besides her complete set of Bishop works, Em kept all my mother's art books, shoved in among anarchic piles of prose and criticism. She also has the only one of Sarah's paintings that survived the fire. It has volcano-red in it, too. One day, when I have a permanent home, or one with a wall big enough, I'll claim it. If I can bear to live with such a vivid reminder of my mother's emotional demise. In the meantime, it dominates the living room in Em's Park Slope apartment.

On the TV screen a photographer from *National Geographic* is talking about a trip to Ngorongoro – technically, it's a volcanic crater, even though it's full of wildlife. Zebras and elephant, lions and giraffe.

Everyone has a *National Geographic* picture. Elizabeth Bishop wrote a poem about hers. She described a volcano, and much more. Six years old, in a waiting room, she paged inside yellow-framed margins to find out what the world was, and discovered that she really wasn't what she'd thought *she* was, in the face of those natives with bare breasts and pointed heads.

My father gave me a *National Geographic* subscription for my seventh birthday. It was delivered to Pittsburgh, then Baltimore, then New York. And so the places where I wasn't, and he wasn't, became our crossing points – points where each one was for the other. *Even though we're not together*, he wrote on the birthday card, *we can share the whole world.*

I had to write to him whenever a new issue arrived, and tell him about my favourite picture in the magazine. The Afghan girl with the blazing green eyes, impossible tigers that looked like fire, a white baby seal clubbed and left to die in the snow. I knew how Bishop felt, finding herself in other places, with people in pith helmets and riding breeches. Desperate people will use any means to escape.

I've got her *Poems* right here, but reading is impossible with the collective restiveness running through the transit lounge like a Mexican wave: disbelief and denial, agitation and frustration, random bursts of anger, a kind of dumb acceptance, cycling around again and again. Our emotions synching like the menses of adolescent girls in dormitories.

Grunge boy is jiggling his foot over the edge of the seat now. Rastaman is fiddling with his volume dial. Asian girl is awake, snapping through the pages of a magazine with a kind of violence. Her soft-pink velour shell suit is covered in tiny hash tags. Twitterati couture. Business Joe has put down his magazine; he's jabbing his fingers at his smartphone screen, the line between his eyes and the straight stripe of his mouth make a kind of inverted 'T' that's starting to freak me out. I really need to move.

It's a calculated risk. I'm already possessive of the small familiarities of chair and windowpane, pillar and light. What to leave behind as a marker? I don't want to lose my small comforts. Don't want to permeate my bubble of solitude, either. But I'll have to.

In the end I leave behind my fleece and *Dona Flor*, one on each seat. Rastaman is gracious. 'Tranquilo,' he says in a soft Brazilian accent: 'I will save them.' Turns out we're on the same flight. If there ever is a flight, if we don't end up marooned here forever. Maybe we're actually caught in some cruel reality TV hoax. *Terminal Survivor.* All the hanging screens could have two-way purposes, spewing false information intended to foment panic and disorder, while recording and broadcasting the reactions of the unwitting players. In these games, people turn tribal fast. The key to survival is to be brutally self-serving while you form strategic groups. In which case, I've already made my first tentative alliance.

Even so, I take Elizabeth with me when I head off to find tea and connectivity. The Soyinka, too – it already feels like some kind of talisman. Maybe because it's so small. Or maybe because I'm more superstitious than I will ever admit. But then life is a continual play of bargaining with fate, even if you say you don't believe in fate.

Step on a crack, you break your mother's back; step on a line, you break your father's spine. How is a small person supposed to walk the world with such frightening omnipotence? No wonder we dream of flying.

The food hall is a droning hive compared to the islands of relative serenity around the useless boarding gates. A place comes free as I get to the first hotspot café – a Starbucks. I grab a bunch of paper serviettes and wipe the table before I put my Bishop down. You might wonder why I bother. Its cover is scuffed, the endpapers grimed, there are dog-ears marking my favourite poems – 'One Art' supreme among them. Many of the pages are smudged with chocolate.

There was a Bishop poem, or a line of one, for every seminal point in my life, and I know the perfect one to share with Em right now. I slip a sugar sachet between the pages at 'Crusoe in England'. My tea, in a cardboard cup, is too hot to hold, never mind drink. The mermaid on the cup is gripping both sides of her split tail in orgiastic glee – the place has run out of some of their 1001 flavours because food vendors, like mobile airtime sellers, are making a killing out of this crisis.

While I wait for my laptop to fire up, I stab the teabag up and down with the blunt plastic needle that serves for a spoon and get pulled into the televised eruption. There really is no escaping it. All the people stranded, all over the world, at all the frozen airports, watching themselves on screen. This airport isn't as bad as some, apparently. The flights that were mid-air when the ban was put in place have arrived. There'll be no more leaving or landing until the airspace is declared safe for travel again.

A wide-eyed, blonde announcer is trying her best to make it all sound terribly exciting, this long, dull pause in business as usual. Would Elizabeth have been at all interested in the gossiping TV screens? Would she have shrunk inside herself, painfully shy and unable to escape from all these people? Or would she have put her hands over her ears and let out a silent scream?

Dear Em –

'A new volcano has erupted.' Well so it has, and here I am, grounded, like thousands of other people, in limboland, and everyone volcano-obsessed.

You may have seen it, if you turned on your TV, which I bet you haven't. Good for you. Don't bother. It's not so much an emergency as inconvenient. Unless you own an airline, I suppose. Or an airport. Or live under a molten mountain. Selfish me, I am none of these. I'm just delayed and waylaid, and I thought I would tell you about it because I saw a thing on TV about how Munch's The Scream *was inspired by the intense sunsets in the wake of Krakatoa. Skies tinted by ash, even a hemisphere away. I should worry about that – the climactic effects, post-eruption. These things are self-regulating in ways that are so much more complex than even the Gaia lovers, who like to reduce all science to linear reductionism, would believe. I'll wait for the scientists to stop arguing about whether it will make us hotter or cooler, then I'll form my own opinion. Not that it will make any difference to the final outcome.*

My tea has gone tepid. I down it in one gulp. When the queue gets shorter, I'll get some more.

I'm on the way to Salvador, btw. The one in Brazil. It's far from Manaus, and I haven't decided yet whether or not to visit Bill. SO DO NOT TELL HIM THAT I AM COMING please. I have some work to do over the next month, and if there is time at the end, I might take a trip up. Not sure if he is even there at the moment. When I get there, I'll write you again. Or, if we are here for much longer, I might be forced to give you a progress report. They haven't run out of tea yet, so we're all right for now.

They have run out of some things, though. Pastries and sandwiches, pre-packed snacks. There's more coming in soon, the cafeteria staff say. They're all bleary-eyed from meeting the increasingly strident demands of the stranded. The guy behind the counter gives me my second cup of tea for free. It isn't as hot as the last one. I pull the sugar sachet out of the Bishop book, which falls open to another dog-eared page. 'The Catheral'd been struck by lightning.' In Santarém.

. . . One tower had
a widening zigzag crack all the way down.
It was a miracle. The priest's house right next door
had been struck, too, and his brass bed
(the only one in town) galvanised black.
Graças a deus, he'd been in Belém.

If Elizabeth was still alive, I could tell her what it's like to be struck by lightning. She already knew what it was like to be raised by aunts and grandparents. She also loved travel and plants –

particularly Brazilian ones. She spent fifteen years in that country. Aunt Em, with her love for words and ideas and sentiments that could not easily be put into words, has never been to Brazil. Em, who makes a living hacking back other people's overgrown prose, and writes her own poetry into slim black Moleskine notebooks, in fountain pen with rust-red ink that looks like dried blood on the page, could never find the right words to tell me the whole truth about my mother. For once, words failed her. But children don't need all the details. They *feel* the truth.

The spine of *Poems* is cracked white where it's been folded open, again and again. There's a picture of a palm tree and windmills on the cover, a watercolour Elizabeth did in Mexico in 1942. Something is written, tiny in the bottom right-hand corner of the painting, but I've never been able to read it; Em's cat Macavity bit through the words while the book lay, irresistibly delicious, in a pile of birthday wrapping-paper.

> *Give Mac a tummy tickle for me, and tell him to go bite a bicycle.*

I hit 'send'.

4
The art of losing in three acts

The mountains were make-and-break territory for Nico and me.

This epiphany arrived while I was hiking up the slope towards the Constantiaberg beacon. My imaginings fell into the rhythm of my steps as I trudged up the white sand trail, letting the city and my briefing at the Institute fall away behind me. The unseasonable heat was already giving way to a foreshadowing cool. The storm building on the northern horizon was not the usual winter cold front; it would be a much rarer thing, a massive thunderstorm.

My built-in lightning sensors were sending alert signals down my spine and into my fingertips. But the storm was a way off yet. A bit higher, and I would be able to see the clouds drawing in energy over the Atlantic. Already the sunlight had an eerie intensity against the gathering grey. It suited my mood.

I was hoping the walk would clear my head, help me deal with the upcoming evening. I wasn't looking forward to Sherman's party. I dreaded making the final cut with Nico. I knew I would get too drunk, regret my excesses the next day. Plus a dull pain in my lower back signalled it was *that* time.

I told myself this was the natural course of things. People have cycles, relationships have cycles, life is a series of wheels within wheels. It didn't help. Only now that it was finally ending, could I admit how much I'd wished we could have turned the mutual vulnerabilities that brought us together into something less fragile.

Vavi burst out of a bank of proteas, a brown and white blur as he crossed the path and dived into the bushes on the other side. I knew I should call him to heel before he actually caught up with a dassie or a porcupine, but we hadn't been out on a proper walk in a while. I let him run.

The russet patches in his shaggy coat blended perfectly with the fynbos. He was a hybrid of his sheepdog mother and an anonymous donor, a 'pavement special' who gave him his colouring and his cocked ears. I love the happy accident of his genes, his joy attacks, his utter dependability. I named him after Nikolai Vavilov, the Russian plant geneticist and champion of hybridity. Vavi for short. Nico thought I'd named him after the former leader of the Congress of South African Trade Unions. He bought him a red collar, and joked about his communist roots.

We were from such different worlds.

The original Vavilov would not have appreciated the joke, either. He dedicated his life to promoting food security through biodiversity, travelled the globe collecting specimens for his seed bank in Leningrad – then starved to death in one of Stalin's prisons.

Now there's an institute and a statue in St Petersburg, a coin minted with his face on it, a crater named after him on the dark side of the moon, and a glacier honouring him in the high Pamirs ... and a skewbald dog trailing his name through the wild flowers on Africa's southernmost peninsula.

The winter rains had tinged everything low-lying with a fresh new green. It was always such a relief when fire season was over. We hold our breath during the hot dry summer, with its relentless southeaster gales, waiting for the inevitable blazes.

Fynbos needs fire to regenerate, but before the city crept up around the base of the mountains, those fires had natural causes.

These days, too many of them are set by bored, pyromaniac hooligans. Or by mindless tourists tossing cigarettes out of rental-car windows. These days, there are too many fires for the fynbos to recuperate; too little time between blazes for the plants to regenerate, mature and reseed. Burned too young, they edge ever closer to extinction.

I felt another hot-iron cramp ripple through my belly, and walked harder. I love the idea that every woman is born with all of her seeds in place. Even in our infant wombs, all possible future children wait. Every month from puberty onwards, one of those future chances, maybe two, will unfurl, reach out and expire. Our bodies signal biological disappointment with sharp pains and raging moods. Ever since I turned thirty, I've been well aware that each cycle brings me closer to my last. This has been my choice. What kind of mother could a motherless child possibly make? That's what I told Nico when he came at me with romantic notions of hearth, home and family. If you need to love and nurture something, I told him, you get a dog.

Vavi's ecstatic bush thrashes had released a honeyed fynbos scent. I breathed it in and felt myself expand in the way that only happens to me when I'm alone, far from crowds and under infinite skies. If ever I need a religion, this is where I'll find it.

From the highest points on the peninsula, I could see both the Atlantic and the Indian Oceans, alternately or together in snatches. The back of my brain was still on lightning alert, but I calmed myself by absorbing the minutiae of the plants in my peripheral vision.

There is a sublime subtlety to fynbos. You can look at it from afar, and see nothing but featureless scrub; get in close and the tiny details are astounding. That day, masses of tiny pink erica balls hazed the grey-green brush. In the lab, I love to lift the erica's tiny seed case with tweezers and put it under the microscope. The seed is a speck to the naked eye; amplified it fluffs up, perfectly round and covered in luxuriant, shockingly pink fur. Such a lascivious little seed! On screen it would be played by a bombshell wearing a fluffy boa and feathered mules; the Marilyn Monroe of seeds, as drawn by Dr Seuss.

I rounded a speckled sandstone buttress, and my chest filled up with candle valley. I call it that because of the way the leucadendrons carpet the bowl; this time of year, their lime-yellow bracts shine as if they'd absorbed all the sun of the day, their cones lit up like candles. Spring was flirting with the mountain. When summer arrived, I would have my work cut out for me. Except that I was going to Brazil. I was going to miss the season my entire year revolved around.

I met Nico in spring, in a high valley not unlike this one, in the Kogelberg reserve. Back then I was part of a team of young botanists in Search and Rescue, identifying critically endangered plants in reserves and urban lots around the city. I was leading a group of city geeks on a nature appreciation hike. Nico was a rising ad-agency writer who'd won a few awards, and was looking for a social responsibility campaign to raise his profile. Fynbos awareness was the one he'd stumbled upon.

At first I thought he was just like the others – if less obviously so than Marilese, his art director. She came all in black, with horn-rimmed glasses and slim pumps that always filled with sand so that she kept having to stop to empty them out. Such an awkward bird, balancing on one leg, swiping her shoes clean with a finger and muttering about how she would rather be sipping a skinny latte – if you told me she'd become the one person I could always turn to for tea and sympathy (or a seriously stiff whisky), I would have laughed in your face. So much for first impressions.

Nico's hiking boots showed real wear and tear, and his faded T-shirt was an ironic local beer logo spoof. He kept up with me, while the others fell behind. We synchronised our breaths up the steep slope, and I remember how his eyes began to shine as the landscape did its work. When we let the others catch up for a water break, they all climbed up on top of a monolithic boulder to get a better view. Nico stayed down beneath it, leaning against the lime and orange lichen on its shady side. He was staring at a *Polygala myrtifolia*. 'It's called a butterfly bush,' I told him, and was going to point out how its purple petals opened like wings, but he shushed me and pointed to a green leaf that morphed into a praying mantis.

I wanted to call the others, but he silenced me again with a finger to his lips. Then he grabbed my hand and pulled me down next to him. What he had found was not one praying mantis, but two. The female was fat, bulbous, her bulging sides stencilled with a racing stripe of dark spots. The male, much smaller, was perched on top of her, his green stick hands clenched around her neck in concentration. We watched him pulse and flush orange, passion blazing his abdomen. Nico looked at me from under his dark blond fringe. I remember thinking, 'So not my type.' Even so, I had to stop myself reaching out to brush his hair aside so I could see more of him.

Afterwards, we called it our 'mantis moment', and made it our mission to recreate it wherever possible. We made love on mountaintops, behind waterfalls, in tea-coloured rivers. We slept on sand islands exposed to the stars, woke up in sunshine and painted each other with zinc sunblock in crazy neon colours from small plastic jars. He always took particular care around my nipples.

Our first Christmas, he gave me a copy of Laurens van der Post's *A Mantis Carol*, Jungian-inspired reflections on the sacred role of the praying mantis in ancient bushman lore. On the inside front cover, he had sketched our mating mantises. I was so touched by the gesture, I almost forgot the cynicism of his parting shot that first day, as he stood up and eased the stiffness from his thighs. 'Enjoy yourself, sucker,' he told the flushing mantis male. 'You're about to become lunch.'

5
The climax

We began in the mountains, and we climaxed in the mountains. Pun intended. Although the middle was really the beginning of the end. I see that now.

We got caught in a storm in the Cederberg. That winter was a particularly wet one. Friends said we were crazy to hike that weekend, but we went anyway – Nico was insistent.

We slept in a cave the first night, watched over by the ghosts of long-ago people who had marked themselves in elongated ochre on the walls. When the fire had burned down to a few glowing coals, Nico pulled out a ring, joked about question-popping, and offered a possible future. I remember the weight of the ring in the palm of my hand. Instead of a gemstone there was a convex pool of pyrite, a bevel of coppery gold speckled with black, like the dense clouds of the Milky Way, obscured that night.

I lurched for something to say. 'This is fool's gold.'

I realised my mistake immediately, as the hurt pooled and hardened in his face, but it was too late to take it back.

He slept turned away from me, cocooned in his sleeping bag. The next morning, as the rain clouds gathered, I put the ring in an inside pocket of my backpack. For safekeeping, I told him. For later, I meant.

There was no lightning in the storm we got caught in on our way down, just wild winds with icy spears of sideways-slicing rain. We couldn't find an overhang to shelter under, so we slid down the slope, soaked and shivering, to a little hut we'd spotted.

It belonged to an old woman, a goatherd whose flock huddled, slit-eyed, under the eaves of a corrugated-iron shed in the backyard.

The goats had bulbs of garlic tied with knotted twine around their necks. So did the crone. There was garlic everywhere – under the eaves, over the doorway and all the windows. I quizzed the woman about the healing properties of indigenous herbs, asked her what other plants she used. I expected 'agtdaegeneesbos' for skin ulcers, or 'kouebos' for coughs and colds.

Instead, the old woman set a speckled red enamel coffeepot over a single gas ring, walked over to a cabinet high in the wall, and pulled out a giant-sized jar of Vicks VapoRub. 'Maak alles reg,' she said, in a rolling Afrikaans brei. Fixes everything. As if to prove the point, she sat down, hoicked up her skirts and began rubbing the pungent gel onto her mottled, skinny legs until the skin shone. When she poured us coffee, it had a greasy whiff of eucalyptus.

Before we left, I walked out back to see where the woman grew her garlic, hoping to find some other herbs there. Instead, I found strange glittering fruit hanging from a tangle of trees. They were CDs, twirling and sparkling in the emerging sun like Christmas decorations. 'Chases away baboons,' the woman explained. She told us the trees were apricots, but they were gnarled and fruitless.

It took us a few hours to hike back to our car. Driving out of the mountains on the twisting dirt road, we came across a young girl running after a goat. The goat was coming straight at us, veering off at the very last minute so Nico had to slam on brakes. The goat slowed as we passed, which gave the girl a chance to stop, hop-skipping on one foot to adjust the plastic shoe on her other. For one long moment we were all paused, connected: the girl, the goat, the two of us. Then the goat leapt sideways up out of the roadside ditch, and the girl began running again, waving and laughing as she continued her futile chase.

'She doesn't seem to mind that there's no point in it,' Nico said. It might have been the first thing he'd said all day.

'Maybe she just enjoys the chase.'

'Maybe,' Nico said. And then, it seemed, there really was nothing left to talk about.

When we stopped at the Clanwilliam Cash-n-Carry, I bought a jar of Vicks. In the car, I twisted off the blue plastic lid and scooped out a big spicy blob. Menthol 2.8mg, camphor 52.6mg, eucalyptus 13.3mg. I put my feet up on the dashboard and rubbed it into the scratches on my own legs, just to feel the heat and burn. I rubbed some on the faint latticework of scars on both my knees, even though the cuts had long since closed up. Skull and horse head – only I knew what the uneven shapes were supposed to be. I rested my chin between them, breathing in the smell of comfort and loss, until we got home.

6
Bowing out

As I walked, planning what I would say to him that night, I teased myself with the faint idea that things might still turn around. Because there had been moments, with Nico, whole ones, golden ones. But the stretches between those moments had grown longer and longer. And during those stretches, when I failed not to think of Nico at all, I felt completely bereft.

We *were* always good in nature. Maybe that's why he chose to confess to me on a mountaintop. Maybe he thought there would be enough space up there to dilute the hurt of a betrayal.

'Did you at least use a condom?' I asked him, on a peak called Judas, where a cave blinked over the Atlantic, glittering and indifferent below. His eyes shifted. 'Jesus, Nico, in this day and age!'

The sun was punishing that day, and I took some pleasure in the thought of it beating down on him after I left him up there to find his own way to the empty car park, and then walk the long road home. Without water, or forgiveness.

The sun was less fierce this day, winter angled and cloud muted. A strange purple glow illuminated everything, and a low clump of everlastings shone out white against the gathering shadows. I bent down to pluck a few, their petals naturally parched and paper-thin. I always keep a few threaded into my car's dashboard grille. They stay there for months, until the first blast of summer air-conditioning sends them flying. Proof that nothing actually lasts forever, no matter what you call it.

There's nothing quite as satisfying as having your strongest fears justified. It took me a while to collect enough coffin nails and last straws. I weathered the first infidelity. But I couldn't stand to be near Nico after the second. I had no idea how many there had been since then. It was irrelevant now, anyway.

We called a kind of truce. When Marilese's tenants ran out on their lease, she offered me her Hout Bay cottage. The time was right for me to move out of Nico's cliff-hanging glass box. *His* house, even though we had been together when he bought it. Three years on, he still couldn't afford it. But it gave him an excuse to push himself even faster on his treadmill.

I was just starting to feel settled now, cocooned in the forest, one huge window framing the greenery of Orange Kloof, and only a short winding road to the Institute. I fantasised about digging a moat, filling it with water siphoned from the Disa River, adding crocodiles. The miniature, nocturnal variety that comes from Central Africa; their pupils are permanently dilated to help them see in the dark, which makes their eyes soft and mammalian. Disney eyes, to distract you from their deadly jaws.

'You only pretend to be inaccessible,' Marilese told me. Her rambling homestead was roughly halfway between the cottage and the Institute. Since having kids, she worked freelance from home. Not so much with Nico anymore. I felt a sudden need for her company. If there was time, I could swing by her place on my way home.

Vavi was barking urgently some way ahead. I could hear no voices, no jangle of approaching cyclists. He must have found something interesting and wild. I hurried to catch up to him before he did any damage.

I still had a key to Nico's glass eyrie. Glass houses were for people with nothing to hide. Or people for whom the mere pretence of having nothing to hide was itself a kind of camouflage. I'd only used the key once since moving out. I had to pick up a colander. He wasn't there. I was a stranger, an alien in his transparent cube. I was free of the strain of looking for traces of other women – in the laundry basket, the bathroom bin, the scribbles on the telephone notepad. I'd hated the straw-clutching person I had become, towards the end. And he like a bug trapped in amber.

Nico hired a decorator just after we moved in together. I came back from a field trip to find 'Soozi' sitting on my worn-out sofa, surrounded by fabric samples. I pretended not to notice how his eyes lingered on her cleavage while they discussed the virtues of uplighting. The smell of her perfume lingered between the seat cushions for days.

One Saturday morning, she picked Nico up in her convertible built for two. They were going to test sofas. Seriously, that's how he put it. How exactly do you 'test' a sofa? I didn't like to think. At the time I was researching the medicinal properties of *Thunbergia alata*, the vine my grandmother called black-eyed-Susan. The afternoon became evening, and still he didn't come back. I thought about the diseases – venereal, principally – that *Thunbergia*'s East African relative was good for. I pictured the designer tangled up in it, pulled down and smothered until only one high heel thrust out of the innocent greenery.

So much happier now, on my own.

I would give him his key back that night. Should have done it long ago.

Vavi's barking grew more frantic. When the barks turned into yelps, I began to run. I rounded the bend and stopped so abruptly I felt my feet sink into the sand beneath me.

A Cape cobra was swaying in front of Vavi, hood unfurled on top of a metre of sleek brown body, still more spring-coiled and ready on the ground. In the long seconds it took me to assess the scene, I registered eyes like two black beads, a cool lemon throat, a flickering tongue. The snake was total concentration. It followed Vavi's movement with eyes and body as the dog darted from side to side, letting out a yelp every time he came to the end of his run and changed direction. He had already churned a groove in the sand. Had he hypnotised the snake, or had the snake charmed him? I opened my mouth to shout, but nothing came out. I took a step forward, Vavi turned his head, the snake struck.

Whether my movement distracted the snake, whether it was a mock strike, or whether Vavi's instinctive reflexes helped him to evade it, I'll never know. I threw ineffectual clumps of sand after the cobra as it slid away into the undergrowth. Then I grabbed Vavi by the collar and sank to my knees, checking his eyes for signs of cobra venom before I buried my face in his soft brown ruff and let the dam inside me burst.

It was only after I had Vavi safe in the car that I saw the spray of old everlastings in the air vent, and realised that I'd dropped the fresh ones I'd just picked. As the thunder rumbled outside, I leaned over to hug Vavi, proud on the passenger seat.

'We'll just consider it a snake offering,' I told him.

In Transit

At first I think the thunder is part of my dream, but when I open my eyes, it's still rumbling.

My skin itches. My mouth is dry. My limbs ache, and I'm numb where my hip is pressed into the space between two chairs. I have a memory of fire, hot orange rivulets and ash.

It takes a while to register the bright glare in the high ceilings, the newly familiar faces bobbing above orange scoop chairs.

I sit up, push off a red blanket. Where did that come from? It's thin and striped with yellow. Standard airline issue. Everyone else in our section of the transit lounge has one. Rastaman's is still neatly folded in its plastic wrap. I hate the way they do that – unnecessary plastic to suggest hygiene. Who knows where these blankets have been? And even if they *have* actually been cleaned, what kind of toxic chemicals are trapped in the process, waiting to escape and hit you in the face when you rip the bag open?

Another low rumble from somewhere beneath the building makes me nervous, even though I know the volcano is thousands of miles away, in another country.

Rastaman is watching me. He's lying across his chairs, using his backpack as a pillow. His smile is one of a man fully aware of his considerable charms. 'You were asleep, but I think you were cold.' He is holding a book – *my* book, the *Dona Flor*. 'I hope you don't mind?' His thumb is keeping his place, well into the story already. He's either a fast reader or I've been asleep a long time. 'In English, it is strange.'

So we've been lying side by side, separated by a thin strip of airport carpet, connected by Amado's story of love, lust and magic in last century's Salvador. The strange intimacy of strangers.

I feel more than a little invaded, but force myself to smile. I chose him as an ally, after all. He still has his earphones in. 'What you listening to?' I'm actually a little curious, since I haven't pinned him down to a tune.

'Kaya N'Gan Daya.' He sits up in one fluid movement. 'Gilberto Gil doing Bob Marley.' He pulls the buds out of his ear and offers me his iPod. I decline. I don't want his music in my head.

'Gil came to Cape Town once,' I remember. 'When he was Minister of Culture. So it was all official business. We didn't get to hear him perform.'

'Brother makes us proud.' His mouth rounds the words so that his English lilts into something soft and sweet. He pulls a card out of a side pocket of his backpack and hands it to me, half-bowing with old-fashioned formality. *Roberto Alvarez da Costa Silva.* I'd forgotten the pleasure of elongated Brazilian names, the way they build on themselves and contain their own bouncing rhythms and attenuated family trees. Beneath his name is a picture of a drum and the name of a store – Os Agogos. On the back, in red, yellow and green: *OLODUM – casa de samba-reggae*. An address in Pelourinho, Salvador.

'Prazer.' I introduce myself, speaking my first stutters of Portuguese in too long. I can feel myself becoming more languid as my mouth stretches around the long vowels. 'I'm going to be staying in Pelourinho, actually.'

'You should visit us.' He motions for me to keep the card. 'I'm going to a conference in Rio, but I'll be back next week.'

'If we're not still stuck here.'

He shakes his head. 'We won't be.' How can he be so sure? He has drumsticks stuck into the netting of his backpack, tied and tasselled in the same fluorescent green and orange as his dread elastics. 'We play Sundays and Tuesdays,' he says, standing up. 'You should come.'

I find myself nodding as I stretch my neck to look up at him. He is tall. The red, black and white beads around his wrists remind me of the ones my sangoma friends wear, signs of faith and practice underneath urbanised exteriors of nylon and crease-free cotton. I promise to watch his things, watch him as he walks off with long, floating strides into the vastness of the concourse.

A bossa nova tune winds up from deep inside my brain. Not a Jobim original, but a parody of it – the cool irony of Beck's 'Tropicalia'. Something about broken guitars and tropical charms ... I can't remember all the words, but the riff has hooked me, is looping through me with the manic whoops of the Brazilian laughing gourd – the cuíca always makes me think of a deranged toucan hiccupping and high in the middle of a song.

I've been shut down way too long.

I start scrabbling inside my backpack for my iPod. Time to tune in again.

An hour later, Roberto isn't back and I'm still tethered to this lookout post. Outside, lighting flashes bounce off the hulks of parked aircraft. I wish they would turn the lights off. Incessant fluorescence is bad for your body clock. Plus I want to keep an eye on what's coming, and the light inside is hazing the window-pane.

From what I can make out, the sky is throwing up puce and green, but it's not yet light enough to compete with the reflection from inside. I've got my iPod set on random, but it seems intent on serving up only the most self-indulgent tunes on my playlist. Right now it's Bonnie 'Prince' Billy moaning that having no one means there's no one there to hurt you. At least he's practical in his self-pity. If I'm going to rewrite my recent history, I need a new soundtrack. Maybe I should have accepted Roberto's iPod after all.

The low rumble travels under the floor again, louder now. I can taste sulphur as the hairs on the back of my neck begin to rise. Might as well face it. I go to the window to look for what I know is coming. When I press my hands against the glass, I can feel my palms tingle, feel the current in me rise. Come and get me already. Please.

Sometimes memories ride in on physical sensations, sometimes they hitchhike with smells. Airports smell of anonymity, metal and dust. But there's something else here now, animal, vegetable or chemical, which takes me back to—

Christmas on my mother's family farm. So different from the snow-scented East Coast Christmases with my father's relatives, where the houses were covered in tiny lights and life-sized plastic reindeer stood thigh-deep in front-garden snowdrifts. Christmas in Africa was hot; not the heavy, dripping heat of our Amazon home, but a dry heat that built through the day and climaxed in dramatic thunderstorms, bringing relief and a coolness that would last through the evening and into the night until the cycle began again the next morning.

My mother's parents farmed cattle in the Natal midlands. Their spread lay at the foot of the Drakensberg range – ragged, beautiful, unpredictable. One day, in the lull between Christmas and New Year, my mother took my father and me on a hike to

Cathedral Peak. She said I was finally old enough to walk most of it on my own.

The day started out clear, but the breeze exhausted itself by noon, leaving us gasping for air that got stickier the higher we climbed. Sarah carried a picnic in her backpack – hard-boiled eggs and red-and-white checked napkins, warm fizzy Appletiser, and cheese sandwiches that tasted of the farm.

The eggs had blue-green rims around their yellow yolks. I didn't want to eat them. My mother told me blue was nothing to be afraid of. But those eggs tasted dry and strange.

We were on our way down the mountain when the air changed. The clouds that had been building on the horizon, bulbous and purple, seemed to grow as they gobbled up the daylight. And then they began to growl.

'The dragons are waking up,' Bill said, trying to keep his voice light. I saw both my parents stiffen, and have an entire conversation without exchanging a word.

'Let's hurry, then!' My mother turned her back on the gathering clouds and took me firmly by the hand. 'Right, Maddy?'

That voice meant business. It meant no more dawdling, I'm-only-going-to-tell-you-this-one-time. But I was already tired. I'd walked all the way up by myself.

'My legs are jelly,' I whined. And before Sarah could protest, Bill had scooped me up onto his shoulders and started striding down the path.

'I don't think that's a good idea,' my mother came panting up beside us, catching his sleeve. She was the one who knew these mountains, had grown up exploring them. The purple clouds were almost on top of us now, although we were still in sunlight. The grumblings were turning into shouts, and when I looked back across the deep valley behind us, I could see lightning bolts being thrown from one peak to another. Without a word, Bill swung me down and they each held one of my hands, making a game of swing-pulling me between them as we ran.

Just before the sun was snuffed out entirely, we came to a rocky outcrop with a large overhang.

'Maybe we should shelter here.' Bill was panting.

Down below, in miniature, I could see the lodge, and the parking lot behind it where the roof of our car glinted.

'I think we should push on.' Slick strands of Sarah's long hair were stuck to the sides of her face. Some had found their way into her mouth and she pulled them out, impatiently. We began to move forward again.

As we rounded the outcrop, I saw a cluster of dry, paper-thin flowers sheltering in the lee of the rocks. Everlastings. I loved the flowers even more after my mother told me they were also called 'sewejaartjies' – 'little-seven-years', which is what I would be soon. It was my first inkling that something could represent infinity, and yet be trapped in a predetermined, finite time.

'Look, Mama!' I slipped out of my mother's safe hand and began to tug at the flowers, taking hold of the stems low down as I had been told, so there was something to tie them together with.

The first loud crack sounded like a tear in the sky, and a keen wind rushed out from that gash.

'Come on, Maddy!'

My own name was the last thing I heard my mother say. The next crack was so loud that it seemed to come from inside us. The earth opened under us and I was flung forward as my father's cry unravelled behind me.

Then the ringing in my ears made everything else go quiet. I could feel rain hard on my skin, but I couldn't hear it. I could see my father, as if through a dim tunnel, sitting with his legs splayed in front of him. He was shaking his head. He looked so silly. Like someone in a cartoon.

The air smelled wrong, and there was a taste in my mouth I would learn to call sulphur. I couldn't see my mother, and when I tried to sit up, I couldn't move. I could only blink, and blink, until my father scooped me up with a sob I felt in his chest but still could not hear, and I saw my mother's body, rigid on the ground, emitting a strange blue light, ringed like the yolks of the eggs we had eaten an hour before. The life left in my mother was otherworldly. The life that had been her, earthly, earthed, was gone, as if the circle of singed grass around her had been burned by her life force, leaving.

'You Will Miss Me When I Burn' is still playing on my iPod. As if I need to be warned about the awful things behind me.

I see his silhouette reflected before I feel his touch on my elbow. 'Okay?' The voice is low, gentle. I realise that my eyes are streaming, my face as wet as the other side of the glass. 'We won't be much longer here, I think,' Rasta Roberto says.

I switch my iPod off, but I don't answer. In real time, this moment would be uncomfortably long. But transit time is different. It seems to have distorted the continuum, so the usual conventions of social discourse – the correct number of beats between a question and an answer, the thoughtful pause not long enough to suggest lack of interest – become meaningless.

Even so, a silence left too long speaks volumes.

I have nothing to say to this person, while lightning flickers over the dead runway. In our reflection, he is much taller than me. I'm tiny anyway, but the difference is even more absurd because of the elongated knit cap he's pulled over his dreadlocks. Broad shoulders. Feet spread wide in the way of tall people, arms crossed in front. Without any music playing in my ears, the forgotten verse of 'Tropicalia' comes to me in a rush.

Maybe I am out of luck, standing here tear-stained, riffing funeral songs of lust and bossa nova. I'm way too jaded for the Brazilian-sex-god-holiday-cure-all fantasy.

But what Roberto is offering is much worse. When I turn around, he is still looking at me. There is no expectation in his eyes. No judgement, no false sympathy. Just kindness.

I leave him standing there, and head off to find a cup of tea, alone.

7
Bolts from the blue

I like to think I don't buy into superstition. But I couldn't shake the feeling that the cobra was some kind of sign.

In my years on those mountains, I'd had near misses with fat, lazy puff adders more times than I care to remember. I'd seen wisps of snake sliding off paths so quickly I couldn't be totally certain what they were. I once saw a yellow cobra pooled like a curl of butter in a rock hollow. But I'd never had to face one down.

Still, if I was going to be superstitious about anything, it should be lightning.

In the United States, you have a one in six million chance of being killed by lightning each year. You have an even higher chance in South Africa, which tops the list of lightning-death countries, along with Mexico, Thailand and Brazil. Statistically, by living in two of the top four, my mother had stacked the odds.

Some people are natural conductors. Look at Roy Sullivan, a park ranger from Virginia who was struck seven different times over forty years. He lost a toenail, hurt his ankle, singed his eyebrows. Once he was knocked unconscious and lost his left shoe. He survived all this, but when a woman broke his heart, he took his own life. Which just goes to show, internal turmoil can be more devastating than anything nature throws at us.

There was a staccato flash and I gripped the steering wheel hard, bracing myself for the thunder crack that would follow, counting the seconds to calculate the storm's distance. Marilese's place was just around the corner. I planned to shelter there, let the worst of the storm pass before I headed home.

I told myself that statistically, the chance of running into a snake on this mountain, on an uncharacteristically hot late-winter day, with the ground baked warm to comfort the cold-blooded, and a dog flushing out the bushes, was pretty high. A lot higher than getting struck by lightning, which I'd already accomplished. Not that it left me feeling particularly special. The lightning bolt didn't grant me any special talents or abilities. Now *that* was unlucky. Why couldn't I be like that doctor who was struck by lightning in a telephone booth and became a musical savant overnight? He gave up a successful medical practice to compose and conduct symphonies.

My bolt from the blue simply gave me an affinity for electricity.

My aunt Bella was the first to notice. I went to live with her right after the strike. I was fresh out of the bath, and Bella was about to dry my hair. But when she slipped the switch, the current leapt from the drier and swarmed in an unholy halo around my head, lifting my long hair straight up like Struwwelpeter's. It was one of the few times I heard my Jesus-loving aunt blaspheme. The next day, I got a haircut I hated. I got used to the hairstyle, but I don't think Bella ever really got over her shock.

For a while, everyone tried to keep me away from electrical appliances. But I learned to seek out the buzz. I think it was a way of feeling something other than pain. Eventually, I got bored playing with domestic voltage. I moved on to pins, then blades. I liked razors and adjustable box-cutters best. I have a fine grass thicket etched on the underside of my left arm, and a pointillist patch on each knee. By the time anyone noticed my scars, I'd found a more private way to punish myself. You'd be amazed how little food a growing girl can get by on. Em was the one who finally called my bluff. But by then, my childhood was practically over.

If Em was elegant and urbane, my father's sisters were at the other end of the spectrum, and so dissimilar it was hard to imagine they shared any heritage at all. Bella was skeletal and blonde, and devoted to her saviour with a fervour that frightened me. Her Pittsburgh home was a shrine of Catholic kitsch. I wanted my flesh-and-blood father, not this bleeding stand-in on a cross, but my father stayed away, hiding his grief behind his work, while my sorrow was left to the inadequate aunts.

Bella painted icons on wood blocks and rubbed the colours with gold leaf. One day she presented me with a postcard detail of Michelangelo's Sistine Chapel fresco, the part where the hand of God reaches down to give life to Adam. She believed that I'd been touched by something divine. But Catholicism didn't agree with me. I found myself bucking the convent school system without even trying. Once, on a dare, I went up to receive the body of Christ even though I hadn't had my first communion. My pious aunt was mortified. Father O'Connor came by the house to discuss my transgression, and left with an armful of her finest painted wares for his vestry.

That wasn't the reason Bella sent me away. The reason was Judd, a Pontiac car salesman who wanted to take her with him to start a new life – and a new dealership – in New Mexico. There would be plenty of desert inspiration – cactus Madonnas and baby Jesuses on burros. She couldn't fit me into the frame.

I was sent to Baltimore to live with Dot – but not before my soul was set right. I was squeezed into a lacy white dress and patent shoes, and what was left of my hair was tortured into curls by Bella's neighbour, Nancy. The fumes of an entire can of

Curvy Curl X-tra Hold trailed me like a noxious veil as I walked down the aisle to become Christ's newest bride, too old already at the tender age of eight.

Nancy's daughter Olive was the one who dared me in the first place. Olive's hair was long and dark and always smelled like Johnson's No More Tears anti-tangle spray. Her mother told me I could come in any time for a wash and blow-dry, even though my newly shorn hair was so straight and fine, there was nothing much anybody could do with it. You would never see me in barrettes with butterflies or bobbled hair ties in glitter colours like Olive had. Bella said my short hair was easy maintenance. *Unlike the rest of you*, she didn't need to add.

Olive knew about all kinds of mysteries, and not all of them religious. One late autumn day, when the leaves had all fallen but the snow hadn't yet, Olive showed me a corner in the disused Bloomfield lot that had magical grey dust. If you drew a shape in this dust, she said, and left it there through winter, it would freeze hard and still be there in the spring and forever after. We spent a sunless afternoon with our fingers in the soft dirt drawing angels, winged and haloed like Christmas decorations. I never found out whether our angels survived the snow season. Before the first daffodils came out, Aunt Bella had gone south with her motorman, and I'd moved on to my second aunt in Baltimore.

The only thing small or pointed about Dot was the fineness of her scrutiny. You could get nothing past her, and so I became determined to hide every salient detail of my real self. It's hard to remember which came first, her strategic assaults or my impenetrability. But we were constantly at war, and abstinence became my armour and artillery.

The only thing we agreed on was smell. Dot had a cupboard full of essential oils that I was permitted, under strict conditions, to smell. I learned that lavender could neutralise the venom of a black widow spider. I learned the difference between fungus-fighting tea tree and antiseptic eucalyptus, both from Australia. Later, as a botanist, I would learn that one nation's treasure was another's alien invader; in South Africa, nothing would grow under eucalyptus trees because they made the soil too acid. I also learned that mood-lifting geranium is actually a fynbos – I still can't walk past a pelargonium without rubbing its leaves to test its smell. I liked the energising effect of citruses – neroli, ruby grapefruit, mandarin and lime – but I shunned the cloying florals. Especially rose; Dot's favourite.

Through Dot's oils I learned the origins and properties of plants. I inhaled the essences of herbs, grasses, bark, flowers and berries. (Later, I could sniff out Em's clandestine drinking by the tell-tale whiff of juniper.) I began to travel, not just through the National Geographic images my father shared with me, but via my nose: Indonesian sandalwood, African rosewood, Arabian frankincense, Somalian myrrh, goaty vetiver from the Philippines ... I would close my eyes, inhale, and imagine forests, or fields, or realms that were neither, where flowers hover in the ether. I didn't yet know what an epiphyte was, but later it seemed natural that I would be drawn to them; nominally attached to a host, in reality the plants live on nothing but air.

The labels of lotions and shampoo bottles became tickets to ride. I'd whiz around the world to find calendula and aloe, white ginger and awapuhi, almond and jojoba. I ignored ingredients like 'Wheatgermamidopropyl Ethyldimonium Ethosulfate', which didn't sound remotely botanical.

I would smell just about anything, but there was less and less that I would eat. And so, finally, I was dispatched to Em, who played it slant and left me to my own devices. I flourished under her benign neglect. It made me feel capable. She gave me space to become restless. I was about to become a teenager. School was too easy, rebellion too obvious. I learned to travel through stories instead of smells.

Em's books were piled up everywhere, sliding out of the shelves, toppling over in huge bedside towers she called 'bally-cumber', cluttering up the otherwise minimalist furnishings. I was free to browse – *Fear of Flying* or *The Second Sex*, Dostoyevsky or Didion, *The Wasteland* or *Paris Review*; proof copies, review copies, signed copies – I just had to put the books back more or less where I found them, because there was, Em insisted, order to her biblio-chaos.

One afternoon my aunt found me in a patch of late-season sunshine, paging through Elizabeth Bishop's Time-Life book on Brazil.

'She hated that book,' Em said, seating herself underneath the 'Rothko Red' – my mother's last painting, which took up most of the living-room wall. 'She said the Time-Life editors completely missed the sensibility of the place.' I turned over the static black and white images emphasising industry and the artifice of a new capitol. The book was written in 1962, and showed a country striving to become modern in every sense. Even then I could tell the story needed more green.

'She went on a boat trip in Brazil with Aldous Huxley, did I ever tell you that?' Em was twisting a cigarette into a long ivory holder. 'Down a tributary of the Amazon, I think.' Despite my self-destructive tendencies, I've never been tempted to smoke. But I loved Em's ritual of tamping and twisting and lighting, loved watching the pleasure of her first deep inhalation. Em was older than my mother, but carried herself like a young woman. She sat sideways in the deep chair, swinging her legs over one arm, holding her cigarette in one hand and a squat tumbler of gin on ice in the other.

'Maybe you should go visit your father in Brazil,' Em said now, on the tail end of a particularly long exhalation. 'Dip your toe in the Amazon, tempt some piranhas. Or what do they call those little razor fish that swim up your urinary tract?' She shook the tumbler at me, clinking her ice. It wasn't her first drink for the day.

I stared over my aunt's head at my mother's painting. Stared long enough to lose myself in the green that floated somewhere inside or behind or beyond its layers of red.

Within the month, I was getting stoned on a pier in Brazil with the boat guy who took tourists out to see small alligators and pink dolphins. I helped him improve his English; he gave me unlimited access to the forest and its waterways, and a steady supply of marijuana. We spent evenings watching firefly lights bouncing conjoined parabolas above and below the glassy water. As above, so below; everything mirrored, and the river the fulcrum of it all.

8
Stormy weather

The sky flashed and I counted the seconds before the rumble. Vavi looked up at me and wagged his tail reassuringly. This is a dog that can stand up to snakes, he seemed to be saying: this dog is not scared of thunder! I rang Marilese's doorbell a second time, and fought panic as I heard the empty echo of nobody home.

The storm broke with such violence that we didn't even have time to race back to the car. We sheltered under the roof overhang, watching hailstones the size of quail's eggs hammer the paving of her driveway. The combination of bouncing ice and rising vapour was hypnotic, and I focused on that small microclimate to distract myself from what was happening in the stratosphere above.

Vavi heard the approaching 4X4 before I did, alerting me with a surge of tail-wagging. Then they were there, electric garage doors opening and dogs exploding out of the car and Marilese shouting 'Bloody hell!' as they splashed through new puddles to greet Vavi and his human sidekick.

'Bloody dogs,' she said again, hugging me as the hounds skittered around the vast entrance hallway, knocking over a stand of raincoats, gumboots, umbrellas and horse halters. The smell of animals and wood polish was deeply comforting.

'Tea?' She peered at me through slightly foggy glasses that magnified her gaze, and pointed me towards the kitchen. 'Start without me, I'm going to get out of these wet things.'

I knew this kitchen almost as well as my own, and quickly found all the necessaries. To get to the milk, I had to confront the billboard for perfect family life that was Marilese's refrigerator door: Tristan's latest work of crayon art, a certificate of merit from a local gymkhana, an invitation to a wine tasting.

'Sorry there was no one here when you arrived,' Marilese was rubbing her hair with a towel. She'd changed into something soft and dark that would take her from a yoga class to a cocktail function, and the fog had gone from her glasses. 'Nkosasana is off sick,' she said, rinsing cups in the sink. 'Tristan is on a play-date – do you know he asked me to stop calling it that? I have to say "arrangement" now – and Coraline is at gymnastics. The place is a mess.'

The air outside was still growling as I picked up the tray and followed her back into the living room. This was my favourite place in the house – possibly in any house, anywhere. The vast glass wall allowed the forest in close, framing mountains to one side and letting the city's southern suburbs slide away into insignificance on the other. A sleek wood-burning stove took the edge off the chill.

'If this weather clears before you go, I want to show you what I've done out back.'

When Marilese and Piet bought the place, it was overrun with Port Jackson, the Australian plant introduced to stabilise the sandy, wind-bitten Cape Flats, so people on the wrong side of the racial classification line could be moved there, freeing up the more pleasant, verdant mountain slopes for those with pale skins and privilege. But *Acacia saligna* didn't believe in boundaries, and was soon colonising the very spaces that the human newcomers prized most. It was also edging fynbos out of its native biome – and there's nothing a botanist likes less.

With a little help from her friends (me), Marilese had ousted the aliens and turned her garden into an indigenous showcase. She'd come a long way since that first mountain walk in city shoes. Every year she paints an exquisite series of fynbos watercolours, turns them into greeting cards, and donates all proceeds to the Botanical Society. If I were a missionary, I'd consider her my most successful convert.

As I was setting the tray down, a flash of lightning lit up the window, bringing the trees inside and sending the dogs under the table. The accompanying thunderclap almost masked the sound of shaking crockery.

'I deliberately move to a place that hardly ever has electrical storms, and what good does it do me?' I put one hand over the other to steady the teapot, but my aim still wavered.

'I don't believe in aversion therapy.' Marilese took over the pouring. 'Buddhism is cheaper.' She didn't believe in any kind of therapy, in fact; instead of 'paying someone to care', Marilese had a savings account she called her 'Inner East'. She'd been twice already, to Bali and Tibet, and was angling for me to join her on her next trip. I watched her scoop extra sugar into my cup. 'You look like you need this. Or maybe something a little stronger?'

'No, I'll save that for Sherman's tonight. But thanks.' I took the tea and sipped it gratefully.

'Ah, the party. I wondered what had you rattled. Besides the storm, that is.'

'It's a whole confluence of events, actually.' I told her about the lucky cobra escape, and the impending trip. The next lightning flash reflected off her glasses.

'Will you see your father in Brazil?'

'He might not even be there.' Through the window, the trees shuddered. 'It's funny, when I was little, I thought my father was a very busy hero, sacrificing his time with me to help water and feed the world.'

And then the mighty man fell. As all mighties must. And we had an argument about the Green Revolution.

That wasn't all there was to it. Of course I was horrified to learn that the dams my father engineered were part of the systems that provided irrigation for monoculture. I was full of righteous disgust about the seed schemes local farmers were pressured to join, the ones that depended on fertilisers provided by the same oil companies who patented the seeds. I accused him of helping tie small farmers into 'soft loans' that forced them to leave their smallholdings and migrate to slums and shantytowns. But that was a cover for my real resentment, which was less noble, more personal.

Now the old feud was the only bridge we had to reach each other, and I wasn't letting it go. In 2006, I sent my father a postcard of the inauguration of the Svalbard Global Seed Vault. I connected the dots for him: sponsored by Ford and the Rockefeller Foundation, Bill Gates and Monsanto. 'They call it the Doomsday Vault,' I wrote on the back of the card. 'Interesting choice of name, don't you think?' I just signed it 'M'. He didn't write back. More than once, Bill had called me an idealistic conspiracy theorist. But I had called him much worse the last time we spoke.

'Parents are only human, you know. Once you have kids yourself, you realise that only too well.' Marilese leaned over and poured more tea.

I envied Marilese her extended family. It wasn't about the financial security that came with her father in-law's vast fortune – if anything, I found too much luxury distasteful. (As is the fashion, Marilese and Piet were married on a wine farm; the difference was, his family actually owned it.) What I envied was the regular Sunday braais with cousins, the family holidays to the beach house where three generations had spent every summer. Much as I liked to pretend otherwise, I really, deeply wanted that continuity. I would have denied it then, but I know it now. There's a part of me that will never stop believing in the squeaky-clean ideals of the TV shows of my childhood. Even though my cynical head knows they are no more real than the tokens on Marilese's refrigerator door. Or the kind of ads Nico makes.

On cue, Marilese asked the burning question. 'Does Nico know yet? About your trip?'

'I'll tell him tonight. At Sherman's.' I tried for nonchalance, and failed. 'I don't see how it will make any difference. It's so over. I'm going to tell him that, too.'

Marilese put on a diva pose and snapped her fingers sideways. 'A storm, a snake up and a break up,' she sing-songed. 'They say drama always comes in threes.'

The leaves on the trees outside began to blur, the greens running into one another, their canvas too wet. I tried to make out all the species: Candlewood. Stinkhout. Yellowwood. Cape ash. Waterberry.

'Oh, Maddy, don't, I'm so sorry,' Marilese said, more gently. 'You know he still worships you. He just doesn't know how.'

'How to what? Stop sticking it to other women?'

'How to reach you, Maddy.' Marilese leaned forward and felt for my hand, but I pulled away. I'd had enough self-pitying waterworks for one day. 'I'm not for one minute excusing any of the things he did,' she said quickly. 'We all know he's behaved like a total prick.' She looked away for a minute as if weighing the implications of her disloyalty. 'But I also know that for a long time, he felt he just couldn't really get *in* there.' Her eyes swam vaguely towards my chest. 'Especially after, you know. The whole proposal thing.'

Oh, that. It always came down to that. Nico the spurned. Nico the victim.

I feigned a sudden urge to pee. In the bathroom, there was a tube of toothpaste for 'Tiny Teeth' and a mug that held two small toothbrushes. One was shaped like the squashed blue character from the latest Pixar movie. I half expected it to jump up and start dancing to a tinny jingle.

Too much TV in your formative years – that's what it does to you. Besides the cartoons and the kids' programmes, there were black-and-white reruns from the 1950s where women bashed anguished fists against the chests of the men they desired. Strong men who would pull them close to silence them, looking away over the tops of their heads at something only they could see, while the women kept their eyes tightly shut. Love was Humphrey Bogart slurring on 'schweetheart', it was Lauren Bacall sucking on a cigarette and refusing to leave. It was *To Have and Have Not*.

I stared at a tube of face cream. *Water, kelp, alfalfa, sasparilla, black cohosh, saw palmetto, liquorice, sage, mullein, fenugreek, hops, peppermint, cayenne, cabbage rose* . . . The letters were tiny and the words were shaking. I realised I was shivering. Maybe it was delayed shock. I wrung my hands under the tap for the comfort of warm water.

The sky was still grumbling when I got into my car. Marilese leaned in through the open window to kiss my cheek goodbye. 'Sure you're okay now?'

'Got rubber tyres, I'm shock-proof!' I'd be driving under trees all the way home, too. I've always felt safer under a canopy.

9
Party games

'Dahling!'

Sherman air-kissed a halo around my head and ushered me into his apartment. The lights were low, and the tang of skunk wafting in from the kitchen balcony made me dizzy before I'd been anywhere near a drink.

I saw Kolade holding forth at a low table designed to be a modern version of the campfire. It had a long line of blue-bellied flame licking out of a slit in the middle of it. I've always hated that table. I'm afraid I'll be tempted to lie down on it and let the heat of that flame slice me open.

There was no sign of Nico, but I spotted Justine wedged into the windowed corner that pointed like a glass prow over Kloof Street. She was talking to the notorious letch who made ersatz Tretchikoff rip-offs. He had positioned himself in front of one of his paintings, a blue-tinged woman with arum lilies. As he bent down to light a cigarette at the table flame, Justine widened her eyes at me, and made gagging gestures.

Sherman was at my elbow, juggling something icy in a silver shaker. He handed me an empty martini glass and poured something frothy and lime-scented into it. The first sip started a frozen fiesta on my tongue and lit a cosy fire deeper down.

'God, I needed that.'

Sherman clinked my glass with a small blue bottle of sparkling mineral water. 'You shouldn't stay away so long, sweetness. You know we're always here to help take the edge off.'

I pulled my face into what was supposed to be a smile, but it's impossible to hide anything from Sherman. He never keeps his opinion to himself, judges ferociously, but lets his good friends off lightly. He'd been fence-sitting on the matter of Nico and me for almost a year now, hoping he wouldn't have to take sides. He's known Nico since their first day of school at the impressionable age of six. But he also harboured a special loyalty to me.

'Nico has some agency thing, said he'd be along later.' Sherman watched me as he took a swig from the blue bottle. It was kind of him to save me asking.

'What's with the water – you detoxing?'

Sherman shook his head. 'Long story.' The door buzzer sounded. 'Later, luscious!'

I turned to face a room full of beautiful people. There was a bare-chested man-boy in a tartan waistcoat – he had a Scottie dog on the end of a lead in a matching mini-version. There were models and actors and artists – a few faces I recognised from television, but I didn't know their names. To get to Justine, I had to push past a woman whining to a famous metal sculptor about how she wanted to do AfrikaBurn in a retro Winnebago, but some guy had bought every single one in the country and put them up on the roof of a hotel in the city centre. There were none of my Institute colleagues in this hipster crowd. This was Nico's world, but it also reminded me of my aunt's New York art scene. I have a distant sense of smoky rooms like this one, only with more brown furniture and 1970s shag.

By the time I reached Justine my glass was empty, but fighting my way back to the kitchen bar felt like too much effort. Justine pulled me down onto the couch, wedging me between herself and the letch artist, who was deep in debate with Kolade about the significance of Die Antwoord.

'Bart,' Justine tugged on his sleeve. 'Go get us that pitcher of punch from Sherman, won't you?' She was poured into a red dress that made the most of her considerable charms, but Bart ignored her.

'What do you mean, Steve Biko said it first?' he blazed at Kolade. His nose was veined from years of supporting South African Breweries.

'Have you even *read* Steve Biko, Bart?' Justine had to lean over me to goad him, and it was making me claustrophobic.

'I bet he never said, "Black, white, coloured – everything fucked into one person"!'

'No,' said Kolade, 'he had a lot more finesse.' Kolade put his hand over his heart as if he was taking the Hippocratic oath all over again: 'For a genuine fusion of the lifestyles each group must be able to attain its style of existence without encroaching on or being thwarted by another.' He lowered his hand. '*That's* Biko.'

Through the window, I could see car lights tumbling down the slope towards the harbour. I watched them cluster around the traffic lights. The pods of privilege would be surrounded by hungry street kids. But the cars had central locking, and the kids were seldom lucky.

'Your Breyten Breytenbach called his own people a bastardised nation obsessed with purity.' Kolade, ever the measured medical man, was still trying to reason with the drunk artist. 'Die Antwoord just usurped gangsta rap to say exactly the same thing.'

When I came to Cape Town, I expected postmodern hybridity. Instead, I found dislocation. A shared sense of displacement that didn't seem enough to bind people together. This collection of tribes, so far from everywhere, seemed permanently unsettled. Nobody belonged here, so everybody did. It made for a *dis*comfort zone, and that suited me fine. Cape Town is a place you can disappear in. That – and the uniqueness of the floral kingdom – was the reason I was still here.

Bart's alternative Afrikaner artistic set had rebelled against apartheid evils by being as eccentric as they could. Now the bad guys were harder to pin down. Struggle heroes had become self-serving politicians or corrupt tenderpreneurs. Ordinary people felt powerless. This place had lost its moral centre, and yet wherever you stood, just by being here, you were taking a stand. Living here was a lesson in the impossibility of the non-position. I longed to escape the incessant self-questioning. Just then, Brazil felt like a nation on the up, in love with itself and its unified hybridity. Of course I knew that racism was just as endemic, if not as systemic, in that country. But Sherman's drink was strong. And I am prone to wishful thinking.

Bart was frowning so hard, he was squinting. 'Sherman, you moffie!' he yelled, startling everyone into momentary silence. 'Bring us some more of that bloody drink!'

Kolade put his hand on Bart's arm to calm him. I could imagine being one of his patients, lulled into serenity while he explained the life-or-death complexities of impending anaesthesia. But Bart shook him off.

'Ag jissus man, you all talk kak!' He stood up and stumbled towards the kitchen.

'Good riddance, Hum-bart Hum-bart,' Justine muttered, pushing me over to fill the space he had left. The seat was hot and clammy. 'Honestly, I don't know why you humour him, K.'

Kolade turned the beam of his smile on me. 'So, Miss Flowers, where've you been hiding?'

'Where is that *drink* hiding?'

And there was Sherman bearing down on us, twirling his shaker of elixir. He squashed in next to Justine and reached over her to fill our glasses. I downed my drink, and immediately held my glass out for another. Sherman filled it to the brim. I was starting to feel much, much better.

'This would work well with cachaça, you know that? I'll bring you some back from Brazil.'

'You're going to Brazil?' All eyes on me now.

'Looks like it.'

'Rio?' It's everybody's fantasy first stop.

'Salvador. Much further up.'

'Little Africa.' There was a wistfulness in the way Kolade said it.

'You've been there?'

He shook his head. 'Always wanted to. I have a friend from there.'

'What's he say about it?'

'She.' He stared into the table flame, his thoughts flickering elsewhere. 'It's a powerful place.'

'There's a plant we're looking for,' I told them. 'It's extinct in Africa now. The theory is it might have been taken over there by slaves from West Africa . . .'

'They used to be a perfect fit, the bulges of West Africa and South America. Used to lie together, like this.' Kolade curved the palm of his right hand to cup his left fist.

'Ooh, spooned lovers!' Justine wriggled and adjusted her cleavage. How much had she had to drink? In my own mind, considerably more relaxed now than when I'd arrived, I saw the continents swirl together into a conjoined yin-yang.

'Alas, poor lovers – continental drift tore them apart.' Kolade released his hands and let them fall into his lap. 'In a perverse kind of way, the Atlantic slave trade linked them back together.'

I wondered again about his 'friend' in Salvador. I followed the little star seed in my mind, crossing the Atlantic in a pocket, or sewn into the hem of a blanket, tipped into soil far away, but not so very different from its home ground. After all, as Kolade said, the lands had once been connected.

Justine was shaking the upended shaker over her empty glass. 'If I go make more, Bart will be back here to take my place in a flash,' Sherman told her. Bart was glowering at the edge of our seated circle, clutching a tumbler as if it would stop him from falling over.

'Please don't go, Sherman.' I offered Justine my own glass. 'Here.'

'Sweet Jesus, this is good.' Justine had all but drained the drink before I could claim it back. 'What are you doing drinking mineral water when you can make concoctions like these?'

'In a way, it was spirits that got me here.' Sherman was not a large man. When he affected an Irish lilt the way he did just then, what with his little goatee and pointy sideburns, he reminded me of a leprechaun. But the story he told wasn't a fairy tale; it was a ghost story.

Sherman had poured his life savings into his new gallery. When the collection was held up in Customs, it threatened to delay the opening, leaving him with all the overheads to pay. 'I was sick with worry. Sick!' Sherman paled at the memory. 'I couldn't eat – but blow me if I couldn't drown my sorrows!' He swigged hard at the water, as if he wished it were something else. 'Then one morning I woke up horribly babelaas, and spoke to my grandma about the problem.'

'Your *dead* grandma?'

'Yes. I did a little ceremony, just me and her.'

'What, incense, flowers, little white candles?' Justine was not one for what she called 'hippy shit'. I shushed her with an elbow in the ribs.

'And suddenly there she was. I mean *really* there. And she told me, "Everything will come out all right, my boy, but you have to stop this drinking."'

I was struggling to silence my own inner sceptic, and clamped down on Justine's leg to stop her saying anything else.

'Which is ironic, because you know what an old piss-cat she was. She gave me my first shot of whisky when I turned ten. My reward for reaching double digits, she said. So I knew she must be serious. "Granny," I told her, "if you help me with this thing, I won't touch a drop for a month. I promise."' He sat back, satisfied, and took another long pull from his water bottle.

'And?'

'And the next day, they released my shipment. That was three weeks ago – as you know, the opening went off fabulously.' He clinked his bottle against Kolade's beer. 'I haven't touched a drop since. Feel rather marvellous, actually.'

Justine's giggling was contagious. There were a handful of white sangomas at the party, but the thought of Sherman the style-merchant practising ancestor worship seemed absurd.

'Maybe I shouldn't bring you that bottle of cachaça, then.'

'Oh, bring back that bottle of firewater, sweetness,' he said. 'Bring ten. I've only got a week of sobriety left.' He leaned in, mock-serious. 'Just don't piss off any ancestors while you're over there. I have a whole new appreciation for their power.'

My late grandmother would have called the shiver I felt just then a goose walking over my grave.

10
Sparks

The narrow balcony off Sherman's small kitchen was crowded, so Kolade and I squeezed together on one of the fire-escape steps a few rungs down. A fog of reefer smoke hung above us like a fragrant umbrella.

It turned out Kolade knew quite a bit about Salvador, thanks to the 'friend' who grew up in the Candomblé tradition. He wouldn't be drawn about the girl, but he told me plenty about the factions within and between some terreiros, and about the influential government and society figures they counted among their members.

He even knew something about their plants. Besides the many shared plants that came from both Africa and Brazil, each terreiro has its own special herbs, Kolade told me, specific to it alone and shared with no one. A terreiro would go to great lengths to protect their sacred plant lines. 'If your seed is so rare,' Kolade said, 'it could well be one of those that are most sacred. What makes you think you can just walk in there and ask them to hand it over?'

'My irresistible charm?'

He rolled his eyes at me.

'Their innate altruism?'

'Even you are not that naïve, flower girl.'

'Look, I'm offering to protect the plant, take it from the brink of extinction and ensure that it survives into the future, whatever that might hold for the plant's natural habitat. That's a *good* thing. Surely they'll see the benefit in that?'

'And what's in it for them? If they are taking perfectly good care of the plant themselves, why on earth should they share any of it with you?'

He was right, annoyingly. 'For a doctor, you know an awful lot about this. What's this, your grandma's Yoruba wisdom?'

'As it happens, my grandmother was full of old-school Yoruba wisdom. But no. My friend got caught up on the wrong side of this, and it was scary stuff.' Somebody passed a reefer down from above. K took a long toke before passing it on to me. 'I'm just saying.' The last part came out in a swallowed rush as he tried not to exhale.

I was starting to feel pleasantly light-headed. 'You're not trying to scare me off with voodoo, are you?'

'Look, it's not about right or wrong or what you believe. You don't have to believe in it, just know that belief itself is powerful juju.'

'I should believe in belief? A hardened atheist like me?' I handed back the joint. What *did* I think about the power of belief? I believe in science. Which includes some unfathomable mysteries. What was it Einstein said? It took me a moment to find the words. '*The most beautiful thing we can experience is the mysterious.* I believe that.'

The look he gave me was loaded with gravitas. 'Candomblé is not just some colourful cultural tourism stop, Maddy. People live and die by it. It's ancient. And it's powerful.' He flicked the roach over the stairwell railing, and we watched its spark flare briefly as it fell into the well of the courtyard below. 'Your science and mine, they are irrelevant in that world. Bear that in mind, and be careful. That's all.'

11
Starting over

Even before Nico arrived, but after too many refills from the silver flask, I started feeling that bittersweet sense of impending loss that comes in the midst of a perfect moment. The way you can be enjoying something so desperately you want to cry, not because the moment lacks anything, but because nothing, ultimately, can fill the gulf of need that lies beneath it, no matter how scintillating the conversation, or how lovely the conversationalist, or how exotic the setting. You just want to cry. But you mustn't, so you turn on the high beams instead. And with enough alcohol, it almost works.

Of course, he made an entrance. Looking perfectly dishevelled, as if he'd forgone basic grooming in the hurry to grace us with his presence – though the clothes were top-end, and the bed-head lovingly gelled. He brought a celebrity appendage; she was tall, willowy and wearing a knock-out dress that seemed to be made of nothing but plastic discs, artfully wired together. Everyone was staring, checking the dress for strategic gaps. The two of them seemed to be glowing with shared fabulousness. Or shared stimulant. It didn't help that the soap star – appropriately named Candy – had recently sunk to a new low to feed her habit. She appeared in one of those excruciating toilet cleaner ads where a minor star knocks on your door and asks to inspect the smears on your porcelain. Suspension of disbelief aside, who would *ever* entertain such a request? To up the celebrity quotient, Candy was usually accompanied on her TV household visits by a rugby flank, an affable giant loved by everyone. He wasn't here now, so she was slumming it with the campaign manager instead.

'Oh my God, it's the toilet queen!' At moments like this, I really loved Justine.

We met on the kitchen balcony, cushioned by the marijuana haze. Nico was drunk, but not too drunk to miss my recoil from his sour breath when he leaned in to kiss my cheek.

'You drove like that?' I hadn't intended to sound so accusatory. When exactly had our every interaction started clanging wrong?

'What's this about Brazil?'

I knew Sherman was a fast operator, but this had to be a new record. And while I searched for the right words, I was overtaken by a sense memory. The thought of Brazil – *my* Brazil, lush and green, a place familiar enough to feel comfortable in and vast enough to lose myself in, *that* Brazil felt safe. I wanted to be unknown. To have the excuse of work and the promise of some kind of homecoming, if I chose. In that moment, I fell from the edge of indifference to a plateau of total certainty. I wanted this escape.

'It's just a work trip,' I lied.

'Nice to be the last to know.'

Thanks for nothing, Sherman. Standing there, I became aware of how profoundly tired I was of the thrust and parry that every conversation with Nico had become. So very weary of waiting to duck the next punch, while planning a pre-emptive jab of my own. I stared at his shoes – he always wore sneakers, even with a suit. Especially with a suit. It was his trademark. An attempt to come across as childlike. Disarming. I caught a whiff of perfume, feminine.

'I see you brought your work with you. Or is she just another expedient exaggeration?' I hated myself for the words the minute they left my mouth.

'*North by Northwest!*' He laughed too loudly. It was – had been – our favourite Hitchcock line. Cary Grant striding between skyscrapers, claiming there was no such thing as a lie in advertising. But it felt wrong, here, now.

His laugh dropped and his mood veered, in the way of the inebriated. 'You're always so fucking evasive. I just don't know where you're at.' He was ducking down, weaving in front of me, trying to catch my eye. How hard was it to understand that evasion was protection, that looking away was my way of angling the feelings away from me? He was trying to be cute, with his ridiculous dipping from side to side. For an instant, he reminded me of the cobra. Had that really only been a few hours ago?

'Look at me.' He grabbed my arm much too roughly. 'Look at me!'

And that was that. I pulled my arm away and stepped back. 'It's over, Nico.'

'You're doing this here? Now?' His indignation seemed genuine.

'I'm sorry.' I reached out a hand to him, but he held a finger up to stop me. Swayed, steadied himself with a flattened palm on the balcony balustrade.

'You're always so quick to cut and run,' he slurred. 'Just remember, every time you cut your losses, you create new ones.'

How could he pull out that bit of wisdom, in his state? I wasn't going to stay to find out. I left him leaning heavily on the balustrade looking at the sky, focusing on something further away than the stars.

As for me, I was starting over again. In Brazil.

In Transit

I'm tired, by now, of running against direction over travelators. I must have traversed five miles of airport, terminals one two three and back around again, past the bad-tempered businessmen corkscrewed from pulling their wheelie bags one-handed, the frayed families who look like they want nothing more than to sever the tethers that bind their brood. Past the snack stands and the perfumeries, the scarf and mascot vendors shutting up shop, relief showing on their grey faces as they pull their steel grids down until morning.

When was morning? I've lost track of time. The featureless grey sky seems to be paused, waiting. And the people slumped in clusters around defunct departure gates are paused, waiting. The empty chairs are paused, waiting, and the waiter L-bent behind the counter at the juice stand with his head in his folded arms, sleeping – he has run out of fruit, and even in his dreams he is paused, waiting. I wish I could sleep again, but I'm fuelled by something I can't shake.

There's no gym in this airport, so I've shouldered my backpack like the turtle willing to win the race and I'm running, jogging, fast-walking, sprinting, down broad passageways too bright with refracted light. And as I come around for the nth time, I can see that some of the waiting passengers are paused, waiting, for me; some seem to be counting off the number of times they see me coming. The first few times they smile and make eye contact, then they look mildly alarmed, and by now they probably wish I would stop pounding past, but have accepted me as part of this long suspended moment. A metronome that doesn't so much mark the passing of time as the inherent rhythm of return contained within it.

Eventually, my way is blocked by an airport guard. He is sympathetic, kind even. Has a kindly little paunch; his tool belt, police issue, has to angle down to accommodate it. No gun here, just a Taser swinging, benign. This is probably like a beach outing for him. Instead of drug busts and bomb checks, he is reuniting wayward children with their families, guiding mothers to places where they can warm milk, managing queues, tempering frustrations, smoothing rough edges. I've become an edge, with my incessant pacing. He understands. But he asks me to please stop. He is very polite. The kind of polite that brooks no argument.

What now? The floor is too gleaming, the fluorescent lights, far up overhead in the vaulted ceiling, are too bright. I feel like the marble in a pinball machine. Dizzy. The concourse buzz is a constant background hum, but I can pick out individual sounds as I career into and away from them – the bleep of cash tills, the electric whine of printers spewing out receipts. Cans clattering against the inside of vending machines, cutlery scraping against plates, voices rising and falling, but mostly muttering complaint. There are occasional announcements, but the signs never change – DELAYED DELAYED DELAYED. *We are sorry for the inconvenience ... Please be patient ... Awaiting update ... No word yet as to when ... Further news to follow shortly.* People gravitate to TV screens to watch the cone-shaped mountain spew smoke with no sign of abating; then wander away, expectations defeated. They will return again too soon, borne on another wave of hope doomed to be dashed.

These huge airport windows are like giant TV screens, but the same nothing is happening out there. Planes hulk like slumbering giants, all lined up with nowhere to go. Why don't the pre-flight safety displays, with their drop-down masks, lifebelt whistles and the head-to-knee crash position, convince passengers of the impossibility of flight? Perhaps they should be shown a mathematical equation for Bernoulli's principle, so that they could see how vulnerable they are to density, how reliant on airflow over wings that defied logic in the first place. Defied logic, but also, luckily, defied gravity. A little like love.

Parked in lines and eerily quiet now, the planes are great silver seedpods, ready to be filled with people who will be dispersed at their destination. Seeds had propellers before planes did, because all seeds are made for travel. Some corkscrew great distances through the air, some gust like ghosts trailing tendrils. There are seeds that hitch rides in the guts of elephants, relying on pachyderm digestive acids to burn chinks in their carapaces; they'll sprout when they finally drop to earth, encased in nourishing dung.

Drift seeds bob down rivers or cross oceans – I have a dark brown Sea Heart on my desk at the Institute. I picked it up on a beach near Durban, far from the tropical Americas where it might have begun. I've rubbed it like a giant worry bead, glossed its brown skin thinking about its adventures on the currents – Gulf Stream, Equatorial, Canary, Brazil, Atlantic, Benguela, somehow making its way around Africa's tip and up to the tropical sands of KwaZulu-Natal. It sits on my desk between a framed photograph of Vavilov, stiff-suited with a sheaf of Mexican corn in his hand; and a postcard from Em, a New England autumn scene with a Rachel Carson quote: *Those who contemplate the beauty of the earth find reserves of strength that will endure as long as life lasts.*

When I'm desk-bound, that Sea Heart has all the beauty of the earth in it, and all its travels. It reminds me of the pips Johnny Appleseed carried in sacks, balancing counterweight on his double-hulled canoe as he travelled up the Mississippi, spreading sweet fruits to pioneer farmers. It reminds me of the seeds carried in pockets, in saddlebags, in tins and barrels and crates. Seeds secreted across borders, traded at market fairs, sent with daughters as dowries. Seeds that beat impossible odds, like the Abu Ghraib seeds. There was a seed bank there, before it became an infamous prison, with thousand-year-old specimens, ancient Mesopotamian grains that were secreted into Syria during the Gulf War. Just like the ones smuggled past Gestapo agents into Vavilov's Leningrad vault, the ones his fellow plant geneticists died protecting during the nine-hundred-day siege. They starved to death, those stalwart seed guardians, in a storeroom of pulses and grains.

And then there's *Newbouldia mundii*. My Saint-Exupéry planet of a seed, ridged with its tiny volcanoes; a tiny time capsule containing everything it needs to tell its tale, when conditions are right. What kind of transit did it endure? What rough sea voyages, narrow escapes, enforced dormancy, what long limbo, before it arrived on new and fertile soil? Whose hands helped it survive? Which mutations, over time, made it more suitable for its Brazilian here and now than its African there and then?

The concrete apron I can see through the huge windows is unfriendly to seeds. It makes me feel small and hard and ineffectual. So what if there are fifteen hundred banks around the world and counting, storing the seeds most useful to humans? What about those we haven't yet identified? What about those that have no apparent use, there just for their own sake, working unrecognised miracles in their ecosystems? I'd be happy not to find them, if I knew they would be safe where they are. If one in five of them wasn't facing extinction.

They've stopped me running, but my mind is still going round and round. I don't care what time it is, it's cocktail hour somewhere. Earlier, I'd run past a relatively quiet bar tucked away on a mezzanine. I start walking in that direction. Now that I know where I'm going, I don't feel the need to move quite so fast.

The bar is dark and comforting. Its back wall is mirrored with ye-olde-worlde signage that could do with some Windowlene. I order a single whisky and turn my back to the mirrors so I don't have to see my pale face through adverts for malt and ale. There's a TV in the corner, but mercifully the sound is turned down. On the other wall, a frozen flight board hangs with its suspended arrivals and departures. What are all the air traffic controllers doing right now, relieved of their duty to plot those flight paths? I don't envy them having to untangle the spaghetti when everything gets going again. Flying is an act of faith: faith that those controllers will make sure their vectors never intersect.

The unpronounceable ash-spewer is still top news, but the ticker-tape running along the bottom of the TV screen tells of other events. Life goes on, it reassures us. A dispute threatens the Pakistan-India one-day international (limited overs). Wild fires are spreading through Russian wheat fields, tinder-dry from drought. Cheers, Vavilov. What would you say to the GM foods infiltrating natural gene pools? Or about 'terminator genes'? What mad scientist dreamed that one up? Do they have a plan, you might ask, if that terminator gene goes rogue? Begins spreading to other plants? If they can't turn it off, you would surely tell them, it would stop the current of life at the mains.

During our last argument, my father accused Vavilov of being a communist plant. ('Ha ha,' I'd said.) I was a bit drunk at the time. We were in a bar in Manaus, and I'd had too many gin and tonics. I drink them in malaria areas for their prophylactic effect, even though gin makes me belligerent. I prefer the amber comfort of whisky. And now there is only ice in the glass sweating on the countertop in front of me. I signal to the barman for another.

Bill was brought up in a family of girls who fed his ego and fostered the selfishness that drove my mother over the edge. That's what I told him. Even before the lightning took her, I said. You made her crazy, even before then.

'It wasn't the lightning, Maddy.'

I hated him for denying it. 'I guess it was just you, then.'

I have a recurrent memory. Not the kind triggered by a smell, or linked to an angle of sunlight on a certain street corner, but one that comes riding in, bareback on a mustang of emotion. It surprises me at random moments. When I remember the back of him, leaving the bar. The vulnerable nape of his neck. My father, the child. I didn't want to feel sorry for him. I needed to be furious.

Because there's something else that always comes riding in alongside that memory. A little pony called shame.

I took the first plane out the next morning. I didn't see my father before I left. That was ten years ago. We haven't spoken since.

It might be time to speak to him now. I'm not sure. Damn this volcano for forcing me to face him, if only in the recesses of my mind.

The whisky isn't helping quell my anxiety, but a few hands of Texas hold 'em might. This bar has wi-fi, so I pull my laptop out of my backpack. While I wait for Party Poker to load, I watch Justin Bieber being lashed with a belt by a talk-show host, and add my name to a petition, 'Protecting Access to Genetic

Resources and the Fair and Equitable Sharing of Benefits Arising from their Utilisation'. A mouthful of marbles, even if I hadn't had a few stiff drinks. So much for seeds being the 'most democratic experience on the planet', as Vandana Shiva so beautifully put it. Try as they might to spread their abundance, plant genes were being straitjacketed, their escape routes blocked, their natural terrains fenced in and tarred over. And the more vigilant governments get about protecting indigenous resources, the more desperate companies become to get their hands on 'exclusive' genes.

I don't believe that adding my digital signature will make an iota of difference in combating bio-piracy, but neither can it do any harm. I always feel a frisson of inappropriate pleasure when I see the word 'bio-piracy' – I can't help picturing my colleagues raising Jolly Rogers in the field as they sit munching trail mix. It might be a dirty word, but even I can see the advantage of bending the rules if it means benefiting a species, rather than a corporation. I can't see any of my colleagues being turned by the lure of money. But if they thought they were saving the planet? They'd hoist the flag.

A thought floats in, lazy on a whisky cloud: If I were a bio-pirate, mine would be the perfect cover. You don't need a visa to enter Brazil, so I'm coming in as a tourist. With a letter from the Institute, and a professor at a Salvador university waiting to introduce me into my first terreiro. From there, it'll just be a matter of getting the state permissions. Kirk should have put in the applications already: 'Just go in as a tourist,' he'd said. 'We'll take care of the paperwork as and when you find the seeds.'

I'm still waiting for a game to start, and my email alert flashes. It's from Em. She's up late. Or early. '*On our earth we are much too small to clean out our volcanoes. That is why they bring no end of trouble upon us.*' All Em's emails have literary quotes in the subject line. This one is from *The Little Prince.* Which is funny, because I don't remember mentioning my little planet seed to her.

> *What a troublesome little berg, and now there you all are, grounded and circling one another like animals in a zoo, with no way out! How perfectly awful. I hope you are taking notes.*

At times like this, I really miss my aunt. Maybe I should visit her on the way back. I have enough money for a quick side trip to New York, thanks to my nest egg of stashed poker winnings.

Em doesn't know about my poker habit. Hardly anybody does. But everybody needs a secret. Mine is my unexpected talent for cards. Poker is the one place where I am infinitely patient. I bide my time and strike when the time is right. If I play tight, curb my tendency to be reckless, the winnings pile up.

The game is about to start. I'll reply to Em later. I get dealt two cards: an ace and an eight. The 'Dead Man's Hand' – my favourite. It's the only hand I allow myself to be sentimental about. It's the one Wild Bill Hickok was holding when he made his last stand in a town called Deadwood. He was shot in the back by a coward with a vendetta while he sat, winning cards in hand. The moral of the story: watch your back. So I'll take some time to suss out the rest of the table before I act. Fold and observe.

I sometimes wonder which is my true nature – the death wish, or the slow, steady hand. But I won't get a chance to test my mettle this time. A wave of excitement is sweeping through the concourse. The flight ban has been lifted. The planes are starting to move.

PART II
INCOMING

I
Colours

Salvador, Bahia

There can be only one first time, before the thrill of the unfamiliar becomes mundane. I wanted to savour it.

Salvador wasn't what I expected. It didn't smell like the Manaus of my early childhood, pervaded by river stench. That sandy settlement, carved out of the jungle, always felt temporary, in spite of its airport and its baroque opera house. This place was different. It wasn't *every square inch filled with foliage*, which was how Elizabeth Bishop saw nature greeting the Portuguese explorers when they landed in Rio's Guanabara Bay. I didn't have to reach for the book to recall the words in 'Brazil, January 1, 1502':

> *big leaves, little leaves, and giant leaves,*
> *blue, blue-green, and olive,*
> *with occasional lighter veins and edges,*
> *or a satin underleaf turned over*

There was little green in this city's tapestry, despite the tendency for a tropical plant to find foothold in any neglected gap. Instead there were concrete jungle flowers. Every spare space was tagged with graffiti, each artist seeming to respect what went before by finding new spaces to fill, rather than writing over the old.

Most of the tags were monochrome, black on grey. It was the people that provided the colour. I remembered how Brazilians confounded their census-accountants with poetry back in 1998, describing themselves in terms more delicious than anything that could be ticked inside a bureaucratic box. *Caramel*, they wrote in the space reserved for skin-colour; *burnt sugar, chocolate, toast, coffee-with-cream*. That year, there were a hundred and forty-three different answers to the question of race – including 'navy blue', 'green', and 'the colour of a fleeing ass'.

Coffee was just one of the smells that came in through the open window of the taxi. The other was oily and spiced. If a smell could have a colour, this one was orange. It reminded me that I hadn't eaten for a while.

'What are they selling?' I asked Fernando, my designated taxi driver. We were passing a group of Baiana women bent over roadside braziers. Their hair was tied up in white headscarves, their full white skirts anachronistic alongside the plastic and the baubles that spilled out of the storefronts. Modest clothes from another era; worn in this one as a mark of pride. *Emancipated from mental slavery . . .*

'Acarajé,' he said over his shoulder. 'Beans, shrimps and spices, fried in dendê. Foods of their orixás.' He pronounced it 'orishas'. The Candomblé deities. Even mixed with smog and diesel, the smell made my mouth water. After three days of eating in airplanes and airports, I needed some real food. 'You will try some,' he assured me, with total certainty. 'Very delicious.'

Fernando had a medallion of St Christopher dangling on a long chain from his rear-view mirror. Every time he took a corner, it pendulumed from side to side. I wondered how he felt about those other gods. *Their orixás*. If he managed to comfortably accommodate multiple pantheons. I didn't know him well enough to ask him, yet. But I would. Fernando was someone I would come to trust and rely on, in the weeks ahead.

I was surprised – and relieved – to be met at the airport. He stood there with my name scrawled on a sheet of paper clutched to his bony chest, a skinny oasis of calm among the throng of taxi hawkers. 'Two days, we waited for you,' he told me without reproach. Senhor Fernando was nominally attached to the pousada I had booked in Pelourinho. I'd arranged a transfer from the airport, but I really hadn't expected it to be there after all the delays.

The traffic congealed around a hub crowded with billboards. Poster-sized families were happy here the same way they were anywhere else – in bright primary colours and with the help of the right kind of cola, followed by the perfect toothpaste to counteract decay.

They were probably much the same in 1951, when Elizabeth Bishop arrived here for a short holiday. She ate the fruit of a caju and became violently ill. If it isn't shelled properly, the seed of the ubiquitous cashew nut can be as toxic as its cousin, poison ivy. Bishop didn't know that. She didn't know she would be one of the rare ones who react to the fruit. But even bloated like a blowfish, Elizabeth was able to captivate Maria Carlota Costallat de Macedo Soares. The Carioca architect and intellectual better known as 'Lota' became the love of her life. Because of her, and because Brazil was Brazil, Elizabeth stayed for fifteen years.

She won the Pulitzer Prize and wrote the Time-Life book on Brazil – the one I paged through that afternoon when Em suggested I play with Amazonian piranhas. That trip launched my love affair with plants. I had Elizabeth to thank for that.

Which was ironic, because that book had so little of the natural Brazil in it. 'Not a single bird, beast or flower – in Brazil!' Elizabeth lamented to her friend Robert Lowell. It was no small thing that my aunt gave me her copy of that book; it was autographed by the author. Bishop had refused to sign it at first, Em told me, because she was so horrified by what the *Life* editors had done to it. Slashing and burning her thickets of words. Excising her love of nature.

Somehow Em convinced her to sign. I used to trace my finger over the scrawl on the inside cover. *Do not believe a word of this false propaganda*, it said, in furious letters, small and slanted. In her own hand, Em had added, *Discover for yourself.* Em never made it to Brazil. She encouraged me to do the discovering instead.

'A Cidade Alta.' Fernando's voice cut into my reverie. A different kind of colour seeped in as we ascended to the high city. The streets grew narrower as we spiralled upwards. Tall buildings leaned in across cobbled lanes to talk about old times. The taxi sputtered and strained to the summit, an open square where Fernando cranked up his hand-brake and stopped to orientate me and, I suspected, to give his jalopy a breather.

Pelourinho showed off its colonial accoutrements like an ageing belle swishing mouldy petticoats. Here the buildings wore ice-cream colours – peppermint and strawberry, tangerine and caramel. Some were faded, some wore the grime of ages in black smoke streaks, mould and fungus. Some had been recently repainted so their white detailing stood out like icing on a Christmas cake. Arched windows looked out with cartoon eyes, lashed with filigreed wrought-iron balconies. And the roofs – covered in curved terracotta tiles in variegated colours, they stretched down the hill to the right like the flank of an enormous calico cat. On my left, the pastel façades culminated at the top of the hill in a tall, pale-blue church. Twice as high as its neighbours, it reminded me of an over-optimistic wedding cake; an ornate architectural triumph of hope over experience.

'Largo do Pelourinho,' Fernando said, jerking his head up the hill towards the slanted square. The whipping post – named for the activity that defined this area at the height of the slave era. A paper wrapper floated towards me on the dark stream that bled down a gutter. Everything looked a little more sombre, through the lens of its history.

It took us another twenty minutes to reach the pousada. It wasn't far from the square, as the crow flies, but to reach it, Fernando had to negotiate a maze of cobbled back-roads and side streets, and plead with a delivery truck whose driver was deep in conversation with a dona in hot-pants on a balcony.

When Fernando finally left me in the lobby of the Lua Azul, he warned me not to venture into the neighbourhood alone at night, and reminded me that he was always only a phone call away. He refused the tip I offered him on top of his fee, and left with a sulphurous backfire bang.

My room was a white cube with blue-painted shutters opening out over the harbour, far below at the bottom of the cliff, and the industrial grey ocean that reached back to where I had come from. I wanted to explore the neighbourhood, find a good meal, stretch out on the wide flat bed under the ceiling fan. But thanks to the volcano's tantrum, I had lost two days. There was a message waiting for me at reception. It was from Ernesto, my terreiro contact. There was a ceremony at the Ilê Axé Bençois tonight, and they were expecting me.

Fernando and his taxi had only just made it down to the lower city when the receptionist called him back up the hill. I barely had time to shower and change. Tonight would be my first introduction to Candomblé. *Wear white*, the message said.

2
Drums

It felt more like a pageant than a religious ceremony. But after about an hour, it started to make sense. I began to recognise the shift in rhythm that heralded the arrival of each new orixá. Before the costume changes, before the colour shifts, even before the drawing inward of a dancer, when a new spirit was about to take over a corporeal son or daughter and spin a new story, I sensed it in the drum beat.

The drumming was relentless and hypnotic. Each change in tempo was also a change in energy and personality, taken in, communally, by all the participants in the ceremony, whether initiate, elder, local, tourist, or 'other', like me.

I sat in the women's section, which faced the men's along one side of the barracão. Towards the front of the hall, where the stage would have been if there was one, a door led to a mysterious space from which plates of food and costumed figures emerged at irregular intervals.

There were two sets of entrance doors at the back of the hall. Men and women streamed in and out, separately, to and from the dark, cooling night. Against the long walls, cement benches tiered from floor to ceiling.

I arrived late, but found a place in the body crush about three tiers up from the floor. A group of excitable blonde tourists, speaking too loudly, sat a bit further along the bench. I distanced myself from them mentally, focusing instead on a row of little girls standing in front of me.

The children were small and nimble, and preoccupied with sharing out a packet of colourful sweets – the candy-coated chocolate button kind.

The little girl directly in front of me had dark hair tightly braided with white ribbons at the end of each cord – her only concession to white. Most people in the hall wore white; a sign of respect to the spirits being honoured here. But this little girl wore a pink and white striped T-shirt over a frilled and faded red skirt. I imagined the rules were different for children.

Every so often the girl would break off her candy negotiation, close her eyes and immerse herself unselfconsciously in the rhythm. She couldn't have been more than seven or eight years old, but she flicked and rotated her skinny hips in a manner way beyond her years, opening a window to the sensuality I was sure she would one day practise with more self-conscious skill.

She was not just pulsing with the beat, not performing an obvious parody of what she must have seen her mother, and countless other women, do as part of their birth right. She had surrendered herself to it, utterly.

So had the spinning women on the floor, dervishes whose long skirts flared out, stiffened by motion and layers of white petticoats. One was decked out in ornate gold brocade, with rivers of seemingly precious gold chains and trinkets, even though they were probably made of painted plastic. She held a hand mirror, preening and spinning and reflecting and weaving, like water.

Facing them, from her two tiers up, the young girl jiggled and swayed, gyrating to the pulse she had taken inside her, eyes closed, fist closed around a handful of the sweets. When she opened her eyes and hand and looked down, they had run into rivulets of colour that coalesced in the centre of her palm like a chocolaty stigmata. She shoved the congealed mess into her mouth, throwing a look of bliss and triumph at her small neighbour, who had long since finished her own handful.

I felt my face crease into a smile, but when the child turned around, I looked away – I had shared this intimacy without permission.

That was when I noticed that I was being watched.

The drummer held my line of sight and didn't falter in the rhythm he was beating out on his tall, carved drum, even as he saw me register him. There were about ten drummers in the drum pit, directly in front of the women's section. They were grouped with their backs to us and turned slightly towards one another, so that a nod or a glance could initiate a change in beat, as they weaved their percussive spell over the terreiro. He was on the far edge of the group, head tilted to keep an eye on his fellow drummers. Except that his eye was tethered to me.

My watcher's left hand palmed slow time, while in his right, he flicked a stick that teased the skin of his drum. He didn't smile. He just looked. And played. I wasn't sure if he was even seeing me.

I felt my own lips pull into a tentative arc.

He was nodding his head – to me, to the beat? – swaying slightly with the rhythm, stroking, beating, nodding.

I found myself swaying and nodding, too.

The little girl in front of me turned again to look at me, then looked back at the man.

She elbowed her friend and said something I couldn't hear. The friend also turned to look.

Senhorita Magdalena?

3
Called

At first I didn't register that the voice was calling me. I'd been away so long, I had to get used to hearing my full name again – Mad-da-LE-na, with a silent 'g', the long emphasis on the third syllable, and a definitive stress on the last that made me feel like I was being underlined. My mother loved to tell me I was named after Frieda Kahlo, whose full name was Magdalena Carmen Frieda Kahlo y Calderón. She made up a little song about it, to the tune of the advertising jingle 'I'd like to Teach the World to Sing'. You'd think I would be addicted to Coke, but I'm not.

'Senhorita Magdalena!'

The voice was more insistent now. It came from the edge of the stand, from somewhere near the door. I thought I saw a swish of beckoning colour moving out into the night, and got up to follow it.

The fresh air cleared my head. The moon had just risen. Fat and nearing full, it cast a cool light on the sandy patch in front of the terreiro. More light spilled out through the open doors into the almost dark, glinting on the metal trim of the cars parked street-side, and on the steel frames of the snack stalls set up for the evening. It reflected blue off a pyramid of Agua Viva bottles, and I felt suddenly, powerfully thirsty.

I was about to take a step towards the water when I was arrested by a figure silhouetted in the open door. He was edged by light, and it made a halo of his floss of white hair. The boom of his voice was anything but ethereal.

'Senhorita Magdalena! We have been waiting for you! I am Ernesto.'

He stepped forward and extended a welcoming hand. Now I could see his face, his eyes creased with smile wrinkles, his mouth framed by a trim white beard. I'd been expecting a bespectacled academic and alderman, not the seraph-in-training from *It's a Wonderful Life*.

Besides being an academic, a poet, and a personage around Salvador, Ernesto de Souza, I learned, was an elder in the Ilê Axé Bençois. He waited while I quenched my thirst, making polite small talk about my journey. He was particularly interested in the mischievous personality of the volcano.

'We are pleased that you could be with us on this special occasion,' he said. 'This is a celebration of the terreiro's ruling orixá, Xangô.' He pronounced it Shan-GOH. 'Perhaps you have already met him. He stands for justice, but presides over volcanoes, as well as lightning.' His eyes were an extraordinary yellow-brown, and enthusiasm shone from them as if they were car headlights turned to bright. 'Tomorrow you can see the gardens. José Carlos will show you everything. But for tonight . . .' He cocked his head, and raised his hand. He was listening, he explained, for the rhythm that would signal his orixá – Oxalá. When the time came, he would need to dance. He took my elbow and guided me towards the door. 'Please, you must come and sit with us inside.'

We walked in on the wrong side, for me, past the stand reserved for men. I felt sure that this was a breach of protocol, and I felt curious eyes burning my back. And then I found myself in the intimate inner circle, where terreiro regulars and luminaries – those who had not yet been called to join in the dance – sat in relative comfort on plastic chairs at the front of the hall, directly opposite the drummers.

I was welcomed warmly, a fold-up chair appeared, and a space was made for me next to Ernesto. Then I was left to orientate myself.

Everyone's focus was on the roda, the ceremonial circle on the floor that became centre stage, where women in their wide, Baiana-style skirts, their hair tied up in white kerchiefs, orbited endlessly. They were all draped in long strands of beads, piled strand upon strand, colour upon colour. I figured there must be some kind of code in the arrangements, but I couldn't crack it.

Then I just let the beat and the colours wash over me, and thought about the gardens. Tomorrow. The Ilê Axé Bençois was honoured to share its knowledge, Ernesto had told me. He talked about community outreach and education, and suggested that I keep quiet about my search for a particular plant, 'to stop people pulling up flowers from here, there and all around to show you'. I had no doubt that there were limits to what the terreiro would share with strangers. Surely there were plants that would be off-limits, too. But I knew how to recognise what I was looking for.

As for whether I would be allowed to take seeds or plant material away – assuming I found my *Newbouldia* – I would have to convince the powers that be that it was a good idea. And at this moment, those powers seemed either to be whirling on the dance floor, possessed, or waiting to attend the newly entranced.

The dancing was monotonous, but I was starting to sense a pattern. Every so often, one of the women would fall to the floor. She would be helped up by one of the circling attendants, and taken through one of the doors into the back. A little later, she would return, costumed to represent whichever orixá had taken residence within her. She would move randomly around the floor, eyes closed, weaving in and out of the circle without missing a step or colliding with any of the others. I watched this happen countless times that night, and couldn't work out how they were doing it. Whenever an 'orixá' approached a section of the audience, the crowd would close their eyes in rapture and lift their hands up, palms forward, as if to capture its energy.

There was a woman sitting on Ernesto's far side. She was nodding to the beat and chatting, every inch the middle-class matron. Until one of the entranced approached her. The two women might have been neighbours in the world outside the roda. They probably swopped recipes, or borrowed cans of condensed milk from each other to make crème caramel pudim. But at that moment, the woman next to Ernesto slipped off her chair, kneeled down and kissed the ground at the feet of her deity.

The power of belief.

I panicked. What if I was approached by one of the whirling, juddering possessed? Would I be expected to prostrate myself, to humbly accept the blessing of the incumbent orixá? I prayed – as much as my allegiance to atheism allowed – that they would pass me by.

And they did. But it wasn't just them I was worried about. Sceptical scientist I might be, but I was starting to sense how easily I might be drawn in, sabotaged by my own need to belong.

The way I was that time, at eight years old, when I shuffled along in a line of other children towards the altar at the St Josephs' school chapel, tipped back my head and opened my throat to accept the body of Christ, even though I wasn't officially sanctioned to do so. The wafer tasted a little like peanut butter, just as my new friend Olive had promised.

I didn't just do it because Olive dared me to. I did it so I wouldn't have to sit alone on that hard pew, looked down upon by weeping saints. I did it so I wouldn't have to endure the nudges and the giggles of the other kids as they passed down the aisle, and the silent judgement of the nuns and teachers sitting at the back of the church. I was new at the school, but at my age, I should already have had my First Communion. I didn't understand the meaning of my transgression. I just wanted to belong.

Now I sat through an entirely different kind of ceremony, face plastered with a rigid smile, willing myself to be ignored, and at the same time, not entirely trusting my ability to remain apart. After all, I needed to ingratiate myself with these people.

At one point I was handed a paper plate of food that was – thank whatever-spirits-were-responsible – a lot more substantial than that Catholic wafer, or anything that I had eaten for the last two days. There was rice and okra, swimming in sweet orange dendê oil, but carrying the dryness of unfamiliar spices. It reminded me of the free plates of Hari Krishna food they used to give out at university. Simple, sturdy, and vibrating with something more than the sum of its wholesome ingredients.

I was impressed by the attention paid to every aspect of the ceremony. While the colour and the pageantry went on, people laboured in the background to keep everything working smoothly, so the audience could focus on the dance. Like the drums, which kept up their beat without pause. I noticed that my drummer was no longer part of the group; he'd been replaced by another. Most of the tourists had left by now. The energy was a little more intimate, a little more intense.

There were many deities on the roda floor now. One was a man – or so I thought; it was hard to tell through the wig-like mask of long grass that fell over his face. Another man in a red loincloth swung a double-bladed hand axe. When he passed in front of us, Ernesto leaned over to me and whispered, 'Xangô!'

The one I'd noticed earlier, with the gold and the mirrors and the blissful expression on her face, was back too, eyes closed, mouth twitching as if she was conducting some kind of inner dialogue. From this close, I could see she was not a young woman, but her body moved with the grace and suppleness of a goddess. Whoever usually lived inside that weathered skin had made way for something else.

'That is Oxum,' Ernesto pronounced it OSH-OON. 'She is goddess of sweet waters. Also of wealth and beauty – she is quite vain.' Now the mirrors made sense. 'We celebrate her in rivers and streams. All over Salvador. You know the song?' He began to sing, 'E toda cidade é d'Oxum . . .': 'The entire city is Oxum's'. I recognised the tune. I had it on a CD at home, but I'd never made the connection.

Ernesto turned away to talk to the woman on his other side, and didn't seem to see Oxum approaching. Swirling, whirling, coming straight towards me, she was a blaze of yellow, a spinning vortex drawing energy – my energy.

My heart was a drum that wanted to leap out of my chest. *Go away*, I thought. *Please go away*. I closed my eyes to shut out the sight of the woman, gripped the seat of my chair to anchor myself.

What if I die here? The thought rose up to choke me. The blood clamoured inside my veins. I imagined them clogged by the cholesterol in the dendê oil. Perhaps this was an extreme reaction to the food – perhaps I would die, poisoned and bloated like Elizabeth after her caju. I couldn't remember the last time I had feared death. I'd been courting it for so long. *You are having a panic attack*, I told myself.

And then it was over. I released my grip on the chair, opened my eyes. The orixá had veered away. The floor, the lights, the rise of stands across the barracão hall, the drums, everyone around me was carrying on, unaware of my panic.

I looked for Oxum in the crowd of circling bodies, saw a glint of gold as a gap opened up. *Did you hear me?* The woman's eyes opened, flashed as they looked straight at me, then folded back, alarmingly white, into their sockets again.

Of course I didn't really see that. I was tired, dizzy, disorientated – dehydrated! That was it. The long trip. The jet lag. The suspended transit limbo. I hadn't been drinking enough water.

I drank a gallon of it back at the pousada, just before I fell into a deep, dreamless sleep.

4
Passion fruit

If you ask me, the alchemy of Five Roses brewed strong, with one sugar, is the potion to dispel any grief, worry or anxiety. As far as self-medications go, mine is a mild addiction.

They say you should only infuse green tea at 40°C – otherwise it burns the leaf. Regular Ceylon is more forgiving. You can boil it for hours, like they do in India, with cinnamon, cardamom and cloves, to make a good strong chai. No chance of that at the Lua Azul. The water in the flask at the breakfast buffet was tepid, and left a line of scum at the top of my cup, which was too small. I had to go back again and again to get my proper wake-up quota of brew.

The breakfast balcony hung out over the haze of the harbour and city, already grown hot. Today I would return to the Ilê Axé Bençois, meet José Carlos, the caretaker of the garden, and talk about plants.

But first, I needed to visit Pelourinho's Afro Brasileiro Museum. Last night's ceremony made me realise how ill-prepared I was for this mission. And I was beginning to suspect that the price of the terreiro's confidence would be more than my scheduled talk on southern African traditional plant lore.

Sonia the receptionist gave me a walking map of Pelourinho, when I passed by on my way to breakfast, and marked out the museum with a ballpoint 'X'. She also handed me a message, scrawled on paper torn from a hotel memo pad designed for the purpose. The night porter forgot to give it to me when I came in last night, she said. Desculpes. I had missed a telephone call.

Now there was a shiny black granadilla seed clinging to the note, which I'd shoved under my breakfast plate. It was short and sweet. *Tempo*: 20h50. *Nome*: Gillermo Bellani. *Mensagem*: A telephone number in Manaus.

How had my father tracked me here? Em, of course. But so soon?

A small circle of passion-fruit pulp stained the paper around the seed. Now there was a plant that wasn't shy about advertising itself. My grandmother had a crazy wild vine in her garden. She called them granadillas; the Brazilians called them maracuja. Their flowers looked like ladies twirling in wide white skirts flecked with purple, their green stamens outstretched arms. Like the women last night.

I had played with the flowers on my grandparents' farm that African Christmas, when I was six and ignorant of the fact that my parents were trying to save their doomed marriage. It took a lightning bolt to finish off what Sarah's burning studio had started a few weeks earlier. The immolation of grief.

Grief my father caused.

The 'Rothko Red' was all that remained after the studio fire. Almost the only thing I have left of my mother. A few other pieces were snapped up by small galleries and now hang in collectors' homes. Maybe one day I'll trace and find them all.

If it weren't for that small scorched corner, bottom right, you would never know what the painting had been through. The mark seemed to complement the painting's blood colour. And you had to look closely to see that it wasn't oil paint, but singed canvas. Blackened in a way that seemed unintentional, even for an artist bent on confounding expectations. It was almost as if the charcoal smudge foreshadowed what would happen a few weeks later on an African mountaintop. But she couldn't have known that.

When I was fifteen, my art teacher gave our class an assignment: choose a painting, from any style or era you feel best represents you. I chose *The Scream*. Before the week was out, the guidance counsellor called Em in for a consultation. I waited on the bum-polished bench in the corridor outside. Em came out wearing a serious face, but gave me a conspiratorial wink when the counsellor wasn't looking. She took me out for a latte afterward (adding a tot of Glenfiddich to hers). She raised her glass. 'To Munch, who was not afraid of the scars of life.'

She told me *The Scream* had been stolen once. When it was recovered, people wanted to restore it to its original state. But Munch knew this was impossible. 'He believed you cannot undo what has been done,' Em said. 'That painting went out and had an adventure and came back marked. That was its true nature.'

I knew what she was trying to tell me. We are all a little damaged. My mother, her painting, me. Even my father – my idealised, absent, inadequate father, with whom Em encouraged me to connect, on that first teenage trip back to Brazil.

We started fighting then, and the fights got worse with each subsequent visit. We pretended we were arguing points of principle, but ultimately, it came down to trust. And faith. He had become devout again, thanks to Lucia, his new wife. Pious and faithful. A little too late, I reminded him whenever I had the chance.

What to do about him now? Just knowing that he knew I was here made my emotional barometer plunge.

On my way out, I checked my email in the reception lounge of the Lua Azul, which had the only reliable wi-fi in the place.

It doubled as an informal gallery, and even though there was no one else there that morning, it felt crowded. Carved masks and elongated statues peered out between oversize ferns. I sifted quickly though junk mail and the countless newsletters I subscribe to but never get around to reading. No mea culpa from Em. I doubted she would feel the need to explain herself. But there was a brief mail from Kirk.

> *Trust you arrived safely. Don't get distracted by Brazil's many seductions! Remember your mission. Our sponsors want results.*
>
> *Find us our seed!*
>
> *Live long and prosper. Over and out.*

And an even shorter one from Nico.

> *I'm sorry, it was a shitty way to part. Can we talk when you get back? (When do you get back?)* x N

Nico's mail had an attachment; a photograph of two furry creatures lying on their backs next to one another, with the heading 'Significant Otters'. One of them looked like it had been squashed flat. Significant road kill.

The Rua do Carmo was a quiet residential street with a smattering of pousadas, a few clothing and curio stores, and a per kilo self-service café that was already gearing up for a brisk lunchtime trade. The uneven cobblestones forced me to keep an eye on the ground, but when I rounded a corner and looked up, I found myself in front of Roberto the Rastaman's music store. Os Agogos was closed. I peered through the glass. The floor inside was crowded with drums, from small gourd shakers to massive djembes that were bigger than I was. On the walls, single-stringed wooden instruments hung like bows waiting to be taken into battle. I made a mental note of the location. It would be nice to see a familiar face once Roberto got back from his trip.

I had a lot on my mind, but as I reached the entrance to the museum, one pressing question clanged through the clamour. My habitual irritation with Kirk's Trekkie tone had masked the question that had dogged me all through Pelourinho's knobbly streets, and finally coalesced in a single word: *sponsors*. Kirk had assured me this was an independent Institute initiative. Note to self: check with him later.

5
Orixás

Exu was the one to watch out for. He liked to hang out at crossroads, demanding tribute. If you didn't pay your respects, you would pay in misfortune. In this, there was no divergence of opinion.

As for the rest, there was some disagreement. Especially between the purists, who liked to emphasise the Yoruba origins of the orixás, and the syncretists, who were happy to have their Catholic saints merge and converge with the African deities. But everyone respected the devilish trickster Exu. You would be crazy not to.

I passed quickly through the ground floor of the old colonial manse that housed the Afro Brasileiro Museum, past the artefacts from Benin, the Niger and Angola, where the majority of the three million plus slaves brought to Bahia originated. (By the time Brazil ended its official slave trade in 1888, the pamphlet told me, double the number of slaves had been brought here than to the future United States of America.)

I found the orixás at the top of a short flight of stairs, in a room set out like a hall of fame. There were charts, drawings and photographs for each deity, with descriptions of what they wore, what they stood for, and what they protected. Each one had a day of the week, a personal colour, and a favourite food. There were helpful models too – dressed-up dolls in glass cases wearing miniature versions of the finery I had seen on the roda the night before.

There were orixás for water, plants, storms and rainbows, for steel and industry and war. There were books of Candomblé stories, Yoruba legends woven in with tales of the Amerindian Coboclo. A set of wall posters explained how Candomblé had evolved, how Mary, Mother of God and Yemanjá of the Oceans could be one and the same.

It was like being inside a kaleidoscope, the colours refracted, some patterns in the repetition, subtle differences between them. I really wanted the pantheon to make sense to me, but there was just too much to take in. And it all felt a little like playing house with dolls.

Except for Exu. Exu made perfect sense to me. Exu was the only orixá that could flit between the material realm of mortals and that of spirit. If you wanted to get a message through to your chosen deity, Exu was your telegraph man. He was also the messenger for all the other orixás, the only one who could travel between them and report to their high god-in-chief, Olórun. It was no wonder people made sure to make good with him. Forget to placate Exu at the beginning of a ceremony, or at the beginning of a new endeavour, or when you were travelling, or when asking any of the other orixás for help and advice, and he could block your message, or your path. He was a mischief-maker, and easily offended. I liked him already.

Before I left the hall, I took a long look at Ossain, lord of magic potions, orixá of leaves, herbs and medicine. He was dressed in green (naturally), wore a short crown and carried a spear with a dove at its apex. 'I'll be seeing a lot of you,' I promised him.

In my hurry to leave, I almost missed the best part of all. I took a wrong turn down an unassuming corridor and stumbled into a vast space. It felt like a cathedral, but instead of stained glass, the walls were covered in carved wood. Each member of the Candomblé pantheon rose from floor to ceiling in polished cedar, accented with copper, metal, shell and bead. They were massive and sensuous. I was alone in the room, and had them all to myself. I could take my time, marvelling at how wood became sinew and skin, carved with exquisite skill into flowing robes and diaphanous cloth, feather and hair. I wanted to run my hands along the grooves, lean in close so that the heat of my breath would release the cedar sap, and perhaps something else.

Then a couple walked in, distracted by their backpacks, guidebooks, water bottles. I sat on the backless bench that allowed a three-hundred-and-sixty-degree view of the carvings, waiting to be alone with the orixás again, revolving slowly on the bench, taking them all in.

It felt like being in the eye of a storm. A still centre away from colour and crass. Here the orixás were private. And powerful. It wasn't just their size, but the element they were carved from – wood that had been trees, alive then, and somehow here still so. Massive pedicels, carrying the ages they had lived through, carved to represent these deities who had lived even longer, if only in human imagination.

In the carvings, each orixá had an animal companion or a familiar. The river goddess Oxum had a small, flat-horned deer. A meek little turtle accompanied thunder god Xangô, whose swinging loincloth was carved with axes, cogs and triangles. Iron man Ogun had his fox; the rainbow weaver Oxumare, an ox. Yemanjá was the mother of them all. The goddess surfed the waves on a fish, listening to the secrets of the sea in a shell pressed to her ear. She had a space carved in her belly where all the other orixás crowded around, waiting to be born.

But the one I found myself coming back to again and again was Xangô. Last night at the ceremony, I'd learned that the patron saint of the Ilê Axé Bençois commanded lightning. But there was something else. It was in the double-bladed axe he wielded, like a tomahawk. He held his left arm raised above his head, and he seemed to be twirling . . .

I saw my mother silhouetted against trees – they were the green trees of a North American late summer, but fire had turned them the colours of autumn. There was a cool carpet of lawn under my bare legs, and people rushing around with water buckets, and my father trying to connect a hose, and my mother standing unmoved, unmoving, watching as the annex to our vacation house in upstate New York – her artwork, everything in her outhouse studio – went up in the blaze. Fallow Farm. After that, it would live up to its name.

I gazed up at the polished figure of Xangô towering towards the high ceiling and watched my mother break into a victory dance, twirling like a Comanche, tomahawk in hand, flaying hair backlit.

The vision could only have lasted an instant – lightning fast – and when it was gone, I was alone in the room again.

For the rest of the day, that vision would dog me, floating at my periphery like a corona, or the afterburn on your eyeball after you look too long at a bright light. Images from the blaze and its aftermath would continue to follow me for many more days. I would see the Navajo woven blanket someone – I can't remember who – put around me when they picked me up off the lawn; the bowl of pale yellow custard they placed in front of me in the cabin kitchen, and the royal-blue table edging. I would remember the smell, through the smoke, of pine or sumac – relative of the poisonous cashew – and mosquito repellent. I would remember the tear in one of the window screens that let the bugs in.

After that, there were quiet nights in Aunt Em's New York apartment, where I waited for my mother to finish resting and come back to get me. When Sarah finally came, she was bright and hopeful, excited about a trip home for Christmas. Back to Africa!

We could not know that the trip was to be my mother's last. Or that it would be a decade before I would return 'home' to the jungle of Manaus. That Bill would not be given the chance to fulfil his promise to stop returning from trips with the traces of other women lingering in the folds of his clothes and around his eyes. The Drakensberg trip was supposed to be a reconciliation attempt. But all it did was let him off the hook.

But I wasn't going to. He should have looked after me, should have kept me close after my mother was gone. And now that he's repented, now that he's comfortably settled with the mild-mannered Lucia, and a monkey tethered to the porch, now that I'm all grown up and there's nothing left to do for me, now he wants a reconciliation? Staring up at the massive figure of Xangô, I felt a surge of emotion that was new to me. Pure blazing anger.

6
Terreiro

The Ilê Axé Bençois looked so ordinary in the flat light of midday, without the shadow possibilities of darkness.

Fernando's taxi dropped me outside the main gate. The short walk up the driveway past the dozing guard seemed to take forever in the humid heat.

I walked past the barracão hall, scene of last night's festivities. It seemed much smaller from the outside, locked up against the noontime glare. What I had not seen, in the darkness, was the compound behind the terreiro's public face. It was walled in and, at the moment, utterly quiet

There was no obvious reception area in this warren of buildings. Some had that startled look of the new prefab, others were clearly very old and settled, but still freshly painted and carefully maintained. One long building might once have been stables; behind it, I could see the tops of tall trees that I presumed bordered the gardens. Ernesto had told me that they were quite extensive, but I couldn't see how that could be – the terreiro was on top of a hill slap bang in the middle of the city, bordered by a busy main road on one side, and with houses and businesses crowded all around.

I wasn't expecting a reception committee, but there was no welcome of any kind. The silence was almost eerie.

A shrill alarm bell sounded behind me, making me jump out of my skin. I felt a rush of relief as the peal of the bell unleashed children's shouts. A schoolyard. The ordinary, everyday joy of pupils escaping the classroom for morning break. I felt the adrenaline subside and laughed out loud.

As if on cue, the terreiro seemed to wake up. A woman came out of one of the buildings carrying a large aluminium urn, its electrical cord looped over her arm. She crossed the empty space and entered another building without seeming to see me. The door she had just emerged from was open, so I headed towards it. Before I reached it another young woman in a skirt – modestly long, but not flared, Baiana-style – ducked out, carrying a small wooden bowl. She didn't look at me either, but disappeared into the adjacent room.

I peered into the open room and found what appeared to be a kind of shop, its long tables weighted with the business end of Candomblé. There were cellophane-packed herb teas, labelled with unfamiliar names. A few promotional books on the lineage and heritage of the terreiro and its mãe-de-santo, Mãe Gabriella. Also carved wooden figas – the small fist clutching its thumb found in every flea market in Brazil, which believers wear to ward off the evil eye. My father once brought me one as a gift, carved out of semi-precious green stone, before he rediscovered his faith.

Mostly there were beads. Separated by colour, they were coiled in rings, heaped in bowls, hung on hooks; they flowed down the walls in translucent streams of turquoise and yellow, deep blue, white and green. I already knew that yellow was for Oxum. White seemed to be for everyone. I wondered about the red and the black – the devilish colours of Exu, perhaps – but my hand was drawn to the clear, cool turquoise. Turquoise for Yemanjá, queen of the sea and mother of all.

'Com licença.'

The woman stood in the doorway, hands on her hips. Masses of springy coils of hair were tethered at the nape of her neck, and her café-com-leite skin was dotted with freckles. Her expression was guarded. 'You like that one?' she asked, in Portuguese. I put the beads down.

'I'm looking for José Carlos. I'm supposed to meet him here.'

The woman didn't move, her expression didn't change, but her silent scrutiny went on a little too long. I wondered if I had transgressed some kind of code. 'I'm Magdalene,' I stepped forward, holding out my hand. 'Senhor Ernesto said I should come today?'

'Luisa.' The woman took my hand reluctantly, as if she was not sure what to do with it, and quickly let it go. 'Prazer,' she said, as if it were anything but a pleasure to meet me. She was pricklier than a saguaro. But even cactuses flower at least once a year. Perhaps, like the *Carnegiea gigantea*, Luisa only bloomed at night?

Luisa continued to stare at me, then nodded as if she were listening to something I couldn't hear. It occurred to me that these were the mind-games people played when they were trying to seem magical and mysterious. I was determined not to let it work. I was feeling uneasy, it was true. But Luisa was just being rude.

'The mão-de-ofá, he's in the garden,' she offered at last.

Ernesto had briefed me about the mão-de-ofá, which literally means 'hand of the herbs'. He or she is the person at the terreiro tasked with tending the garden. Besides knowing which plant should be harvested for what medicinal or ritualistic purposes and when, the 'hand' held the knowledge of the terreiro's signature herbs, the kind known only to its inner circle. I couldn't wait to find out if *Newbouldia* was one of theirs.

'Can you show me where that is?'

'First you will meet Mãe. Then I can take you.' Luisa slipped out, and I heard low voices from next door. Then Luisa was back. 'Mãe Gabriella says you can come.'

She must have seen me glance down at my frayed cargo pants – force of habit, wearing khaki bush pants, with lots of pockets for samples – and T-shirt. I had dressed for the field, not for the cloister.

'It is okay,' Luisa said. For the first time, she smiled. The effect was extraordinary. Her cheeks dimpled and her eyes shone. I had never seen a face go so quickly from fierce to captivating. With that small bit of graciousness, I was almost willing to forgive her earlier unfriendliness.

I followed Luisa into the adjacent room. It was dim and cool. The mãe-de-santo, high priestess and head of the terreiro, sat in a high-backed wicker chair, as regal as a throne, despite patches of frayed and broken cane. The proportions of the chair made her appear even tinier than she was, but there was nothing small about her presence. Even though her eyes were blue-grey and rheumy with age, and her hair almost as white as the headscarf tied over it, she exuded authority. Around her neck she wore every bead in the colour spectrum, the long strands running over one shoulder, crossing in front and looping down under her opposite arm.

I was unsure of the protocol, so I crouched into something between a bow and a curtsey, like a deferential Japanese acolyte.

'Welcome, daughter,' the mãe-de-santo said. She nodded at a nearby chair. 'Sit, please.' She watched me closely as I settled myself. 'You are from Africa.'

It was as much a statement as a question. I reminded myself that this information was common knowledge, not gleaned from mysterious sources.

'I am.'

'But you are not black.'

'No.' I didn't think an explanation of South Africa's racial complexities was required here – Brazil's colour-coding was at least as complex, if perhaps less fraught. Still, it felt safer to play on my African connection than my American one.

'You were born in Africa?'

'No, here. In Brazil.' I wanted to add that my first memory was Amazon green. But I kept that to myself.

'Catolico?'

I was tempted to confess my atheism. But I remembered that Einstein called himself a 'deeply religious non-believer'. That had always appealed to me. But the answer the mãe required was a lot more simple. And, technically, I had had my First Communion. Eventually.

Mãe Gabriella continued to watch me, without expression, as I struggled between honesty and expediency. Nico would call it a Hitchcock moment. 'My father is Catholic,' I said eventually. Might as well get some mileage out of his reborn piousness. 'My mother was born in Africa.'

Mãe Gabriella nodded as if to say, *finally*.

Then she started to speak, so softly and rapidly that I had to lean forward to hear her, my mind scrambling to translate the Portuguese. I didn't catch all of it, but thought I heard: *Tambem morreu la*. She died there, too. *Sinto muito*. I am sorry.

Then there was something about Xangô, the god who threw thunderbolts and lightning. My thoughts began to spin. Electricity prickled my extremities. I felt my blood slow, my head filled with cotton wool.

Mãe Gabriella was muttering down into her hands, clasped in her lap.

And I was small again, and the green grass was bending under purple clouds. I heard thunder, smelled sulphur, and my peripheral vision was tinged with blue.

Then it was over. Mãe Gabriella thanked me for my visit, wished me well, and told me to come back for a cleansing ritual when I was ready. Then I was out in the yellow sunshine, following Luisa through the compound, returning to myself through fug and static.

I hadn't had a chance to tell Mãe Gabriella why I was here – although surely Ernesto would have told her? Declaring my intentions would have been the right thing to do. After all, this was the woman I would have to convince to let me take the seeds, if I found any. But I was thrown by the lightning stuff.

All in all, not an auspicious beginning. Unless that was exactly the way they wanted it? Mess with my head, let me know who was really in charge here?

Then again, maybe I had misheard the part about my mother? As for Xangô, he was the patron of this terriero. Wasn't it natural that the Mãe would offer a prayer to him whenever someone came to pay respects?

'Let's go,' Luisa was peering at me. I had stopped in the middle of the square and was staring at the ground.

Suggestibility, that was it. This whole terreiro thing just had me a little bit spooked. I would think about that later. Right now, I needed to map the terrain, remember what I was here for. Play the modern-day Mata Hari, even if it meant selling off a bit of my non-believing soul for the good of the planet. Biodiversity was my agency, and my cause.

7
The garden

Behind the compound's last outbuildings, a low stone wall demarcated the beginning of the garden. The ground dropped vertically down a steep hillside, tumbling into a green space that seemed to go on forever. The green I had seen from the terreiro gate came from the tops of massive trees that had their roots way down below. Over the treetops, I could glimpse the city high-rises, the heat of steel and concrete floating beyond the oasis of foliage. It would be so much cooler down in that green.

Luisa stopped at a wrought-iron gate. Its bars were twisted into leaves, spears, tridents, doves and axes. She called out.

'Zé!'

'Falou!' the muffled reply drifted up from below.

Luisa swung the gate open and stepped back, pointing me down the rough concrete steps that dropped into the trees. Then she turned and left.

Three steps later, and I was in another world. The garden's perimeter was held by a few buttressed ficus trees, with wide white ribbons tied around their trunks. I walked on and down, through towering Bahian myrtles and fat-fruited jaca trees – originally from the Far East, now so common in Brazil they're practically a national institution. I passed white jacarandas and trees heavy with cacau fruit. Mangos and avocados mingled with Atlantic rainforest trees that I didn't recognise.

Bahia's rainforests are floristically unique and spectacularly diverse. Half the plants here grow nowhere else, and the other half have roots in Africa. About eighty per cent of them host ethereal epiphytes. Here, at last, was Bishop's first idealisation, her leafy tapestry:

> *monster ferns*
> *in silver-gray relief,*
> *and flowers, too, like giant water lilies*
> *up in the air – up, rather, in the leaves –*
> *purple, yellow, two yellows, pink,*
> *rust red and greenish white;*
> *solid but airy; fresh as if just finished*
> *and taken off the frame.*

I tilted my head back and looked up into the canopy. Breathing in the ozone, I let myself get dizzy with green.

The slope made it difficult to sense how far I had gone by the time the terrain eventually flattened out and the trees began to thin to let in light. There was no obvious order here. Herbs and grasses grew together haphazardly, but I began to make out rough beds bordered by striated bamboo. Tendrils of bottle gourd snaked among castor beans, and around tall sprays of mist-grey *Artemisia* – the old-world witches' favourite. A morning-glory type of flower curled around the trunks of juvenile kola nut trees. Flat tobacco leaves vied for space with spreading *Plectranthus* and the jasmine-like *Hedychium coronarium*, which I knew well from its home continent. But I saw no sign of *Newbouldia mundii*. Or of the mysterious 'hand of the herbs'.

I could hear him though, or at least the rhythmic thwack of his blade. The sound drew me forward into a clearing. He was standing with his back to me, hacking at a tall stand of speared bracts.

I suppose I had expected some priestly vision in white. But there was nothing special about him. His pale shorts were an indiscriminate colour. His sweat-marked vest had once been white, but had faded to an over-washed grey. His feet splayed sideways out of plastic flip-flops as he anchored himself for each swing of the blade.

I didn't call out, just stayed on the edge of the clearing. I told myself I was savouring the moment before he knew I was there, before my work had to start in earnest. But in truth I was enjoying the way each swing rippled through his shoulder muscles.

Then his blade snagged on a thick stem, and in the turn of his body as he tugged it free, he registered my presence. He turned to face me and I recognised him – the man from the drum pit of the roda last night.

If he recognised me, he didn't show it. With deliberation, he laid down his blade and lifted the hem of his vest to wipe the sweat from his eyes and forehead. His belly was banded by a thin braid of woven grass, a shade lighter than the taut brown of his torso. I was still staring at it when he lowered his shirt, and said, 'Thursday.'

Quinta feira. So it was. So what? All I could do was concur. 'Sim?'

He had caught me staring. At least he couldn't know I'd been thinking he would look much better if he wasn't wearing any clothes at all. I could feel my cheeks flushing, and couldn't think of anything to say.

He gathered up the leaf spears he had just chopped, and offered them to me.

'This is peregun,' he said. 'Herb of Oxossi, and also of Ossain, who is the orixá of leaves, protector of the forest.' As I took them from him, I caught the peppery smell of his sweat.

The leaves were succulent dark green and rigid, striped along their length with lighter green. 'And Oxossi is the hunter, isn't he?' I was showing off, making my quick visit to the museum pay off. If he was impressed, he didn't show it. He maintained a rigid, almost courtly formality. I decided he was full of himself.

'Thursday is the day of the forest. It is the day of Ossain and of Oxossi. You have arrived on an auspicious day.' He ran his hand along one of the leaves. 'Peregun in the home keeps away bad spirits. It is a small gift.'

The cynic in me wondered: was he giving me the leaves for my own protection, or for his?

'Thank you.' I extended my hand. 'Magdalena.'

'And I am José Carlos,' he said, ignoring my hand, and leaning in for the conventional beijinhos, one on each cheek, instead. 'My friends call me Zé.'

In Transit

Thirty-nine days later

13:50 13:50	BUENOS AIR	ESTM63	ON TIME
14:15 14:15	FRANKFURT	LH5873	ON TIME
15:00 15:45	GUADALAJARA	MX439	DELAYED
16:20 16:20	NY JFK	AI796	ON TIME
16:45 17:25	LISBON	TP4036	DELAYED
17:10 17:10	SINGAPORE	SQ342	ON TIME
18:20 18:20	JOHANNESBURG	SA349	ON TIME

I add extra sugar to what might be my last cafezinho on Brazilian soil until who knows when. The thought carves a lacuna deep in my centre.

It all feels so different. *I* feel so different. One month, two moons, and a lifetime later, I feel changed.

The airport, on the other hand, has returned to what passes as normal. Planes flying more or less on schedule, defying gravity, fate and death wishes. As if all that engine-clogging volcano ash had never been.

I have a six-hour layover in São Paulo. I would never actually choose to spend that long in a shopping mall, but that's effectively what this is. A casino of consumerism. *Distraction is the only thing that consoles us for our miseries*, Blaise Pascal said four centuries ago. *And yet it is itself the greatest of our miseries.* What would the philosopher think of the lack of contemplative space in the information age? Personally, I'm grateful for it. The last thing I want to do right now is think. I am trying very hard *not* to think …

So I focus on what's outside my head, my perceptions weirdly heightened. I can feel currents in the artificial air. I watch the barista fix a cafezinho, pouring water. *See* the water. *Feel* its flow. *Iron, earth, air, fire, water.* How could I not have noticed these elementals – in everything, in myself – before?

Get a grip.

And there are the voices. Not 'get thee to the asylum' kind of voices. I'm not hearing Jesus or Jim Jones or Yosemite Sam. Not even Yemanjá, Oxossi or Xangô, although by now they've all visited me in my dreams. This voice is in my head, urgent. It's me and it's also not me, it comes from within, and from someplace else. And it's telling me—

Go.

The swimming air feels crowded, makes my skin prickle with claustrophobia. I need to get out, get going, get away. I need to leave, NOW.

Now.

I down the coffee in one swift gulp. Heft my backpack onto my shoulder. Check my passport, boarding pass, money, yellow fever certificate (they won't let me back into South Africa without it). Pause at the unopened letter. Move on. I adjust the moon bag, precious cargo strapped close to my belly. Check the clock again. Five and a half more hours. Three hundred and thirty more minutes before I'm out of here.

8
Toucan

Ernesto's veranda hovered in a rare patch of suburban rainforest high over the ocean. When you look out over the Atlantic in Cape Town, you face sunset; in Bahia, you face sunrise. And moonrise – it would be full tonight, but it hadn't yet appeared above the horizon. There were twinkling lights under the forest canopy, though; fireflies in a frenzy of bioluminescent lust. I used to call them 'lightning bugs' when I was very small. How is it that I had forgotten that? Something else lost in the elisions between places, and ways of speaking. Even within the same language (English), there were differences in intonation, pronunciation and the actual naming of things, so that ways of speaking became ways of seeing, and eventually ways of remembering – or forgetting.

I was disappointed to discover that Zé would not be coming to this dinner party. It would be three days – three slow days – before I could meet him in the garden again on Monday. What to do with myself during that time? Without Zé, there was no access to the garden. Without access, there was no chance to look for the seed.

Our first meeting had been frustratingly brief. He didn't have time to take me around the garden. He had commitments most afternoons, he said. Better to meet in the mornings.

'All things in their time,' Ernesto refilled my shot glass with expensive cachaça, and soothed my impatience to get back into the garden. 'We all have our responsibilities, so to say.' I knew it was rude of me to press. I had only meant to praise the abundance in the garden – and thank Ernesto for his introduction to it. But cachaça had made my tongue reckless.

It was an expensive brand, and we drank it straight up, not mashed with lime, sugar and ice like on the streets. It was my second night here, and I still hadn't had a caipirinha. I resolved to rectify that over the weekend.

Ernesto's house was a rambling Portuguese-style manse, with white stucco, dark carved woods and calico roof tiles. Fringed white hammocks floated along the length of the balcony, draped between tropical plants. The air was thick and warm.

There was a toucan in a large cage, grooming his feathers with an outrageous multi-coloured beak that seemed to glow in the fading light. I walked over and peered at him through the metal bars.

Elizabeth Bishop was gifted a toucan when she first moved in with Lota, to a house in the cool hills of Petropolis, above Rio. She called him 'Sammy', after Uncle Sam, because his colours were red and blue. When the bird slept, Elizabeth wrote to a friend, it lifted up its tail and curled under its arm 'so that it looked like an inverted comma'. This one didn't look sleepy. I wondered when he would retire for the night; I wanted to see that comma curl for myself. I plucked at his cage and made vague clucking noises. The bird stopped his prodigious prodding, stared at me balefully for a moment, then resumed his grooming.

The stars were just beginning to show themselves, and I looked in vain for the Southern Cross and its pointers. In Cape Town, I'd learned to draw a sight line between them and down to the horizon, to find due south. I figured that if I faced the pole, then shifted my body forty-five degrees to the left, there would be nothing but blue space and ocean between me and Nico's house. But I couldn't find the stars.

It would be after midnight where he was. I wondered if he might be having a nightcap out on his balcony, what he would be seeing as he stared out over the sea. Who he might be with.

'Saudades for home?' Ernesto was at my elbow with another refill. Without the cut of lime, the cachaça's sweet petroleum whiff was even more potent. Its warmth spread through my body.

'No. I'm very happy to be here,' I said, and it felt true.

'And we are honoured to have you visit us.' He raised his glass to me. 'Have you met Eduardo?' A young man stepped up, offering his hand and a shy smile. Eduardo had a head of tight curls, round wire-rimmed glasses that made his eyes seem much smaller than they were, and a staggering knowledge of contemporary Brazilian music. He told me he was busy mapping the influence of hip hop on Salvador's youth. He wanted to practise speaking English, and asked me to call him 'Ed' – he pronounced it 'Edge'. Which sparked a conversation about U2 and an enthusiastic air guitar display.

The crowd around Ernesto's dinner table was lively. Besides Edge, there was a lawyer, a photographer, and an academic – I didn't catch exactly what she did, just that she had been a colleague of Ernesto's at the Federal University of Bahia before he retired. They were all connected with the terreiro. Some had been introduced to it as children, and had never questioned its centrality in their life. Others had found their way there through circumstance or need.

I was struck by how the terreiro served to integrate so many layers of Bahian society. But Teresa, the lawyer, disabused me of my rainbow nation romanticism. 'There is still a lot of prejudice against Candomblé in middle-class society,' she said. 'People have not forgotten the days when it was a force for uniting the slave underclass.' Thin and intense, she fired off words with staccato rapidity. 'Of course the African slaves and their descendants played up to that fear. When you've been stripped of all ostensible power, you find other ways to exercise it. The Portuguese slave owners were terrified of black magic.'

'And what are they scared of now, this prejudiced middle class?'

'The ones who reject Candomblé?' Teresa stared into her wineglass as if searching for bourgeois tendencies, swirling the claret with such vigour I expected it to slosh out over the side. By some sleight of physics, it stayed in the glass. 'Chaos. A disruption to their sense of order.'

'Anyway, that order is a fallacy.' Ernesto's remark set off a chain of knowing glances around the table. If I had been among familiar friends, I would have suggested that there is no randomness in the universe, that if you look hard enough you will find an elegant order behind everything. But I guessed that Ernesto wasn't talking about quantum theory, but about local political machinations, of which I knew less than nothing. So I kept quiet.

'They cling to the notion of order with both their hands, nonetheless.' Teresa put the wine glass down to shake thin hands in front of her, as if she were conducting a symphony without a baton. 'It stops them from acknowledging or addressing the real problem, which is the systematic exclusion of the poor from culture and full citizenship.' She dropped her fists into her lap and stared at them as if wondering how they got up into the air in the first place.

'An exclusion that our practice serves to address, by removing itself from the periphery that is a construct of the very centre that defines itself against it.' Clara, the academic, was soft and spectacled, her hair bleached pale orange from years of chemical assault. Her soothing voice contrasted with the ideas she expressed. She turned to me and added, 'It is not the unknown they fear. It is their fear itself.'

Wine after cachaça had loosened my thoughts. I struggled to follow the remarks that flew across the table in melodic Portuguese, batted back and forth over the highly polished dark wood, lace doilies, crystal and silverware that looked as if they'd been passed down through generations. On the wall was a heavy silver balangandan, which I recognised from my museum visit. It was a type of charm necklace worn by slaves. This one was hung with caskets shaped like flowers and fruits, with figas and birds – symbolising freedom, I had learned – all tarnished with age. Or age-old sweat. The founding De Souzas stared down from the wall above it, their high collars and dour expressions a Bahian version of American Gothic. I wondered how Ernesto's ancestors dealt with their fear of the chaos lurking in their slaves' quarters. Perhaps miscegenation was one way of taming it. Every person here carried the genes of slaves and colonisers and indigenous natives in them, to one degree or another. Aren't we all part random mutation, part miracle?

At some point, Darwin stopped believing in miracles. I doubt whether Einstein, Eddington or Hawking ever even entertained the notion. But they all left loopholes to accommodate phenomena that defied human understanding. 'Life would be stunted and narrowed,' Eddington said, 'if we were only to use science to understand mysticism.' If I could play the fantasy dinner-party game, he's the one I would invite. But any of them would surely admit that it is only natural – or only human – to put our own face onto unknowables, in order to fit them into some kind of narrative. And so the wonders of the universe were anthropomorphised into the gods and goddesses of the ancient Greeks – or the orixás celebrated by the people sitting around this table. I had no doubt that some of the dinner guests were wearing beads under their elegant blouses and cotton shirts.

No one asked me about my beliefs, let alone my work, or what I hoped to achieve here. Which seemed strange, since I was the newcomer. And then I realised that I was being presented with a pageant, a display that told a story about who and what these people were. Or, what they would like me to see them as.

Everything had been carefully arranged and beautifully presented. A spectacle orchestrated with careful attention and proper regard for protocol, and oiled with good alcohol. The guests represented music and culture, art and law, letters and ideas – it was the intellectual face of a deeply superstitious sect. And Ernesto was the perfect host.

He'd seated me next to Alessandra, the photographer. She looked as if she had stepped out of a Pre-Raphaelite painting. She had heavy-lidded boudoir eyes and an armful of silver, and had just published a book on the photographs of Pierre Verger. She worked at the institute run from his old house in a Salvador favela. I sipped water and tried to focus while she told me how the French anthropologist became fascinated with Candomblé in the 1950s, travelling to West Africa to document the original Yoruba stories. 'He did a lot of work with Carybé,' she said, bracelets jangling as she indicated a series of framed original pen-and-ink drawings ranged along Ernesto's dining-room wall.

Carybé – the artist who had carved the marvellous wooden pantheon. 'I saw his carvings today – at the museum,' I told her. 'They really are wonderfully . . . alive.' I recalled the cedar scent, timber made diaphanous.

'Que maravilhosa!' Alessandra clapped her hands with genuine delight. 'Uncle, did you hear?'

Ernesto nodded his approval. 'Together with Jorge Amado,' he said, 'Carybé and Verger are the holy trinity of culture in Salvador, so to say.'

There was a rush of advice about books and music I had to get, restaurants and bars and street performances I absolutely could not miss.

Clara had left the table, but now her melodious voice came from outside, trilling with excitement. 'Come out to the balcony,' she called. 'Rapido!'

Scraping back our chairs and gathering glasses, we emerged just in time to see the moon rising, full-bellied, over the horizon. Ernesto proposed that we take our coffee in the moonlight.

I found myself gravitating towards the birdcage again. The toucan was still awake, looking grumpy as his feathers were ruffled by the cool breeze. The cool didn't bother me. I felt flushed and warm with bonhomie. My mission didn't feel impossible. We could all benefit if I found the star seed. Zé would be my closest ally. Ernesto too, had offered to give me Salvador on a silver platter – he'd actually used those very words. But now the tray he held out to me was crowded with tiny coffees.

'I was just admiring your bird,' I told him. The toucan's earlier grooming had had little effect. He was looking decidedly disgruntled.

'Ah, Lupe!' Ernesto said. 'My daughter named him. After the bird on the cereal box. He is a real gentleman.' He put the tray on a nearby table and inserted a crooked finger between the bars of the cage. The bird hopped over and arched his neck, cat-like, to rub his ear on the old man's knuckle.

The transcontinental power of the brand. I hadn't seen a Brazilian Froot Loops commercial, but the bird in the ad of my childhood was voiced by Mel Blanc – as were Bugs Bunny, Daffy

Duck, Tweety Bird, and just about every other Loony Tunes character that had kept me company on lonely weekends and winter afternoons. This particular Lupe hadn't uttered a sound all evening.

'Elizabeth Bishop had one,' I told my host. 'She said he had skin the colour of blueberries. As if he had blue jeans on under his feathers.'

'Ah, the American poet,' he said. 'She loved everything about Brazil. Of course there are things that, even with the best of intentions, foreigners cannot understand.' The bird shifted to offer the other side of his neck. Ernesto obliged by twisting his finger around to hook the other way. 'She killed that bird, you know.'

He withdrew his hand and the bird retreated, shaking himself out and looking more disgruntled than ever. 'She was not to know. She took the advice of someone she trusted and cleaned him with a potent insecticide. Found him dead in his cage the next morning.' He picked up his coffee cup. 'Ignorance can be a dangerous thing when you are in unfamiliar territory.' He drained his cup and set it down on the tray. 'Such a terrible waste.'

His words echoed in my head through the long taxi ride back to the Lua Azul. The thought of Elizabeth's dead blue-skinned bird cut a cold current through the warm river of my evening.

9
Walking

I filled the doldrum days that followed by getting to know my neighbourhood. I spiralled my way through the bairro's small streets, returning again and again to the confluence at the Largo do Pelourinho and its cake-blue Igreja da Nossa Senhora do Rosário dos Pretos. Each time I passed it, I had to duck the touts waiting on its steps with armfuls of multi-coloured ribbons. They claimed that Nosso Senhor de Bonfim had blessed the fitas, which were machine-inked with his name to prove it. Quick as lightning, they would grab the wrist of an unsuspecting tourist and tie on a ribbon with a torrent of words; by the time the knot was fastened, the deal was done. Who could then refuse to part with a handful of grubby reias? Untying the bond with only one hand was impossible. And why risk inviting the wrath of the saint, or lessen the chances for good fortune that wearing the ribbon was supposed to bring?

So far I'd avoided being tagged, partly by scowling at anyone who approached me bearing ribbons, and partly by speaking Portuguese well enough to pass as a local. You could pick out newbies by the number of fresh bands on their wrists – ribbons they would cut off with nail scissors in their bathrooms back home, on the morning they returned to work. Seasoned travellers and career itinerants wore only one or two fitas, softened by time, salt, sea and showers. They were an enduring symbol of superstition; to ensure that your wish was granted, you had to wear them until they fell off on their own.

After a day of walking in circles, I gathered my courage and took the Elevador Lacerda direct from the Praça da Sé down to the small harbour market below. Somewhere between a subway and an elevator, the elegant art-deco box was a claustrophobe's nightmare. Even so, commuters lined up all day long to cram into it for the fifteen seconds it took to drop the seventy metres from cliff face to street level.

I looked into dozens of churches – each more gilded and ornate than the next. The winner of this pageant of excess was the Ingreja do Carno, where a life-sized Jesus lay in state in a glass casket, waiting to be resurrected and carted around the city on festival days. A slave named Francisco Xavier das Chagas had carved him in 1730. He had crushed two thousand rubies in whale oil so that the blood that poured from the stigmata on the statue's hands and feet would glisten. The image of that slave, crouched and crushing to create verisimilitude for something he didn't believe in, dogged me as I walked. Was he, at the end of his long labour, at all convinced, let alone converted?

I started re-reading Jorge Amado's *Dona Flor*, wandering the same streets in which Flor was stalked by the capricious spirit of her dead husband. The more I walked, the more it became obvious that here, the impish would always win over the staid and respectable. The first time I read the book, I'd sympathised a little with Dona Flor's second husband, the stiff-collared chemist unaware that his marital bed was being shared with a ghost. But treading Pelourinho's old stones, breathing in sea breezes and steamy city perfume, I found myself rooting instead for the Dionysian cuckold spirit of Flor's first love.

I bought a pair of havaianas, patterned with black and white Ipanema undulations. I imagined 'Girl from Ipanema' playing under me as I walked, giving my habitual fast-forward a new kind of swirl. I'd always associated the rubbery plack – plack – plack of a havaiana tread with the indolence of beach vacations, or slow labour in hot climes. A rebellion against – or nonchalance in the face of – exertion of any sort whatsoever. Here, it was the hard-working person's footwear. But it was also the sound of warm days and wandering ways.

On Saturday, I revisited Os Agogos. Roberto was there this time, his dreads splaying crazily out of a neon-yellow hair tie.

'You arrived.'

'You were closed.'

He nodded, unapologetic. 'Wednesday night was a late one.'

There was only one customer in the store. A large, sunburned American tourist – the Stetson was a dead giveaway – thumping inexpertly on a small drum.

I told Roberto about the entrancing drumming during the Candomblé ceremony, and he gave me a quick tour of the instruments. Low throaty rums, smaller drums called rumpi and rumpilé. 'And these,' he lifted up a pair of conjoined metal cowbells, 'are the agogos.' He thrummed out a samba rhythm, high and sweet. 'Tonight we play on the Igreja do Passo steps. You should come.'

I had already agreed to meet Edge and Alessandra on the steps that evening. I told him I'd see him there. I needed a nap first.

I'd passed the Passo steps many times on my way home to the Lua Azul. The wide stairway led up to a weathered, Gothic-gabled church, and was bordered by buildings on two sides to form a natural amphitheatre. The church at the top of the steep steps was on the same road as my pousada, but I opted to take the longer route home. From the bottom, a narrow cobbled lane sloped gently up to the top road. It was better suited to my jet-lag lethargy. Two late nights out had helped my head adjust to the time zone, but my body hadn't quite caught up. My cachaça hangover wasn't helping.

The warren of side streets exuded the smells of centuries past and dinners to come. Tonight's menu: chicken and beans, laced with spices and diesel fumes from the mopeds spluttering up the hill.

Midway up the rise, I fell into step behind a woman whose rubber soles beat a hypnotic thwack, thwack, thwack. She held a small child by the hand, a boy whose own havaianas scraped and slapped double time as he hurried to keep up. I started playing the beat in my head along with Roberto's rhythms, but my syncopation was interrupted when the woman veered without warning, tugging her child to the other side of the street.

I was almost on top of the pile of feathers and bones before I noticed the circle of red and black candles around it. Not road kill, but an offering. Something in a cup. *Blood?* Oh superstitious mind – it was probably cachaça. Sleeplessness had increased my suggestibility. But I followed the example of the woman and hurriedly crossed the road. The image of the offering lingered over my left shoulder.

My small room was frigid from air conditioning – the cleaner must have put it on while I was out. Didn't they think about global warming? I switched it off and opened the doors onto the balcony.

Far out over the sea, clouds muttered as they darkened the sky. Ordinarily I would be on alert for lightning, but I was too sleepy.

I left the doors open, curtains billowing as I lay down on the bed and stared at the only piece of artwork in the room: a small block-mounted acrylic in the naïf style I had seen replicated in every art shop in the city.

Two elongated figures drawn in spindly black lines, long arms twisting around and through one another. The one in a skirt looked out – faceless, impassive – the other danced around her. Behind them, a tall red drum. The figures stretched like taffy-pulls, the arcs of their arms leaving trails through the picture, tracing blocks of colour, imprinting the air with their obvious desire. There were tiny cracks in the paint that divided its surface.

I stared at the picture for a long time, at the long limbs cutting through canvas and light, until the molecules began to move and blur. From a base in my belly, vines began growing. They reached up and tangled around my rib cage, finding my heart, the vine tips probing and dividing and covering me with thick green arms, twining and budding and blossoming to fill me until I couldn't breathe. I gasped for air and sat up in bed.

Gloaming. I could barely make out the picture across the room. The two figures, perfectly still, black tendril arms frozen. And only one leaf-sized patch of green between them.

10
The steps

Three hours later I was sitting on grey stone steps as cold as tombstones, with a caipirinha in a plastic cup balanced between my knees, drawn up close to accommodate the people packed around me. My backside was chilled, but the bodies were warm, and the scent of lime crush was waking me up. I pounded the lime and sugar with a short straw in time with the Afro-Brazilian groove.

Roberto gyrated on the stage at the bottom of the Passo steps, dreads bouncing as he drummed his band members and the crowd into a frenzy. An ample man jived on the side stage – he was Gerônimo, a local legend who organised these free concerts every week. Roberto's band was tonight's guest attraction. I knew this because Edge was filling the glaring gaps in my musical education. He told me Gerônimo was the one who composed 'É d'Oxum' – the unofficial anthem of Salvador, the song that had been connecting me to this place for years without my even realising it.

Edge tried lecturing me about bossa nova beats – something about hi-hat and ostinato techniques and paradiddle left eighth notes – until Alessandra elbowed him in the ribs and told him to give me a break. Anyway, she said, the act on stage was more samba-reggae.

Someone bought another round of caipirinhas. In front of me, the canopy of heads looked like a sea of hair undulating towards the shore of the stage. One man with a pair of googly antennae eyes bouncing on the top of his head worked the crowd, handing out pamphlets. I wondered how he managed to find footfall in the crush. Some way down and at the edge of the crowd, I noticed that ridiculous Stetson again. Did Roberto invite all his customers to his concerts?

Edge and Alessandra had to leave before the gig was finished – Ale's mother was babysitting their infant daughter. They offered to see me home, but I assured them that I would find my own way – I was having way too much fun to leave just yet.

And then, with the inevitability of the sea retreating at low tide, it came to an end. At the music's last crescendo, people began melting away, taking their warmth and their candles with them. I joined the cluster around the bandstand to congratulate Roberto. He looked even larger, up on stage. He introduced me to his band mates, and to Gerônimo, who was full of burly bonhomie. They invited me to join them for a few drinks. I hesitated. I was so close to home, but the heart of Pelourinho, where they were headed, was in the opposite direction. Plus my second wind was fading fast.

'Next time,' I told him, and waved them off as they lugged their gear to a waiting van.

I decided to take the shorter route home – straight upwards. Halfway up the steps, I began to regret my decision.

Now that the crowds had gone, the light from the tall wrought-iron lamps seemed dimmer, as if the crush of bodies had somehow amplified and refracted it. The light pooled in lonely circles, leaving long spaces in between. I counted the number of steps from light edge to light edge – seven. I looked back down to the dismantled stage area – perhaps I could still catch them? But Gerônimo and Roberto and their gear were gone. There were only a few stragglers left, and they all seemed to be walking in the other direction.

I was suddenly mindful of crime warnings. A woman. Alone after dark. The pousada might not be far away, but distance meant nothing. Time has a way of telescoping. A lot could happen in an instant.

If I had gone back to town with the others, I could have taken a taxi to my doorstep. But … I squared my shoulders and shrugged off negative thoughts. The idea that energy follows thought is a quasi-quantum notion that fits into my scientific 'don't know' category. Still, I couldn't shake the memory of the candle-ringed pile of feathers and bone not far from here.

At the top of the steps, in the shadowy lee of the church gate, three young men had formed an impromptu roda. Their capoeira moves were clumsy and aggressive, a parody of the reverent fight-dance practised by white-clad acolytes all over the city. These guys were more gangsta-rap; baggy pants and trainers, plastic bangles and metal chains. If I conjured them a backbeat, it wouldn't be the bow-like berimbau, but Edge's favela-flavoured hip hop. I concentrated on making myself inconspicuous.

One of them kicked out high towards the other's head, his neon trainers flashing apple-green. The other ducked and jibbed, parried with a few quick boxing feints. A third one leaned against the fence with his arms crossed. He was looking straight at me. He said something quietly to his buddies, and they stopped their jousting and fell in next to him.

I was almost level with them now. I was hiking fit, so I couldn't understand why I was so out of breath. Jet lag and caipirinhas notwithstanding, I was keenly aware of my disadvantage.

The one with the trainers said something to the other two, and they laughed without looking away. I didn't see the signal, but I saw its effect; the three congealed, and began to advance.

I had reached the top of the stairs. If I turned down my road now, I would have my back to them, which would only make me more vulnerable. I had to stop and face them.

They split up and surrounded me. One stood directly in front of me, the other two on either side. The drop of stairs loomed vertiginous behind me. Green shoes resumed his battle rolls and feinted, left to right, like a cobra sway.

'Quer dancar, garota?'

Wanna dance, girlie?

Suddenly he fell back, his face twisting in annoyance. I felt, rather than heard, someone come up behind me.

It was Zé, who had emerged from the shadows below. Without a word to the young men or to me, he took my arm and steered me back down the steps. I heard the hoick and splatter of spit hitting the stones behind us.

At the bottom of the steps, Zé dropped my arm and climbed onto a motorbike, motioning for me to get on the back. He still hadn't said a word. And I felt too foolish to say anything.

I swung my leg over the machine and put my hands around his waist. I could feel the cord he wore there, underneath his T-shirt. As he gunned up the hill, I had to lean in and hold on tighter. As sheepish as I felt being rescued this way, I couldn't help smiling into the back of him. It felt that good to hold a man.

There was no chance to speak over the engine on the short road home. And he didn't invite chit-chat when we reached the arched doorway of the Lua Azul.

'I'm sorry,' I started to thank him, but he stopped me.

'You must take better care.'

'I know.'

'I might not be there next time.'

'I know,' I said. 'I don't even know how you . . .'

He put up his hand. 'I was at the concert. I saw you there. Lucky I came back to check.' He gunned the motor. 'Until Monday.'

I stood in the street for a long time, listening to the splutter of his engine grow fainter until it disappeared.

In Transit

What is it with airports and greenery? There is not a living plant anywhere here. Once, in transit through Singapore and in search of fresh air, I stepped out into a garden of sunflowers on an observation deck. From inside, the yellow heads swaying in the jet breeze looked so enticing. Turned out it was a popular smoking area, the sunflower roots all tangled up in Marlborough and Stuyvesant stubs. Unlucky Strike. And not a bee in sight.

Right now, I'd welcome any bit of green, no matter how distressed. If I close my eyes, my mind fills with forest. A certain garden in the middle of a forest.

Don't go there.

Across the hall is another kind of smokers' bar, open at the sides, with a roof extractor fan. Travellers huddle underneath it, sucking in their poison with naked desperation while they down sweet caffeine shots. If Em was here, she would wrap her legs around a bar stool, her lips around her cigarette holder, and the barista around her little finger. She would give him the full Lauren Bacall treatment. She would take her coffee with a shot of Absolut on the side. And extra sugar.

Tobacco. Coffee. Sugar. Three plants that drove the slave trade. How many of these were necessary for human survival? None. How many were highly addictive? All of them. Three addictions that changed the world.

I wonder if people could have done what they did in pursuit of those plants if they hadn't been in the grip of a chemical obsession? Souls uprooted, families broken, villages razed, hearts wrung, children torn from parents, people treated worse than animals, animals treated like slaves, all because of a desire – a desire, not a need – for certain plants. Who but people mad with drug-lust could have conceived of such things?

The Starbucks I'm sitting in is proof that empires are still being built around such cravings. I was tempted to resist this particular empire, but the table is tucked away and seemed a discreet place to hunker down for a while. Not that I'm hiding, or anything.

Watch your back.

Plus the mermaid logo reminds me of Yemanjá. I'm pretty sure this mermaid used to have breasts. And you used to be able to see the fork of her tail where it split in two. She was much more lascivious before she was cleaned up to suit coy America's ideal of its own innocence. Now all you can see are the ends of her tail, which she holds offstage like two limp fish, and the stylised zigzag of hair that hides her bosom.

Thanks to international brand bland, I could be anywhere. But the coffee, at least, should be local. I want to feel Brazil for just a little bit longer.

Coffee took over in Brazil's south. In Salvador and the rest of the northeast, sugar reigned supreme. It couldn't have been done without slavery.

People followed seeds, and seeds followed people. In sacks and boots and bedding, in crates and pockets and cloth, some accidentally, others intentionally. Like my *Newbouldia mundii*. I don't believe its journey was an accident. I'm sure the first person to take the little star seed to Brazil was mindful of what they were doing.

Or maybe the plant was the one doing the directing? We always assume that plant cultivation was directed to suit human tastes and desires. But what if the plants themselves had something to do with it?

That's what Michael Pollan suggested in *The Botany of Desire*. I felt like I'd found a kindred spirit when I read his theory. Poor busy bees, they thought *they* were deciding which flower to choose and which to avoid, but Pollan said the flower traits those bees 'selected' over evolutionary millennia were designed by the plants themselves to manipulate bee vanity.

Is it so crazy to suppose that we, too, are controlled by plants, and not the other way around? Just look how long it took us to come around to the fact that it was actually the sun, and not 'our' earth at the centre of everything.

So did I pursue the star seed, or did the seed call me? Had I been summoned to bring it home?

If the plants have the power, then it was they that found ways of enticing, captivating, addicting us, to the extent that we'd move mountains, conquer lands, trade people, betray loved ones – in order to possess them.

Coffee, sugar, tobacco, spices, cotton, tea, rubber, cocoa. Plants gave us the fixes that fixed places in our collective consciousness – Darjeeling, Durban Poison, Virginia Leaf, Arabica Bean, Bogota Powder. They caused revolutionary 'Tea Parties'. They created entire cities – if not for nutmeg, there would be no New York, at least not in the form that we know it.

Miss Starbucks stares at me from the curved paper cup, and tells me my ravings are lunatic. I could blame the caffeine. But I think the plants are blameless. Interesting that the crops we feel we can't live without provide no real sustenance. And in excess, they pose the potential for serious harm. Hypertension and diabetes, anyone?

It isn't fair to blame our weaknesses on plants. Lust, greed or addiction – which weakness convinced me to come on this expedition in the first place? And which of them is calling me to turn around, to stay?

My mission is accomplished. There's no good reason not to go home.

Where might that be, exactly?

It's true that there are places here in Brazil that have become addictively familiar. One place in particular. It smells of pepper and coriander and pine. Of sweet, sweet sweat.

Perhaps home can be a person, after all.

Stop it!

My coffee finished, I really need to pee. I can see the ubiquitous stickman signs on the far side of the concourse. To get there, I'll have to pass a man in a blue-grey uniform, and his sidekick of brown fur. Man and dog. Trained to sniff out contraband.

Can they sniff out fear? Or sadness? Or guilt? They say dogs can detect cancer. What about confusion? Loneliness? Despair? If that were the case, everyone would be a suspect. And the crime its own punishment.

My need is urgent, so I run the gauntlet. The bathroom is white, sterile. They say coffee is more diuretic than tea. My Five Roses ran out halfway through my forty days here, but even so, coffee doesn't usually have this effect on me. To which orixá do I appeal to save me from spending my entire flight queuing for the toilet?

At least this restroom isn't as crowded as the ones I remember from the outward trip, when we were all volcano-trapped. Then they were full of families bathing in basins, and all the towel and toilet roll dispensers empty. I remember one desperate woman holding her screaming baby, bottom up, under the blast from a wall-mounted blow-dryer.

The stall seems clean enough. Still, I hover so as not to touch anything.

I stand up too quickly, because the wall spins. I put out a hand to steady myself. Damn – touched something after all.

I feel so diff-er-ent ... For a second, Sinead O'Connor is in the bathroom with me, her voice so clear I actually open the cubicle door to look for her. Earworm, Nico would call it. He doesn't even know I'm on my way back. When did I stop writing to him?

You know when ...

Strange that that song pops up now. Lately, I've had nothing but the songs of Salvador going through my brain. Gal Costa, the Tribalistas – Arnaldo Antunes with his basement basso profondo, Marisa Monte and Carlinhos Brown – they're all in my suitcase, along with Caetano Veloso and Bebel Gilberto, Olodum and Os Mutantes. And the CD from the guy who was playing in our café one night. He burned his own recordings, slipped in a photograph of himself and scrawled his name on the CD in permanent pen. The recording was tinny and awful. But ...

Our café.

There's a boto in my luggage too, a rosewood carving of the small pink river dolphin. A gift for Marilese, for looking after Vavi all this time. And a book on Brazilian legends for her kids, with the story of the shape-shifter to go with the carving.

As a child, I saw botos flash their pink flanks in the Rio Negro and was told their story. When the moon is right, they say, the boto changes into an irresistible man, in a sharp white suit and jaunty hat. He appears magically at social gatherings, blends with the moonstruck crowds, and lures an innocent young girl into a night of unrivalled pleasure.

By daybreak, he would be gone. Dissolved back into the river, pink and naked, with the dolphin's knowing smile. 'But, papai,' the hapless young girl would say when her new pink baby began to grow inside her, 'I could not help it, it was the boto!'

I'm not sure this story teaches children to take responsibility for their actions. But then, how many of us ever really learn to do that?

11
Akokô

I was so looking forward to my first real day in the garden, I could hardly get through the three tepid cups of tea I call breakfast. At the appointed hour, I found Zé drinking coffee with a small group on the veranda of the terreiro's canteen kitchen. Their chat and banter stopped as soon as I approached.

Zé introduced me hurriedly. Not for the last time, I wondered what it meant for him to be obliged to extend his hospitality to me this way. Whether he resented the intrusion into his world. He drained his cup, and signalled me to follow him. I felt the eyes of the group on me, prickling between my shoulder blades as I walked away. Their voices started up again as soon as we passed out of their field of vision.

Zé walked in front of me, sliding down some of the steeper parts of the path without waiting to see whether I was keeping up. I wondered why no one had made access to the garden easier. Perhaps not that many people came this way. Perhaps they kept it intentionally tricky to discourage visitors. Or maybe Zé was just so used to it that it didn't occur to him to do anything about it.

He didn't mention the incident on the Passo steps.

The temperature dropped as soon as we entered the trees, and the air felt richer. I breathed in new oxygen, decay and regrowth.

There's something deeply comforting about tree contours. My eyes slipped over rounded canopies, compact cones and umbrella tops; the tree I was looking for was slim and narrow. If *Newbouldia mundii* was here, it had some serious competition. In floristic terms, Bahian old-growth forest was as diverse as the fynbos back home. One researcher plotted four hundred and fifty tree species in a one-hundred-square-metre patch of this forest – that's more than occurs in the whole of North America. I had my work cut out for me.

Zé led us deep into the centre of the garden. We passed the clearing with the peregun where we had first met, and continued winding through thick undergrowth until we came to a natural amphitheatre where the forest opened up to let in light. There were rough stands of herbs and vegetables, bordered by bamboo fences draped with sun-loving vines. A maracuja in full flower displayed an indecent amount of white petticoat. At the far edge of the clearing, a fallen ficus provided a natural log bench. Zé motioned for me to sit, and squatted down in front of me.

'Today I will introduce you to the garden.' He rested his elbows on his thighs, his hands clasped in front of him. He wasn't uncomfortably close, but I was intensely aware of him. He was more formally dressed than last time, all in white. His collarless cotton shirt had a tracing of embroidery at the neckline. He wore green and red beads around both wrists.

'We grow more than one hundred plants here,' Zé began. 'Many of them originated in Africa. Some were already here when our people came.' His toes clenched and released the thong of his havaianas as he rocked on his haunches. A few inches from his left foot, a small column of red fire ants marched in single file and disappeared under the log.

'Each one is associated with a different orixá,' Zé continued, 'depending on its healing properties, or the colour of its flower, or whether it is hot or cold – these things tell us if its essence is of a particular orixá.'

Over his shoulder, I saw a stand of tall, slim trees. They stood like sentinels at the clearing edge. Glabrous leaves, dark green and waxy, clustered racemes of flowers, tinged with mauve. *Newbouldia laevis*. I felt my breath catch.

'Akokô,' he said, without turning around.

'It's the cousin of one I'm interested in.' I knew my voice betrayed my excitement, and I wasn't sure how much Ernesto had told him. 'In West Africa it's also called the "boundary tree"; people plant them between properties . . .'

'The Yoruba people also planted them in sacred places,' he said, his tone casual. 'You would find them outside the homes of kings. It is one of Xangô's trees.'

His body unfurled in one easy motion as he stood. He walked over to the tallest of the akokôs. 'This one was brought by Pierre Verger, you know of him?' I nodded, grateful for the primer I'd got at Ernesto's house. 'At the beginning of last century, there was only one of these sacred trees in the whole of Salvador. So in the 1940s, Fatumbi went to Nigeria and brought back some cuttings. He gave them to the most important terreiros in Salvador.'

'Fatumbi?'

'That is what we called him – Pierre Fatumbi Verger. It's an honorary name.'

Zé reached up to grab a small branch. He had to stretch to pull it down. Despite my excitement at being one step closer to *Newbouldia mundii*, I enjoyed the way his muscles moved underneath the thin cotton shirt. He came back bearing a stem of flowers, and I told myself to focus on them.

I had only seen the flower before in photographs. It was tubular-shaped, its lip split into four slightly crumpled petals, tinged with pink. He handed me the bract, and I breathed in their sweet smell. And something else; musk and pepper.

'The leaves of the akokô are worn for luck. And to attract money.' He was squatting in front of me again. I'm not a foot fetishist, but his were beautiful. Long, jointed toes, elegant, even with a blue patterned Band-Aid on the littlest toe of his left foot. It had a yellow cartoon character on it.

His flip-flops were strangely feminine for someone who oozed so much testosterone; light purple with – I would find out later – a gold twirling pattern on the upper soles, covered now by the pad of his foot. Under his pants, his leg bulged where the long thigh joined the knee. I made this bit of muscle my point of focus. I could look at this neutral space and take in the rest of him, subliminally, without seeming to stare.

'It is of Xangô, but usually the flowers of Xangô are more red. He is a hot orixá.'

'The flowers of the version I am looking for are like this, but red . . .' It occurred to me that if my star-seed tree was to be found in any terreiro, it was likely to be one ruled by Xangô. Maybe I was getting the hang of this.

'Tia Betinha remembers the day Fatumbi Verger brought the cuttings here. You can ask her about it. I will introduce you.' And then he added, 'Most of Xangô's plants are tall trees. They are the ones that attract lightning.'

I must have caught my breath. Nobody ever fully recovers from a lightning strike. Some die. Some are maimed for life. Some walk away, keeping their scars inside. But everyone who lives remembers that long nanosecond between ignorant hope and the final knowledge that hope, no matter how fervent, cannot bring back what has been and is now gone. Which is why lightning and grief are the same.

Now Zé had my full attention. I needed to stop ogling the man like a teenager and listen to him.

I followed him around the garden, his introduction taking on the feel of ceremony. He started at the edge of the clearing, moving in widening circles, pointing out flowers or herbs, naming their gods or goddesses, paying homage to each orixá, and following their naming with the soft exhortation: 'Axé!'

Ash-eh!

He was presenting the garden to me as a host would a stranger to a dinner party of old friends: with utmost care and courtesy. But I soon realised he was only introducing me to the common plants, ones I was already familiar with. Camomile and mint for Oxum, small wild strawberries (Xangô again), a fragrant lemongrass-like reed for the hunter, Oxossi. And he was going so fast that I struggled to keep track of all the sacred connections.

The last flower he showed me looked, with its frilly gyre, like an upturned wedding skirt.

'This one we call cornet. It is of Oxalá, the orixá of peace. All white flowers belong to him.' He twirled the stem so the flower spun gracefully. 'If he was your orixá and you were sick, the mãe- or pai-de-santo would mix you a remedy that contained the herbs you needed. Or she might mix you something to change your energies.'

We were back at the log now. I checked before I sat back down, but the red ant column was nowhere to be seen. 'This one is of Ossain,' he continued, pointing at a clump of swaying narcissus nearby. 'He also rules the almond tree, and the dendê.'

'But doesn't Ossain rule *all* the plants?'

He cocked his head. 'Ossain is the only one who knows the secrets and uses for all. But as I have shown you, each orixá has his or her own plants also. There is a reason for that, but it's a long story. Perhaps it should wait for another time?'

'What I'd like to know more about is how you propagate the seasonal plants, and store them. How you keep the seeds.' *And where.*

His demeanour changed, a cloud passing over the sun. I had blundered. He had carefully choreographed this lesson, constructing a circle of story that I had thoughtlessly broken. The man was hard work.

'The seeds are kept secure.' He hadn't moved, but it felt like he had withdrawn to the other side of the clearing.

'At our seed bank we can keep seeds for fifty years, in refrigeration,' I pressed on. 'But we still have to grow them every fifteen years or so, to make sure they are still viable. I would imagine that you have some kind of system for the older seeds?'

'This is a living garden.'

'Yes, but I mean, they can't all be on the vine, as it were . . .'

'The mãe-de-santo takes care of them. She keeps them safe.'

Safe from fire? I wanted to ask. *Safe from flood?* How to make him see that I was interested in the greater importance of what he had here, above and beyond the arcane ritualistic dance of the orixás?

'Some of the plants here are endangered where they came from,' I said. He regarded me blankly, as if what I was saying had no bearing on him or what he did. 'Some of them might even be extinct,' I pushed on. 'Without the seed, you can't have the plant.'

'And without the plant, *you* can't have the seed.'

He rose abruptly and walked to a dense cluster of bushes on the eastern boundary of the glade.

He stood a long time with his head bent down, talking to the plants. When he returned, he was holding a leafy spray dotted with what look like small peppercorns. Nigerian malagueta pepper.

'I made a grave mistake.' It was the first time I'd seen him look anything other than arrogant. 'I neglected to begin by introducing one of the most important orixás: Exu, who rules communications.' I noticed that there were gold flecks in his hazel eyes. The colour of sun shafts penetrating the water in a Cederberg mountain pool. Then he grinned. 'Exu does not like to be ignored.'

I felt a sharp sting in my left buttock.

'Damn!' I jumped up, swatting at my pants. The red ant column was on the march across my seat.

Zé laughed. 'Come with me.' My rudeness appeared to have been forgiven; he offered me his hand to step me over the log, and led me across to a patch of vegetables. He squatted down next to a bottle gourd plant and picked up a small green squash, still immature. 'This we call cabaça. It symbolises the connection between the earth and the spirit world.' He rolled the green calabash between his fingers. 'When our people arrived here in Salvador, it was already here, exactly the same as in Africa. As if the orixás knew we were coming.' He laid the squash gently back down on the ground. 'It is also said to be the magical container of Ossain. Remember this when you hear Ossain's story.'

I realised with a sinking sense that I would not be hearing the story from him today. Our time in the garden was over.

I followed him back up the steep path, keeping my eyes on the tricky footing, and all my other senses on the man in front of me.

I wished it was tomorrow already.

12
Iroko

I expected Zé to leave me at the garden entrance, but he walked me through the compound to a flat-roofed building near the main gate. 'Wait here,' he told me, and ducked inside.

It was one of a number of houses dotted around the grounds. Some were small, surely no bigger than one room, and seemed to be dedicated to the orixás. Each one had the name of its resident deity over the door, and was painted in the associated colour. None of the doors were open.

Other houses had washing hanging out to dry, or some other sign that real people lived there. This one had a door painted red. Zé had left it ajar, and I could hear kitchen clatter and TV chatter coming from inside.

The sun was baking the top of my head, and I was beginning to long again for the coolness of the forest when Zé emerged from the doorway.

'Tia Betinha says she will see you. She remembers when Fatumbi Verger brought the akokô. You can ask her.'

He walked me past a warren of rooms down a short dark passage, which opened into a crowded living room at the back of the building. A small boy slouched at one end of a dining table, watching an episode of *The Simpsons* dubbed into Portuguese. When Bart cackled at someone's expense, he sounded exactly the same as he did in the American original. Maybe laughter doesn't need to be translated.

There was a long bench under the window, and on a chair next to it sat Tia Betinha. She must have been at least eighty years old. Her hair was tied up in a patterned scarf, and the beads that hung over her white cotton shirt were red and white, green and blue. There was a woman of about my age kneeling at her feet, who seemed to be reeling off a long list of problems and/or requests.

The old woman looked over her supplicant's shoulder and indicated for me to sit on the bench while she attended to the woman. This gave me plenty of time to take in my surroundings. The near end of the table was crowded with devotional dolls like the ones in the museum, dressed to represent the various orixás. They reminded me of those Spanish flamenco dolls with their flounces and their fans that every little girl seemed to have when I was growing up. Every little girl except me, that is. There were red and green and turquoise dresses, made with loving attention to detail. I wondered if Tia Betinha spent her evenings sewing those fine seams.

I counted at least four clocks, three on the walls and one on the mantelpiece. All of them were set to different times. None of them seemed to be moving.

The smell of stew reminded me how long it had been since breakfast.

Eventually the supplicating woman kissed Tia Betinha's hands and thanked her. On her way out, she ruffled the hair of the young boy. He raised his eyes from the TV long enough to ask his grandmother when they would be eating. I guessed it wasn't the first time he'd asked the question that day. There was a clock hanging over the door, and Tia Betinha looked at it for so long that I wondered whether she had lost her train of thought, or was calculating time. The clock said five past seven, but judging by the angle of the sun outside I knew it was barely past noon.

'In a little bit,' Tia Betinha told him, and turned to me. 'What can I do for you, my daughter?' Her voice was gentle. She radiated love, and not a shred of resentment that I might be keeping her from her meal. Now that she had turned her attention to me, I found I wanted to ask her if I could just stay there, quietly, and rest in her presence. Instead, I started talking.

I explained where I had come from, my work with plants, my interest in the terreiro garden. I told her about the presentation I would give here in a few days' time. She expressed polite interest, and assured me that she would attend.

I explained about the cousin of the akokô tree that had been lost in Africa. I described the seed that looked like a star. I even shared my hypothesis that it might be one of the plants beloved of Xangô.

Tia Betinha was quiet for a long while, and when she began talking, I had to lean in close to hear her above the noise of traffic outside and the excitable TV commercials.

'Iroko,' she said. 'If you cut a branch from Iroko, you lose an arm. If you cut his trunk, you will lose a leg. There are those who are afraid even to look at Iroko for fear that they will be struck dead.' My wide eyes must have conveyed my confusion, because Tia Betinha pointed to a picture on the wall. A man or god standing in front of a tree, his brown skin blending with the trunk, his face obscured by a crown of leaves, a white loincloth for modesty. A tree orixá, of course! I recalled the thick white ribbons tied like cummerbunds around the trees at the edge of the garden. Iroko?

'We should hug a tree every day. Every day, we should hug a tree!' Tia's smile made her look like a young girl. She reached out and took my hand. 'And always keep your promises to Iroko.

This is most important. His realm is time, he rules over life and death.' She kept hold of my hand in her small dry one, and stared into the middle distance. At that moment, it made perfect sense that none of the clocks worked.

'I remember when pai brought the akokô here,' she continued, eventually. 'I was a very young girl, only five years old. He arrived with the branches in his arms, like a baby. They were wrapped in his shirt, which he kept wet, all the way from Africa.' She shook her head as if she still couldn't believe it, seven decades later. 'They had leaves sticking out, some of them. The leaves were still on. All the way from Africa.'

'José Carlos – Zé – told me that the akokô is one of Xangô's trees?'

Tia Betinha nodded. Her next words were drowned out by the roar of a passing bus. I spoke louder.

'And the akokô's cousin, *Newbouldia mundii*? I don't know if it has another Yoruba name. But the flowers are red and the leaves a little ...' I made the shape with my hands. Tia Betinha regarded me for a very long time. I was not sure if she misunderstood me, or if I had transgressed some kind of boundary. Again.

'There are many stories,' she said eventually. 'Many, many stories that you will need to hear. So much that you need to learn.' She closed her eyes and sat there, holding my hand. She held it so long that I thought she might have fallen asleep. There was a screech of brakes as Bart Simpson dodged a car. The old woman's eyes snapped open, and she released my hand.

'Gracas ao poder – Axé! – que possui sobre elas,' Tia Betinha said.

Thanks to the power – Axé! – he holds over them.

My response was automatic, involuntary: 'Axé!' It was like a sneeze, this 'amen' to the orixás. It was the first time I invoked the name. It was the moment I stepped fully into the game.

When I emerged back into the bright sunlight, I was surprised to find Zé sitting on a low wall, waiting for me. He stood up.

'Okay?'

I nodded. 'She told me I should come back tomorrow afternoon when I'm finished in the garden, so she can tell me stories.' I grinned at him. 'I'm joining her for lunch.'

'That's good,' he said. 'Maybe she likes you.' The school bell rang to signal the end of the learning day. 'As for me, I'm not sure yet whether I like you.' He didn't appear to be joking. 'Let's have dinner tonight and find out.'

13
Lightning

'Don't tell me you're falling for that voodoo mumbo-jumbo?'

Kirk's voice was harsh over the phone line, distorted by distance. The connection in my room wasn't robust enough for Skype. Which was a relief – I didn't feel like speaking to him face to face.

'It's a very closed community, Kirk. And so far they've been incredibly welcoming and helpful, thanks to Ernesto opening doors. I'm just doing what I need to do to earn their trust.'

'But still no sign of the tree.'

Outside the grey clouds were massing, as they did every afternoon.

'I've been in the garden precisely twice, Kirk. It's a jungle out there, literally. Saw lots of boundary trees, though.'

'*Newbouldia laevis* I can find down the road.' I'd glimpsed his petulant side before, but it was usually directed at someone else.

'It's actually very interesting, the way they categorise the plants for healing and "magical" work.' He couldn't see my air quotes, but I knew he would know I was making them. 'All according to these deity archetypes. If I was an ethnobotanist, I'd set up a display in Kirstenbosch, link it to the traditional African healing garden ...'

'This is not a touchy-feely playing-in-the-garden mission, Maddy.'

'Until you get those permissions, that's exactly what it is.' A gust of wind billowed the curtains and the balcony door swung on its hinges. I stretched the phone cord as far as it would go and managed to reach the door to shut it. 'How long until we get those?'

'There's a slight hitch.'

I let my long silence ask the question.

'Turns out there's been a significant change in Brazilian legislation in the last ten years. Permission needs to be applied for *before* the researcher arrives in the country.'

Had he really not known this? A squall of rain spattered against the windowpane. Out at sea, long rays of sunlight forced the clouds open, reaching down to light up patches of water.

'You there, Maddy?'

'I'm processing what you're saying.' The squall was already passing, and sunlight lit up the droplets on the balcony railing. 'So I need to leave, come back home, re-apply, and then come out here again?'

Or they might just send someone else to find the seed. Strange that the thought filled me with such dismay. I'd only just got here – I was hardly even over my jet lag. And I was already fond of the little star seed, and invested in the idea that I might be the one to find it and save it.

'No, no, we're working on it from this side. You just carry on there. When are you doing your dog-and-pony?'

My laptop was open on the bed, showing a slide from a PowerPoint presentation. It was a close-up of the orange *Leonotis leonurus* flower, also known as 'wild dagga'. I always got a laugh when I advised audiences not to smoke the plant. Despite its name, and a slight similarity in the hand-shaped, serrated leaves, it had no biochemical relation to marijuana. What you *can* use the herb for, I would tell people, is treating snakebite and scorpion stings. Its African name was 'umfincafincane', and it was traditionally planted around huts to keep away vipers and adders. I had masses of it along my own veranda. I liked the way its flowers attracted bees. And sunbirds – or *beija-flor*, as they called them here. *Kiss the flower*.

My presentation consisted of a photographic tour of the African medicinal garden in Kirstenbosch. It had pictures of the plants in situ and in their traditional settings, being used by rural and urban sangomas, and a few remote farmers still in touch with old Dutch medicine. For a moment I was taken there, to the jewel-green lawns and wooded slopes of the amphitheatre formed by the back contours of the Table Mountain chain. I could see the view Kirk would be looking at, from his office. Did I miss it? Not a bit. Perhaps I should have been more surprised. Through the earpiece, I could hear the impatient drumming of Kirk's pencil on his desktop.

'The presentation is next week.'

Outside my window, on this side of the Atlantic, the sunlight burnished the steely surface of the sea. My 'dog-and-pony', as Kirk called it, wouldn't be any match for Zé's performance this morning, his tightly choreographed show. He'd been tasked to give me something in exchange for what I was, supposedly, bringing to them. He was fulfilling his side of the bargain. And I'd been so intent on my *actual* mission that I'd been impatient and ungracious. Even if Zé was a stuck-up pain in the ass.

Was tonight's dinner part of the deal?

'What exactly does Ernesto think I am after?' It was the first time I'd thought to ask the question. Kirk's drumming stopped.

'I told you, as far as they're concerned, it's a cultural exchange. They know, of course, that we are looking for *N. mundii* as part of our interest in rare seeds. But they don't know that our interest goes beyond saving the tree from extinction.'

'And that's all it is?'

Kirk's pause was a little too long. 'Well, let's just say if they knew about the pharmacological interest, they might do a deal with someone else, and not give us access. But once we get the go-ahead from the Brazilian ministry, and as long as you convince them that our motives are pure, the local people will fall into line.'

I wasn't so sure. Terreiro members knew all about conflict with authority. The freedom to practise Candomblé openly and legitimately had been hard-fought. They were unlikely to roll over and allow those traditions to be messed with by any outside 'authority'.

I could understand why. It was like colonisation all over again. Except that the new imperialists could tell themselves they were doing it for the greater good of the plant. When I'd questioned his mention of a sponsor at the beginning of our call, Kirk admitted that some funding for my expedition had been provided by a company called SeedCorp.

'It's all perfectly normal, part of their social responsibility programme. No need to be paranoid.'

I hate it when people call me paranoid. And I'm not a good liar. Neither, I was discovering, was Kirk.

'So why does this all have to be so clandestine?'

'Oh, come on, Maddy, we're the good guys!'

For the first time, I wasn't so sure.

I took a shower and threw the balcony doors open again. I could feel the humid air on my naked skin. The storm had moved far out to sea, stabbing it with forks of lightning. Zeus wrestling with his old rival Poseidon. Or perhaps it was Xangô inviting Yemanjá to dance.

I'd spent the rest of the afternoon reading the book Kolade gave me – Wole Soyinka's *The Seven Signposts*. The spellings were different – he talked of 'Orisas' and Xangô was called 'Sango'. But there he was, the lightning man, with the same godly qualities. Standing for justice and wielding his axe. 'Can mere brick on brick withstand the bloodied cries of wrong from the aggrieved?' I read. 'No more than dark withstands the flare of lightning, roofs of straw the path of thunderbolts. Sango restores.'

Xangô restores. The images of my mother, the tomahawk, the lightning strike, burning buildings. It was all a little too coincidental. There were only a handful of Orisas in the book, but Sango was a major player. Maybe he had something to do with it all. Maybe I was going mad. The call with Kirk hadn't helped. I wanted so badly to believe in something. Xangô restores.

I stood on the balcony and watched the lightning far out at sea, thinking about the many times I'd climbed to high places and invited those electric fingers to reach out and claim me like they had my mother. But they never did. They never do. And every time they don't, I feel exultant – I'm still standing!

And then I feel the other side of victory, which is shame.

Lightning doesn't strike twice, they say. It doesn't have to. Once is enough.

The young night porter stopped me on my way out. He was lanky and chronically shy – possibly because of the craterous acne that scarred his neck. That, and his almost painful deference, made him an odd choice for a job with a public interface.

'Desculpe,' he said, handing me another blue message without looking me in the eye. 'The man from Manaus, he called again. Your phone was busy.'

'Thank you.' I took the blue note, glanced at it, and crumpled it up.

I felt him watching as I leaned over the reception desk and tossed it, in a perfect arc, into the wastepaper basket.

14
Dinner

We'd arranged to meet at the Praça da Sé. I was early, so I bought a coconut. The vendor trepanned it with his machete, and I sipped the cool water through a straw while I waited next to the statue in the middle of the square. The sombre Bishop Pedro Fernandes Sardinha (1496 – 1556) seemed unimpressed by the lively activities around him. Perhaps he disapproved of indulgence. Or of the way his dark cowl had been anointed with pigeon shit.

'You know why he is famous?'

I hadn't heard Zé come up behind me, but I felt his warmth and recognised his scent as he leaned in close and whispered with exaggerated melodrama into my left ear. I felt strands of my hair moving against his lips as he breathed: 'They ate him.'

I jerked back, hard, and felt my head connect with his nose.

'Nossa!'

'Oh shit, I'm so sorry.' Serves you right for sneaking up on me is what I wanted to say.

'It's okay.' His eyes were watering, but they were also laughing. I couldn't help smiling back. 'Nothing broken.'

'The first drink is on me, then.'

'As long as it's something stronger than *that*.' He relieved me of the coconut husk, and tossed it into a nearby trashcan. He seemed more playful away from the constraints of the terreiro.

'And who is "they"?' I fell into step beside him.

'Caeto Indians.' He nodded a greeting at a dona selling pastéis on the far side of the square. 'You know Jorge Amado?'

'Of course.'

'He says it is typical of the Bahiana, that this person should be celebrated here, in this famous square, when all he did for Salvador was provide one dinner!'

I wished I'd paid better attention to our route through the maze of side streets. When we arrived at the small Bahian eatery, I realised I would never be able to find it again on my own – and I could already tell by the smells that the food would be excellent.

The owner was a large woman with an immaculate white apron over her full skirts. She clasped Zé Carlos to her bosom, planting possessive kisses on each of his cheeks, and appraised me from a safe distance. I could tell I was being measured, but I had no idea by what yardstick.

Only two other tables were occupied this early. At one, a middle-aged couple; at the other, a thin old man who ate alone, completely absorbed in the yellow mound on his plate. He was missing the two middle fingers of his right hand, but this didn't seem to affect his dexterity as he forked food methodically into his mouth. He nodded a greeting at Zé, but didn't pause in his eating.

On the wall above our table, a yellowing Veja magazine cover in a plastic frame showed a feather-headed young samba queen bursting out of yellow and green sequins. 'Dona Marta's daughter,' Zé said.

There was a blue vase of fresh white flowers under the only other picture in the place, a faded tapestry of Yemanjá – obligatory for any establishment serving fruta de mar. Only this Yemanja, with her long blue veil and sanctimonious gaze, looked more like a middle-European Mary than an uncompromising African sea goddess.

The portable television set high on the wall showed the rolling credits of a telenovela. The next one would be starting soon, so Dona Marta kept an eye on it as she came over with menus and bread.

'Tell me more about the guy in the statue,' I said. And wished I hadn't. It was hard to concentrate on food descriptions while listening to the bishop's gruesome story.

'The Caeté Indians were sometimes cannibals, so it was not so special for them to eat the first white man they ever saw.' He tore bread into small pieces while he spoke. 'Of course, this was all the provocation the Portuguese invaders needed. The governor of this new Brazil, Mem de Sá, used it as an excuse to make the Indians into slaves. But they were not suited to it. Which is why they began to bring slaves from Africa.'

'I wouldn't have thought anybody was "suited" to slavery.'

'You are right, of course.' Zé shoved bread in his mouth and chewed. 'Although it seems my ancestors were among the "suitable" ones.'

Dona Marta was back with our drinks – Antarctica beer for him, caipirinha for me. While Zé ordered for both of us, I closed my eyes and breathed in the high-octane promise of lime and cachaça. When I opened my eyes, he was waiting with his beer, and one eyebrow, raised.

'Saúde.'

I think I moaned out loud at that first kicker sip, and Zé laughed. 'Caipirinhas suit you!' His eyebrow was up again. It went so far up his forehead it looked like it was marching, caterpillar-like, towards his scalp. His other eyebrow stayed exactly where it was. Extraordinary.

'What?'

'That thing you do with your eyebrow – I think you're laughing at me.'

'Of course I'm laughing at you. But you will forgive me, because I forgive you for almost breaking my nose.'

By the time our second round of drinks came, we'd found our flow. We floated between English and Portuguese – he didn't get much chance to practise English, he said. And my Portuguese was like an old jalopy that's thrilled to be running again, until it remembers that it's left half its parts behind on Grandpa's lawn. But the talking was easy.

Zé told me he was part way through a degree in philosophy and comparative religion – which explained his attention to detail in matters of the gods. He also ran a gardening service outside the terreiro, tending the lawns and verges in the richer neighbourhoods: Itaigara, Brotas and Pituba. It was from this, rather than his terreiro gardening, that he supplied basic medicinal herbs to sellers in the city's Candomblé leaf houses, which in turn sold them on to the terreiros and practitioners for their rituals. For the most part, the homeowners of the gardens he tended were unaware of the healing properties in their herbaceous borders.

But it was his real money-making activity that delighted me the most: honey. He called it his liquid gold. 'Didn't you see me talking to the bees in the garden?'

'I thought you were talking to Exu!'

'Same thing.'

Dona Marta arrived just then with steaming dishes that smelled of sea and spice, and we ordered another round of drinks. I raised my glass to the picture over the blue flowers. 'I used to think Yemanjá was just about fish,' I told him. 'But I'm beginning to see worlds beneath worlds.' I was already a little bit drunk.

He returned the toast. 'To worlds beneath worlds within worlds.'

We talked about bee behaviours and colony collapse, and Michael Pollan's desire-centric universe. (Zé dubbed it bee-centricity, which I thought was rather good for someone who didn't speak English very often.) He also promised to take me to a leaf house to see the business end of Candomblé medicine.

'I can take you this weekend, no problem. Next weekend I will be in Cachoeira.'

'Where is Cachoeira?'

'Sometimes I travel out of Salvador to get certain plants,' he said. 'In Cachoeira, there are beautiful forests. And rivers. Lots of different trees.' For a moment I thought he might offer to take me there, too. Instead, he launched into a story about a remarkable sisterhood based in the small town: the Irmandade da Boa Morte. The Sorority of Our Lady of the Good Death.

'The Irmandade was founded by freed women slaves who worked to help others buy their liberty,' he said, as we scraped the last morsels of rice, moqueca and farofa from our plates. Dona Marta appeared to clear the table, and gave Zé a fierce look. He returned it with one that was openly defiant. The eyebrows were all in a line, this time. 'My great-great-grandmother was one of them.' Dona Marta grabbed his empty bottle and walked away, muttering something about the tongue-loosening effects of beer.

Zé's ancestor had been brought forcibly to Brazil in the early 1800s. Back home she had been a curandeira of great repute, and on this side of the Atlantic, people had continued to come to her for herbs, healing and advice.

'Her name was Oni,' he said. 'And her reputation became such that the governor of Salvador called on her to attend to his sickly daughter.' The girl had been weakened and depleted by conventional bloodletting and toxic concoctions of lead and mercury. 'Oni's herbs cured her. So the governor rewarded Oni by granting her freedom.'

Dona Marta came back with some acarajé that we hadn't ordered. Compliments of the house, she said. I had seen the fried dumplings at the Baiana stalls and – surprise, surprise – they were a food of Xangô. Zé paused his story for a mouthful of bean, shrimp, chilli paste and salsa. They were that good.

'Oni's husband was already a free man,' he continued at last. 'But he died in the 1835 rebellion. Flogged to death in the central square of Pelourinho for his part in instigating the uprising.'

The whipping post. For all its picturesque charms, I kept having to remind myself that this is what Pelourinho was named for.

'That's horrible.'

Zé nodded. 'After that, Oni went to Cachoeira and became one of the founders of the Irmandade da Boa Morte.'

I thought about how the history of these streets was alive for José Carlos and others like him, whose people had lived and died here over generations. Did he think of his grandfather when he walked through the Largo, past the Casa de Jorge Amado and the urchins tying ribbons on wrists, where the hands of new arrivals were once bound in chains? I was suddenly ashamed of my romanticised reconstructions, my whistle-stop museum visits, my meanderings through myth.

'Oni's husband,' he added, as if in afterthought, 'he could have been the one who brought over your seed, the first time.'

He had acknowledged the seed. My seed.

Dona Marta slapped a bill down on the table. The meal was over.

'Let's go somewhere else,' Zé said.

15
Arch

I held my questions – and, it felt like, my breath – until we were at a table with a blue-checked cloth overlooking a square called 15 November in the centre of Pelourinho. The café was named the Beija Flor. Under its awning, a five-piece band played a brassy choro. I liked this café. I'd stopped in here a few times on my wanderings to drink coffee and watch the capoeiristas in the square. And I'd spent one evening here, alone, near the painted hummingbird over the door, working on firming up my caipirinha legs. They served a good one.

We sat inside, in a secluded corner. Outside was too noisy to talk, and too distracting, Zé said. It was true – he seemed to know everyone. But I missed watching the crowds, and the cats. Dozens of strays gathered in a courtyard opposite the café. Through the wrought-iron gate, which always seemed to be locked, some kind soul put out saucers of food and milk for them each day. I'd counted eight cats last time I passed.

When our drinks arrived, I asked Zé to tell me more about his great-grandfather. I reckoned this was safer than asking directly about the seed. If nothing else, I'd learned my lesson about pushing for information sooner than he was willing to give it.

'He was a trader, not in people – food and fabrics, that kind of thing,' Zé said. 'He worked alongside the slavers. He travelled back and forth to Africa and brought back the things the slaves needed.'

'So in a way, he supported the slave trade?'

'And profited from it.' Zé took a long swig of beer, wiping his mouth on the back of his wrist. There was a glisten of foam left in the horizontal fold that creased up over his top lip whenever he smiled. 'He was not always a good man, before he met my grandmother.'

'Oni.'

'Yes, Oni.' His smile was more like a grimace. 'He was not so good before he met her. And he was not always good after.' He held the cold beer between flat hands and twirled it back and forth, back and forth. 'But that was the bargain he made with the slave traders. His freedom in return for aiding them.'

'People do what they must do to survive.'

He gave me a long look. And then he wanted to hear more about my work. 'Tell me about what you do, as a seed hunter.' I liked the way it sounded in Portuguese. I pictured the title on a business card, in a filigreed font: *Caçadora dos sementes.*

So I told him about the seed bank under the ice at Svalbard, a thousand kilometres from the North Pole. About the seeds kept there, in cryogenic limbo. Preserved for future generations, secure enough to survive the most devastating human-made disaster.

I told him about Kew's Millennium Bank, and my own small contribution to the two hundred million seeds – and counting – that were there.

'What does it cost to keep these seeds frozen?'

'In the region of two thousand dollars to seal, pack and protect each seed.'

He let out a slow whistle.

Even in my inebriated state, I made a point of telling him about *hoodia*, and the efforts my colleagues had made to secure the stake of the communities that traditionally used the plant. I told him how they had shielded it, and them, from the rapacious interest of the pharmaceutical industry.

Of course by that stage, I couldn't actually say 'rapacious interest'. You try doing that after four – maybe five? – caipirinhas.

But I did tell him my favourite Institute success story, about a delicate yellow bulb that once grew in a tiny area on the mountain behind Kommetjie, a bay in the south Cape Peninsula. The *Gladiolus aureus* was thought to be extinct until a few years ago, when a few seeds were tracked to a blood bank at Groote Schuur Hospital, where Chris Barnard had pioneered the first heart transplant several decades before.

'Don't you mean a seed bank?' He thought that I had made a mistake, that my Portuguese was confused.

'No really, a blood bank.' I loved this part of the story. Because the way those seeds were brought back from a fridge full of body fluids was even more amazing than the fact that they were there in the first place.

In the 1970s, before Kirstenbosch had facilities to store live seeds, a forward-thinking botanist realised the lily's future was precarious. So he took some seeds to the nearest large refrigerator, which happened to be the one in the university's medical institution. There they stayed, cold and forgotten – no one even knows what became of the botanist – for a quarter of a century, until they were discovered during a routine clean-out of the blood bank vault.

'They were in a brown envelope, with *Gladiolus aureus* scribbled on the front of it in ballpoint pen, and piled up with the rest of the junk headed for the garbage bin,' I told him. 'So that would have been the end of the line for this particular gladiolus, if not for the ward supervisor, Mavis Pieterse.'

Mavis was a keen gardener. Seeing 'Gladiolus' on the envelope, she opened it to find a thimbleful of tiny seeds, in their paper-thin yellow skirts. She pocketed the envelope, and when she got home that night, she planted the seeds in pots in her small kitchen garden.

The seeds took. Come spring, delicate yellow flowers bloomed, and continued to seed and bloom each year under her care. Until one day she had a visit from a representative from the Botanical Institute. They had traced the plant, now officially extinct in the wild, to the blood bank. They were dismayed to hear that the fridge had been cleared out. But since Mavis talked often and freely about her garden, one of her colleagues had pointed the botanists her way. Mavis was only too happy to give them some of her pots to take back to Kirstenbosch. There they were propagated and reintroduced to the Kommetjie mountain slope, where they bloom again today.

'Brought back from the brink!' I finished with a flourish. He was looking at me with a strange expression.

'You really do love your seeds, don't you?' he asked.

Had I told him too much? I was definitely having too much fun. I had forgotten why I was here. I was a modern-day Mata Hari, after all. If the right music came on, I was even willing to get up and dance to prove it. But Zé's next question sobered me up.

'Would you die for a seed?'

Would I? I doubted it. I hardly knew him, but I already knew that he would risk his life to protect the terreiro. He would defend its sanctity, its right to privacy, its secrets, its rituals and its resources – I felt sure of it.

He moved quickly, turning my hands palm-upwards to expose the network of small scars laced into the soft skin of my inner arms. It was too intimate a gesture, and I tried to pull away. But he held my hands there, flat on the gingham tablecloth. His grip was firm, but gentle. He didn't say anything, only looked, his thumbs pressed into the centre of my palms. I tried to relax into the feel of my hands resting under his, but I wished he would stop staring at the evidence of my youthful self-hatred.

'It's strange, what some people are willing to die for.' He let go of my hands then, and I pulled them back, hiding my inner arms. I was done with story time. And suddenly sober.

'Do you think I'll find the akokô cousin?'

'A semente estrelinha,' he said. And even though he wasn't touching me anymore, I felt a tingle start at the centre of my palms and shoot all over my body.

Little star seed.

He knew exactly what I was looking for.

I felt as floppy as a rag doll on the way back to my pousada. The cobblestones rattled under Zé's motorbike, and I rattled right along with them. This time I wished I didn't have to keep my arms around him to hold on. Too much had passed between us already, and I needed to figure out where things stood.

But my tongue was still loose enough, when he let me off at the arched doorway of the Lua Azul, to ask a reckless question.

'So have you decided?'

'Decided what?'

'Whether or not you like me?'

He didn't answer for an uncomfortably long time. During which I started to hate him. Then he shrugged a shoulder. Über casual.

'Goodnight, Caçadora.'

He leaned in to plant a beijinho on my right cheek, and stayed there. He was pepper and pine and cardamom, and I breathed him in, and neither of us disengaged to move to the other cheek until one of us did, and our lips met in the middle.

We stayed there, under that arch, for a very long time. And I got my first taste of what it could be like to be loved by a goddess-loving man.

In Transit

I'm in the forest. Someone is after me, and I need to hide. I climb into the lap of a sturdy, spreading tree, with small leaves and buttresses like thick thighs flanged into the earth. Its roots cling to the soil like prehensile toes – I know this because when I climb into the tree, I become the tree. The roots are my toes, the branches my arms, the buttresses my hips and thighs. My head is crowned with leaves, and I feel the power of the sap running through me. Heartwood and sapwood.

And it is nothing at all, it is simplicity itself, to unclench my root toes, pull them from the forest loam, flex my cambium like a supple skin, heave my trunk and swing into a stride, heavy but graceful on thick root legs.

I gain momentum, feel a surge of pure energy. I am a jungle of vascular bundles. My sap pumps through xylem and phloem, my corpuscles are powered by chlorophyll.

Slipping through the other stationery trees, I have the grace of a dancer. I'm a sylph, disturbing nothing, leaving no trace of my passage on the forest floor.

When a looming power line threatens to tangle in my topmost branches, I contract, shrink down and skim under the cables unscathed.

As the green gives way to grey asphalt, the sound of my pursuers returns. I'm in a parking lot, sanded over with fine dirt. I am no longer the tree. I stand and hold it in my hand, now shrunk to bonsai-size, my protector needing protection.

I cast around for a place to put my tree self, until I can return it to the forest. Ahead of me a rusted car – once a sporty classic – with one empty headlight socket staring blind, but just the right size. I put my tree in there, scooping in grey dust, packing it around the roots, aware that this will not be enough to feed this tree. But it will have to do for now. I do my best to disguise the tree so no one will notice it until I get back.

I promise that I will come back.

'Brought to you by CNN,' the voice says, and I open my eyes to find the television screen hanging side on. It is raining sideways on a weather chart, and the mermaid is smiling stiffly at me from my paper cup. She looks as if she is lying down, but I'm the one with my head on the table, back at my old bench.

How can I have slept after all that coffee?

Nothing is predictable anymore. The TV meteorologist striding in front of a map of northern Europe points out an unusually severe low-pressure system. I wait for her to show Cape Town, but she doesn't.

The first winter storms always hit Cape Town on the Easter long weekend. The north wind brings rain, and the summer southeaster turns the seawater icy. That's how it always was. But now these season changes come later, or earlier. There are freak storms and hottest years and 'worst droughts since'. The climate feels wilder, on edge.

People tune in to the weather with a different kind of attention these days. Everyone knows the jargon of global warming; we can all connect the dots between the floods, the droughts, the heat, the blizzards – talking about the weather is no longer small talk, but survival talk. As it once was. Memory is short.

What was it Neruda said about forgetting?

Love is so short, forgetting is so long . . .

The weather map indicates a heat wave in Salvador.

I should mail Em. I left Salvador in such a hurry, nobody except for Kirk even knows where I am.

My father doesn't know I've left, either.

When will Zé?

Do. Not. Think. Of. Zé.

I could fire up my laptop right now, but I think I'll just stay here for a little, lying with my head on the table, watching anonymous travellers walk past sideways.

I know how Eddington felt, when he sat at his table contemplating his elbow and the essential permeability of things. Which table is real, he wondered, the one your elbow doesn't go through, or the one it theoretically could, if you could only enter the realm of spaces between molecules?

> *Like a long-legged fly*
> *upon the stream*
> *her mind moves upon silence.*

Em inscribed those words – Yeats's words – in the copy of Eddington's *The Nature of the Physical World* she gave me to take on that Amazon trip. How did she know it would be the perfect place to read it? I thought I knew then, what it was like to feel so insubstantial that you could balance on the thin meniscus between two worlds, two states of being. But I had no idea.

The mysteries of science were so comforting when I was sixteen. On an Amazon outing with Carlos the boat guy and his jungle marijuana, I decided I would always try to know, to understand, to measure, to deduce: if not by observation alone, then by a different, perhaps quantum, set of rules. My one rule was that there would always be rules.

I organised my own life around predictability and routine. I left very little room for randomness in my everyday. I wanted to be my own constant in the chaos.

I thought I could hover above the mysteries, looking down on them from science's lofty eyrie. Well, that little fantasy just imploded, didn't it?

Maybe I'll just stay here forever, in this coffee diner with the mermaid logo and the international beans. Even a coffee bean is a seed in transit. Between worlds, destined for fertile soil, or the roaster-grinder-percolator.

Oh god, I wish I could unspool these last days, last weeks – how far back would I go? To white sheets crumpled at the bottom of the bed during a thunderstorm? To a flat brown rock by a river? To a red story in a green garden? To an indigo song on churchyard stairs? To a yellow skirt swirling in a terreiro? Could I stop at that point, or would the spooling continue, unwinding me further and further back? Do I have to keep going back to everything that went before?

Time is a one-way ticket. If you feel your consciousness going backwards, Eddington said, you had better consult a doctor.

Better to stay here in the limbo space, where I've always felt safest. Limbo. A word stretched evenly between two poles. Not slack, like saudades. It's a tight high-wire and a safety net all in one.

But even here, how can I know that other entities aren't waiting in the wings to enter when the time is right? How can I be sure that Yemanjá isn't watching me, disguised in the logo of a multi-national coffee brand? Or that Oni isn't waiting to infiltrate my dreams when I least expect her?

16
Gringo

Halfway across the compound on my way to meet Zé in the garden, I was waylaid by Luisa. I had taken a little extra care getting dressed that morning. There was nothing overtly provocative about the shirt I was wearing – I was having lunch with Tia Betinha later, and was mindful of the terreiro dress code. But I knew it showed off my stuff. And Luisa noticed.

'Zé can't see you this morning.'

'Why not?'

'He has another guest.' I could almost hear the unspoken words – *what, did you think you were something special*? I followed her eye to the canteen veranda. Zé was sitting under the tin-roof overhang with two other men. One of them wore a Stetson.

'Him?' I couldn't believe it. What was the American tourist doing muscling in on my territory?

'You know him?'

'No. I've just seen him around. He's hard to miss.' That ridiculous hat.

'Gringos!' Luisa's laugh was scornful. The two of us stood side by side, watching the men drinking coffee from tiny cups. I felt a moment of solidarity with her – and absolutely no urge to defend my native country.

'What is he doing here?'

'He is from Texas. His church sent him.'

'He's some kind of missionary?'

Luisa shrugged. 'Many people are fascinated with our ways,' she said. 'Most of them don't last long.' I might have imagined that the look she gave me was meaningful. 'Why don't you go and say hello?'

I wanted nothing less than to have an audience when I spoke to Zé this morning. Not after last night. I felt molten just thinking about it. But I could hardly say no. 'You coming?'

Luisa declined. 'I have met him enough,' she said.

'Bom Dia, Magdalena.' Zé's manner was brisk and business-like, his beijinhos, one for each cheek, entirely perfunctory. There was no outward sign of the spark that had ignited between us last night. But my internal pilot light was still flickering. 'Come and meet a fellow American.'

The Texan tipped his hat at me, but didn't stand up. He looked the epitome of a good ol' boy. He wore the kind of suit jacket you saw on rodeo announcers or crooners at the Grand Ole Opry, with a fancy clasp on his bolo neck tie. Big-boned, apple cheeks flushed too red. He was probably older than his bland baby face suggested. His ham hands curled awkwardly around the small cafezinho cup.

The third man stood up and introduced himself as Dom Cas. He was small and ropey, and looked vaguely familiar. He offered me his seat and poured me a cafezinho from the urn. I hoped the cowboy was taking notes.

'José tells me you're here to learn about plants?' The American pronounced Zé's name all wrong, rhyming it with 'day'. But I wasn't going to correct him.

'That's right. And what brings you here?'

'Doing the Lord's work.' He reached into his breast pocket and pulled out a card. *Atticus P. Jones*, in curly script. On the other side: *Mainline Ministries – Taking the Word to the World.* No address or contact numbers.

'You here to spread the word, or learn something new?'

'I always try to do a bit of both, every day.' He beamed at me, this Atticus P. Jones, but the smile didn't come from his eyes. We already didn't like one another.

'Nice hat.'

He tipped it back. 'Keeps me shady,' he said. 'Think I was born wearing this hat. Don't feel right without it.'

Dom Cas put the cafezinho down in front of me, and pulled up another chair for himself. I noticed that he was missing the two middle fingers of his right hand. Before he sat down, he offered the cowboy another coffee.

'No, obrigado,' Atticus said. 'I think I've had about all the caffeine I can take for one morning.' And then, to me, 'Mr Cassy-muro here's been showing me around the terreiro.'

'Dom Casmurro?' I asked. 'As in the Machado de Assis story?'

Dom Cas flashed me a smile of teeth crowding to get out of his mouth. 'Exactly so!' he said. 'Only I am much more cheerful!'

'Dom Casmurro is a character from a classic Brazilian novel,' Zé explained to the American. 'The name translates as "Sir Taciturn".'

'There you go. I've learned something new already!' I didn't like how Atticus directed his comment at me.

'I am nothing like my namesake,' Dom Cas said, twirling the last of his coffee around in its cup. 'That man could not get away from his jealous fantasies. In the end, he caused the very thing he feared most to come to pass. I, on the other hand, will do anything to protect my wife.' He looked at his missing fingers. Yet another story waiting to be told.

'Dona Marta runs the best Bahian restaurant in Pelourinho,' Zé said. Something in his look told me not to say anything about last night. 'Dom Cas takes care of all the buildings and the grounds here at the Ilê Axé.'

'But not the garden,' Dom Cas said. 'That's Zé's domain alone.'

'I'd like to see it,' the American said.

Zé stood up. 'I'm afraid that is not possible today.' At least the cowboy wasn't going into the garden.

Zé took his coffee cup over to the counter near the urn. When the others weren't looking, he motioned for me to join him there. I drained my cup and went over on the pretence of a refill.

'I'm sorry, Caçadora,' he said softly. 'I'll see you tonight?' He put his coffee cup on the tray of empties, and left without waiting for my reply. The scent of pepper, pine and cardamom lingered.

17
Stories

With my morning in the garden cancelled, I was early for lunch with Tia Betinha. She put me to work in the kitchen, cutting up chicken, washing rice, rinsing beans and slicing tomatoes for salad. From time to time people would pop in to visit, or ask for her advice and counsel, and so I also learned something of the rhythm of the terreiro.

As in any small community, there was gossip. And since only a thin wall and an open doorway separated the kitchen from the living-dining-consulting room, I felt like I was eavesdropping on a telenovela.

Almeido wanted to apply for a new job and needed the orixás' blessing. Patricia wanted good fortune for her tests at the academy. Rebaldo had asked Sonia to marry him, but the foolish daughter was keeping him on a string. 'And he would make the *perfect* son-in-law! *So* considerate …' At times I wasn't sure if they were talking about their own lives, or the latest episode of *Passione*, which flickered in the background. In between visitors, Tia Betinha told me stories of the orixás.

Their lives, I discovered, were followed just as avidly, and retold with as much relish, as the soap stories. That night, while I waited at the pousada for word from Zé, I tried to capture some of it in an email to Em.

Let's see … the steel warrior Ogun battled his incestuous longings for the beautiful river goddess Oxum – who was also married to his brother, the stubborn hunter Oxossi, who was once drugged and captured by Ossain because he trespassed into his forest. Are you following? Oxum and Oxossi were both too strong-willed to bend to the compromises of marriage. They had a child called Logum Ede. Typical child of a broken home, he was destined to live half his life in the water and half in the forest, and because of this double personality, he – she – grew up to be part man and part woman. (Which, I imagine, takes care of any transgender members of the terreiro community.)

There's a stiff competition for the melodrama prize, but I'd give it to Obá: Consumed with jealousy over Oxum, she cut off her own ear and gave it as a gift to her husband, Xangô.

I was tempted to go into detail about the lightning god, but decided against it. My aunt would understand my attraction, and then she would worry that I was getting caught up in morbid fantasies. Which couldn't be further from the truth. I was having the time of my life.

I peered through the ferns and past the masks to the clock that hung over the reception desk. It was coming up to six o'clock, and I was getting hungry.

You'll probably tell me I'm being lulled by bedtime stories, and I'll admit there is something strangely comforting in them. Although it's not all soap opera stuff – some of it is really sad. If it hasn't arrived already, you'll soon receive a postcard of Omolu – he's the one completely hidden behind a grassy mask. Today I found out why. The poor guy was UGLY. When he got sick, he was cast out of his home and left to wander destitute, begging alms and accompanied only by his faithful dog. He was shunned by everyone, scratched by thorns and pitted by pox. Then he recovered and was given the gift of healing, I'm not sure by who. First thing he did was return to his village and cure it of plague and pestilence. After that, he was everybody's best friend. As long as he wore the mask, so they didn't have to look at his blighted face. It seems both humans and orixás can be deeply fickle.

I didn't get around to telling her about the gourd – the one story Zé really wanted me to hear. I could see how for him, being a plant person, it seemed to pull all the others together. And as usual, at least where I was concerned in matters of Candomblé lore, Xangô featured right in the middle of it.

'It is because of Xangô that all the orixás have their own herbs,' Tia Betinha told me as she stirred a pot of brown beans. 'I will tell you the story of his battle with Ossain.'

And so she recounted how Xangô was jealous of the power the plant god Ossain had over the leaves. Ossain was the only one who knew which plants could calm, and which could excite and stimulate; he knew which ones brought luck, or glory, or honour. He also knew which ones brought misery, sickness and misfortune. Because no other orixá had any power over any plant, they all needed Ossain to help them maintain good health, or to guide their initiatives towards success.

Xangô couldn't stand this disadvantage. (Some would say the lord of justice felt it to be unfair, but given what I was learning about the orixás, I was tending towards the more petulant motive.) So he hatched a plan with his wife Iansã, the impetuous orixá of the wind and storms and stars, to usurp Ossain's power over the plants.

On certain days, Ossain carried a gourd containing all the most powerful leaves, suspended on an iroko branch. 'On one of these days,' Xangô told Iansã, 'you must conjure a tempestuous wind to scatter these leaves.'

Iansã was only too delighted to help. On the appointed day, she called down a ferocious wind. It blew with such force that it lifted the roofs off houses, uprooted trees, and tore the gourd off the branch on which it hung. The vessel fell to the ground and was taken by the wind, rolling and tumbling. And as it turned, so the leaves were scattered.

The orixás were quick to take advantage – they seized whatever leaves they could as they blew about in the wind. Every one claimed one or another of them.

But still, only Ossain knew the secrets of the leaves. He alone retained control over their virtues, and over the words that had to be incanted over them to provoke them into action. And so, in this way, he continues to reign over the plants, and remains their true guardian, with absolute power.

There was a rustle in the ferns. I looked up to see Alvaro the porter clutching another blue note. Before I looked at it, I said a private prayer to Exu. *Let it not be from my father, or from Kirk …*

It was from Zé.

Caçadora, there are seven cats in your courtyard. And they are asking for you.

This time I didn't throw the note away, but slipped it into my back pocket. Like a charm.

18
Sete Portas

In a tropical climate, everything seems to bloom at the same time, the cycles of life overlapping.

We fell into a pattern for the rest of that week. Mornings in the garden, planting, pruning, harvesting. I taught Zé a technique for grafting soft woods, and he initiated me into the secrets of the plants and the spirits they served. I learned that there were certain days, or hours, when you could cut certain plants, depending on for whom you were collecting the leaves, and for what purpose. Zé did the cutting, offering silent thanks and vocal incantations.

In the garden, our conduct was chaste and strictly professional at all times. Outside of the terreiro, it was different.

In the evenings we met at our café with the checked tablecloths and the faint whiff of cat. We drank and ate and talked, still mindful of our public personas, but there was an invisible undercurrent between us. The rhythm of our interaction became a gentle ebb and flow. He would open up and play, then retreat and observe. Whenever he retreated, I found myself wanting to follow, to draw him back out and close to me. When he came in too close, I pulled back just enough for him to gather himself like the tide.

There was music everywhere in Pelourinho. No matter how small the bar, if a band could fit in it, there would be dancing. We crowded in with other bodies, pushed together between a table and a window, using the crush to press together.

Every night we said our long goodbyes in the hidden shadow of the archway, astride an invisible line I couldn't see and he wouldn't cross. He never came up to my room. When I tried to ask him why, he silenced me with his lips. I didn't know you could get to know a body so well, fully clothed, standing up. I had never known such a wanting.

Whenever I came in from the arches, Alvaro bade me an excessively polite goodnight. I detected something of a knowing smirk across his pimply mug, and mentioned it to Zé across the blue-checked tablecloth. That night, instead of leaving me at the arch, he walked me inside. At the bottom of the stairs he asked me to wait, and walked over to the reception desk. I never found out what he said to Alvaro. But from that moment, every time I came in late, the porter lowered his eyes. I still felt them following me as I made my way up the steps, and I caught him watching me once, as I turned on the first-floor landing. The longing in his look was not unexpected. It was the fear in his face that unnerved me.

Saturday morning, as promised, Zé took me to Sete Portas, the labyrinthine downtown market that sold herbs and leaves, powders and grains, as well as the beads, candles, effigies and other paraphernalia of Candomblé.

It was a crazy mix of medicine and kitsch. I bought a little mini orixá fridge magnet in a yellow lacy dress that reminded me of the Carmen Miranda doll I'd had as a child, with a basket of fruit on her head.

The orixás were omnipresent, and none more evident than Exu. His statues ranged from garden-gnome size to handbag miniatures. They were usually red and black, and often horned. My favourite was a busty, red-caped version of Wonder Woman.

I tried to imagine the more devilish ones in a different context – like someone's living room – and decided some of these worlds beneath worlds were better left alone, by me anyway.

We didn't venture deep into the market, where the light was dimmer and the trade more intense. But as I followed Zé along the fringes of the maze, I was included in the affectionate greetings he drew – everyone was a darling, a sweetheart, a querido. There were kisses and gifts. One stall-owner handed me an extraordinary flower, painted blue. Another gave me a garlic clove to keep in my purse, to ward off who knows what.

Roberto was impossible to miss, his colourful dreads bobbing above the crowd. Of course he and Zé knew each other from 'around'. Roberto invited us to join him for lunch, and I had to hide my resentment. I wasn't quite ready for our cosy duo to include another.

Saturday was feijoada day. Every eatery worth its salt had started its signature version of black-bean stew bubbling away before sunrise, ready now to dish out over white rice, with dark green kale, tomato salsa and orange wedges on the side. And farofa, of course.

Funny how you don't realise you've missed something until you find it again. As a child, I used to sprinkle the golden toasted manioc meal on everything. I rediscovered it on every return – along with soft white cheese for breakfast and the sweet perfection of pudim, the pooled caramel on top hinting at how close it had come to burning.

At my father's house, they used to tease me about my farofa infatuation. The teasing was less barbed than Lucia's jibing about tea. Tea was foreign, manioc was indelibly of here. Maybe all she'd ever wanted from me was a kind of acceptance.

Roberto watched me ladle farofa over my beans. 'She eats like a man,' he told Zé. It's true – for someone with a small frame, I have a monstrous appetite. Maybe I'm making up for all those years of wilful self-deprivation. I'd piled my plate high at the buffet.

The two men had an easy bantering rivalry. 'I met her first,' Roberto had joked. Zé was at such pains to keep our relationship private, Roberto didn't feel he had to hide his proprietary interest. I didn't want to be reminded of my moment of airport vulnerability. Or to feel like a prize in some kind of funfair ring-toss game.

'Do you know why Jesus is like manioc?' I waited for Roberto to deliver the punchline, but it wasn't the start of a joke.

'Tupi legend,' Zé explained.

I'm sorry to admit that I rolled my eyes. I wasn't in the mood for another fairy tale. But I played along. 'Okay, why is Jesus like manioc?'

'You'll like this one,' Roberto insisted. 'It's our Amazon version of the Virgin Birth.'

'As long as it doesn't put me off my lunch.' I reached for the farofa bowl. Zé excused himself from the table – I guessed he'd heard this one before.

Roberto affected a mock-serious narrative voice. 'Once upon a time, the Tupi king's daughter fell pregnant, and insisted she had been with no man,' he began. 'The king locked her away to punish her. But a gleaming white warrior angel appeared to the girl and told her not to worry, because the child she bore would be a great gift to her people. Sure enough, a beautiful white-skinned baby girl was born. But she soon died.'

'What, no persecution? No crucifixion?' I don't know why I was being so mean.

'Please, show some respect.' Roberto was only half joking. 'They named her Mani,' he continued.

'Let me guess, as in, mani-oc . . .'

'Exactly – the manioc were the white tubers that grew on her grave.'

'So manioc is some kind of holy host?' I asked. 'Tell me, was it the sweet cassava, or the bitter one?' I was feeling rather bitter myself. Zé was over at the counter talking to a woman who was thrusting out one hip and then the other, dipping her chin in a parody of come-hitherness. Her coquetry was raising my blood pressure. Roberto followed my eye line.

'The girls love him, that one. I don't know what it is.'

I knew. But I wasn't saying. Instead I thought about how the cassava tuber contains a deadly amount of cyanide, and needs to be soaked thoroughly before being cooked. Cassava grown in times of drought has higher levels of cyanogenic glycoside, just when there is less water available to soak and ferment the tuber properly. Many Africans have been afflicted with goitres and konzo paralysis, thanks to this gift from the Amazon. It had never really occurred to me before: perhaps a river tuber was supposed to be eaten by a river?

'Did you know,' I told Roberto, 'that it takes just forty milligrams of pure cassava poison to kill a cow?'

After lunch, we joined the crowds at the edge of the square watching the capoeiristas fight-dance. Two by two, contestants dropped into the circle, summoned by the drums, the twang of the berimbau, the call of voices and hands.

I don't think anyone ever wins a round in the capoeira roda. The contestants just seem to flow and parry until one drops out, or someone cuts in from outside the ring. It's hypnotic to watch, the slow gathering of energies, the repetitive high kick, split and twirl, pivoting from the waist, the limbs and torso splaying like gravitational spokes. It looks deceptively easy, but requires the physique of a gymnast and the stamina of a steam train.

We watched the opponents ease around each other, searching for openings. Each strike was a feint, anticipated and parried by the other, the energy of the empty blow taken, held, and passed back again.

And then one of the combatants bowed out, and Zé was no longer next to me. He handed me his T-shirt before he dropped into the ring to shouts of encouragement. Roberto nudged me. *Watch this.*

I was taken by a mix of pride, amazement and desire as Zé became one of a fluid two. Here was the source and expression of his graceful athleticism as he moved around the garden.

Ebb and flow.

Zé's opponent swung one leg up, and Zé crouched, turning to duck underneath it, then springing up onto his hands and into a slow cartwheel. He seemed to defy gravity as he hung, an inverted X, then he was up again and thrusting forward. The other stepped back to absorb the 'blow'. Zé returned the favour, and they stepped and rolled, bobbed and weaved like boxers. But instead of putting each other off-balance, they were drawing each other in.

I almost couldn't bear to watch.

Then, by some invisible signal, it was finished. Zé rejoined us, taking back his shirt and using it to wipe his face and the back of his neck. A little rivulet of sweat trickled down the muscles of his stomach and under the braided band. I looked hard at the ground. The grey rounded cobbles. The dust that held them together.

'I'm late,' I heard him tell Roberto. I didn't know he had somewhere else to be.

'No problem,' Roberto said. He turned to me. 'I need to get back to the shop. It's on your way. We can walk together?'

And with two quick sweaty beijinhos that didn't slide to the middle, Zé was gone. I watched him walk away, completely thrown off-kilter. Then I turned back to Roberto. On his face was a look of mock horror.

'Oh no, you too?' he asked.

19
Bluffing

Em had a knack for being there when I needed her, and her email was waiting when I got back to the Lua Azul. It started, as was her custom, with a quote:

> *'For the notion of homeland, with all its emotional power, is bound up with the relative brevity of our life, which allows us too little time to become attached to some other country, to other countries, to other languages.'*
>
> – MILAN KUNDERA, *Ignorance*

I am impressed with and amazed by your ability to segue from one culture into another, with such apparent ease. It is a rare talent and one that proves Kundera wrong. (Not for the first time, and surely not for the last.)

I sense that you are rekindling real connections in Brazil. Old ones and new ones. This is good.

But it also seems to me that being a child of so many countries, while it fosters adaptability, comes with its own perils. Might encourage one to take comfort in unsafe harbours.

Any port in a storm, they say. But you, my love, are precious cargo.

Tell me my auntly antlers are wrong, but I have a feeling there may be something brewing with this man you are spending so much time with – Jose of the Garden? How is that? Is he worthy? (How could he possibly be?)

I am, of course, thrilled for you, and your great adventure. I just have to sound a note of caution, don't I? Isn't that my job?

I imagined the clink of ice as my aunt took a sip of her customary succour.

Enough! Any minute now, I'm going to start wearing purple and reading poetry on street corners. Write me more. You are too, too quiet in your urban jungle. Think how many letters Bishop managed. (Loved the story of the toucan, by the way . . .)

And now, no more beating about the bush. All this talk of home is not random or coincidental. Your father wants to know where you are, and he has been pestering me. I don't know what's got into him. Old age, guilt, regret – you know better than I how this Catholic thing works. Please just call him. Get him off both our backs.

Thank you, darling, take care.

Aunty Em

PS: Homeland be damned. Home is where the heart is. What I really mean to say is that, come what may, if you ever need to come home, you have one here.

Oh, Em! My heart filled with love for my aunt. I knew I should acknowledge the mail immediately, but for once, I couldn't conjure even a Bishop poem to suit the occasion.

Then again, much as Em enjoyed looking for subtext and hidden meanings, we both knew communication by quotation could just as easily backfire – two people could look at exactly the same thing, and read something totally different. What was brewing with Jose of the Garden? I wished I knew.

And then a line of song floated up. It was from John Prine's 'Angel from Montgomery' – Bonnie Raitt's version was the one playing in my head.

> *If dreams were thunder, and lightning was desire, this old house would have burned down a long time ago.*

I fired off my reply, pleased at finding a response that was exactly accurate, but also avoided the question. And then I realised I hadn't acknowledged the most important part of the mail. The invitation home. I added a PS:

> *When I find my ruby slippers and click my heels together, Aunty Em, the storm will surely blow me back to you. xxxx*

It occurred to me that, in another telling of the tale, Iansã, who was tempestuous and favoured red, would have been the one who conjured up Dorothy's twister.

The rest of the afternoon yawned ahead. I knew just what I needed.

Fernando spent his off-duty afternoons at a table in a streetside café a few doors down from my pousada. If I saw his taxi parked there, he told me, I could call him to take me anywhere, anytime.

I had seen him playing solitaire while he waited for fares to call in. He was often alone, but occasionally played with a group of three or four others. That's what I was hoping for today. I couldn't shake the uneasy feeling the afternoon had laid over me. A few hands of poker would see me right.

I was in luck – at least as far as finding Fernando up for a game.

'It cannot be right that three threes and two twos beats an entire royal family.' He complained after I won my first hand. I loved the way he pronounced full house – 'fulause'. I liked playing poker in Brazil.

'If only they had all been from the same suit,' I consoled him, as he dealt us each two new cards.

'Pfsh. The rroial flesh,' he said. 'You should know in Brazil we prefer to mix our families up. What you want to do?'

I had a pair of jacks, both black.

'I'm in.'

'My favourites,' he went on, shoving two matches – ten centavos each – into the middle of the table, 'are the queens.'

'The more the better,' I said.

'Four queens and I could die a happy man! Although—' he dropped his voice, noted my call, burned the top card and dealt three face-up on the table, 'too many women can be the thing that kills you.'

The flop was scrappy. A five of hearts, an eight of clubs, and a three of diamonds. 'Check.'

'Very good.'

The next card was a queen of hearts.

'There she is, my darling!' he cried. His delight seemed genuine. But I was going to call his bluff. I pushed five matches into the middle.

'Okay.' He met my five. 'Let's see how many queens I get today.'

The next card was the nine of clubs.

'Too bad,' I said, pushing everything I had into the middle. 'I'll put you all in.'

'You sure?' Fernando left his cards face down on the table, with the tips of his fingers resting on their blue-and-white patterned backs. My pile was much bigger than the one in front of him. He counted up his 'chips', and nodded for me to divvy mine to match.

'Let's see what you've got.'

He turned over a six and a seven of spades.

I bowed out graciously as he raked his winnings towards him. 'You didn't really think I had the queens?'

'I was willing to let my jacks take their chances in the royal court.' It was the inside straight I never saw coming. 'Thanks, Fernando. See you on Monday.' I scraped back my chair and stood up. Balance had been restored.

20

Pageantry

Now that the ceremony was not so strange and new, now that I understood some little bit about the orixás, now that I knew and trusted the people here, I became totally entranced.

Not literally. I never let myself get pulled in the way I had been that first night. No matter how hypnotic the drums, or how long the proceedings – and it could take forever just to get through the preliminaries, with at least thirteen orixás to acknowledge and honour – I was always careful to hold myself together, and apart. So shielded (or so I thought), I got into the groove. And fell in love with Candomblé.

I loved the sense of occasion, the pageantry, the care and seriousness that accompanied each part of the process.

I loved the casualness at the beginning, when the circling women greeted friends on the sidelines, helped each other with fallen headdresses or tangled beads, or hurried into the back for some forgotten item.

I loved it when I started to recognise the hand signals that showed which orixá was being honoured as the women did their slow circle – the ocean wave motion for Yemanjá, the arrow for Oxossi, the mortar and pestle grind for Ossain.

I was no longer surprised when familiar people – people I shared coffee with, or greeted in the courtyard outside – would suddenly drop their heads and go rag-doll limp as one orixá after another incarnated.

Only some people were qualified to fall into trance; the others helped hold and contain the ceremony. Helpers would be there to catch the newly entranced, guide them to a seat, or out of the door, if that's where they needed to go (the wind warrior Iansã tended to wander). It was always a challenge when a member of the audience succumbed. They would be taken into one of the rooms at the back and cared for during the ceremony, but without the proper training and inductions, they wouldn't become a regular member of the circle.

I never went into the roda. But I was allowed to help serve and prepare the food, so I got a good look at what went on in the back rooms. In many ways, it was like being backstage at a pageant, with a combination of dressing rooms, rest rooms, kitchen and ablutions.

Sometimes it was hard to believe that what went on 'front of house' wasn't scripted. But I never saw any evidence that it was. One moment a person would be circling slowly, to the rhythm of the drum, adding their voice to the call and response of the song. The next minute they would begin to spin, or shake, or slump down to the ground with their eyes closed. Sometimes they folded their arms back like bird wings while their mouths worked thoughts that were no longer theirs, but came from some other realm. As if they were chewing on the essence of the orixá that had taken residence within them.

Whatever happened to Maddy the hardened atheist, you might ask? Was I suddenly credulous? Not exactly. It wasn't about my belief; it was about theirs. It was about having respect for this living, breathing, dancing, enfolding practice. And about the way it held a community together – a community that had welcomed me, seemingly without suspicion. (With the stubborn exception of Luisa.) A community I was beginning to feel part of.

Which is probably why I felt so proprietary when Atticus P. Jones came to a ceremony. Or maybe it was that his being there reminded me that I was an outsider, too.

At first I didn't notice him on the men's side of the stands because he wasn't wearing his hat. I went out for some air, and found him standing in the parking lot, sipping water, alone. There was no moon that night, and his face was shadowed where the light from the open door didn't reach it.

'Cowboy Jones,' I said. 'I didn't recognise you without the hat.'

He started and turned towards me. His hair, now that I could see it, was sand-coloured and plastered to his head where the band of his hat would have been, but puffed out a little under the brim line. He'd left his jacket at home, and was wearing a white button-down shirt and string necktie. The clasp of his tie, an ornate letter 'P', was polished to a high shine. P for pious? Maybe it was his middle name.

'Well, I saw you working away there. You really seem to have made yourself part of this place.' Whether he said this with admiration or suspicion, I couldn't tell.

'These are good people.'

'Don't I know it. Their faith runs strong.'

Without asking, he bought another bottle of water from the vendor, opened it and offered it to me. I was thirsty, so I accepted. We drank in silence for a while.

'You know what,' he said, 'when I first met you, I thought you were one of those new-age groupies that hang around religious centres, looking for a quick-fix solution because they've forsaken the God they were born to.'

'Ha!' (I actually snorted.) 'Far from it.'

'Oh, I can see that now. You're doing the work.'

He had no idea. But I didn't want him pressing me about what I was actually doing there. 'You've had a lot of experience in these things?'

'Some.'

'And what is it that you actually do?'

'I'm an evangelist,' he said. 'My mission is to help people find faith. Or re-find it, if they've lost it. To do that, I have to understand what draws them to a place like this.'

'If they're actually looking for something.'

'Everybody's looking for something, darlin'.'

I didn't like him calling me 'darling'. Something about the guy didn't ring true. But then I find all religious fanatics scary. By fanatic, I mean anyone who tries to convince someone else that theirs is the best or the only way. Live and let live, I say.

'You're not trying to steer any of the people here away from Candomblé – or Catholicism, for that matter?'

'Not at all. But there's plenty people here who are just plain lost. And if I can help them find their way home ...'

'How can you know where home is for anyone else?' *Especially*, I could have added, *if people don't know where that is*. But to say that would have been to admit that I was lost. I wasn't about to do that.

I knew what he meant by the new-age types, though. Spiritual tourists passed through here all the time. Eclectic adopters of symbolic paraphernalia, they surrounded themselves with white light, went to a few ceremonies, got a new tattoo, stopped eating meat (or only ate white foods, or foods beginning with 'C') – then got bored and moved on to the next thing.

'I did a lot of wandering myself when I came of age.' He reached up as if to finger his hat brim, then dropped his arm down when he realised it wasn't there. 'Only to learn that those

Iowa corn fields were the sweetest home-sweet-home.' I could see the next platitude coming, clearer than if it were lit up on a neon billboard. 'But of course, home isn't just where you come from. When you accept Jesus into your heart, home really is where the heart is.'

Right. I was officially bored. I made my excuses and turned to go back inside. Then I remembered something.

'I thought you were from Texas?' Something – doubt, annoyance – flickered in his eyes.

'People make assumptions,' he said, pointing again to the hat that wasn't there. I felt him watching me leave. 'Anytime you want to talk, I'd be truly happy to,' he called after me. I had the feeling he was taunting me.

At the end of the evening, not long before dawn, when all the orixás had been honoured, when the tourists and the casual onlookers, including Cowboy Jones, had gone home, when only the faithful (and I) remained, I thought of home again. The drums were still beating, and every person in the terreiro was invited onto the floor to be encircled by the ring of celebrants. A huge white sheet appeared, held at the periphery by twelve men, who stretched it out to cover and protect everyone under it. We were all drawn together into the centre of the hall, pulled by a gentle vortex where orixá and ordinary mortals, the entranced and the exultantly tired, came to rest. In the middle of that warm, enveloping huddle, I got my first sense of what it might mean to really belong.

21
Plant medicine

I gave my presentation to a small gathering in the main house at the Ilê Axé Bençois. Giving something back to this community helped me forget, for a short while, that I was actually there to take something away.

Mãe Gabriella was there, and Tia Betinha. Ernesto, of course. Clara with her orange peroxide halo, Dom Cas and Dona Marta, Zé (naturally), and Luisa, who hardly ever left Mãe Gabriella's side. She was civil, but still regarded me with spiky suspicion.

Even Alé and Edge were there. Edge had their sleeping daughter strapped to his front in one of those kangaroo carriers – when he bent forward over her to kiss my cheeks, I smelled baby powder, milk and soft dreams. Alé's bangles chimed musically as she handed me a gift: *Lendes Africanas dos Orixás*, stories compiled by Pierre Verger, with illustrations by Carybé. Line drawings, like the ones on Ernesto's wall. On the bright yellow cover, Xangô danced with a double-bladed axe in each hand. I hugged her in speechless thanks.

The talk went okay. Everyone loved the wild dagga story, predictably – Marta wanted to know how exactly it was used to repel snakes, and I had to admit that I didn't know (faker alert!), other than growing it around a homestead. Then the slide came up that I wasn't quite prepared for.

I knew the picture of Vavi was in there, but I didn't realise how it would make me feel, seeing him larger than life, projected on the wall at the Ilê Axé Bençois. He was sitting next to a lemon bush, all russet fur and trust. '*Lippia javanica* and *Canus lupus familiaris*', the caption said. It was my prompt to talk about how the herb is supposed to provide protection from both dogs and crocodiles, after which I would joke that Vavi demonstrated the exception to the rule, and move on. But I couldn't. 'That's my dog, Vavi,' I said, and then the picture on the wall started to ripple and blur, and somebody passed me a tissue, and everyone started talking at me to help me over my sadness. How cute he was, they said, how old was he, what did his name mean, who was looking after him ...? All reminders of that other life. He was fine, I told them (and myself). My friend Marilese was taking care of him, and he had a lot of friends to keep him company. I felt a twist in my gut and I struggled to push it down. Then I clicked through to the next slide – wormwood – and pressed on with plants.

The women all leaned forward when I described *Artemesia afra*'s efficacy in treating menstrual chills. I was on autopilot now, and while I was speaking to them I was telling myself that I was already halfway through my trip, and that I would be home before I knew it. Home – that word again.

Every person there was interested in the love charms of the fire lily *Scadoxus multiflorus*, or blood flower, which Zulu warriors traditionally used before battle to make them more potent. I made sure to avoid Zé's eye while I showed the sign next to *Athrixia phylicoides* in the Kirstenbosch garden: *Incholocholo tea is believed to have aphrodisiac properties & is not recommended for bachelors.* 'You should have brought us old-timers some of that tea,' Dom Cas called out from the back of the room.

Over coffee afterwards, Clara admired the gift from Alé, and told me about a book she had written on the religious lineage of the orixás. She'd been too modest to bring a copy along, she said, but if I was interested, she would give me one next time we met. It seemed that Clara had no trouble integrating her background in Catholic theology with the cosmos of the orixás and its complex levels of existence. 'Candomblé is uniquely Brazilian,' she said, as if inferring that Brazilians were more complex and interesting than anyone else in the world. I wasn't inclined to disagree. 'Our society is made strong because of its hybrid nature, because our followers move between church and terreiro with ease. This is what makes it so powerful. It is both very old, and very new and vibrant.'

One god, or many, or none? For the first time since I'd arrived here, I felt the need to confess my atheism. I turned my back to the room and almost whispered it to her. The look she gave me conveyed so much compassion, it made me feel ashamed.

Clara was one of those people who radiated goodness. Soft and spectacled, her scholarly absent-mindedness suggested a constant preoccupation with other realms. 'You see that woman over there?' she said, and I looked to where Mãe Gabriella sat, head wrapped in a white scarf, torso wrapped in beads, engulfed by her high-backed cane chair. So slight, but so strong. There was a young girl sitting at her feet, leaning back against the old woman's legs, eyes closed, while Mãe Gabriella played with her hair, running the strands between her fingers as if the braids were Braille. I tried to imagine what it must be like to be that child, safe there, cradled in the chatter of the room, with the wise woman's fingers in her hair.

'Mãe Gabriella is the fifth successor to the nineteenth-century founder of this terreiro,' Clara said. 'You cannot even count the honours she has received for her cultural works. She has started a school for girls, a museum and a library here at the terreiro. She is regularly called on to speak about Candomblé in the media. She speaks out internationally against racism and xenophobia.' There was real reverence in her voice. 'God is not a theory or a belief,' she said. 'God is about the good that you do in this world.'

I was surprised to see Zé approaching. He had maintained a casual but deliberate distance from me all evening. I composed myself while he kissed Clara on both cheeks, but was almost undone again when my turn came. Pepper. Pine. Him.

'I've been thinking,' Zé said to Clara, 'that we should make a document of the terreiro's sacred herbs. I thought perhaps Maddy might want to help us.' He turned to me. 'Do you think Vavi would let you stay a while longer?'

I couldn't believe he had only thought of this now. And I was annoyed that he had chosen to spring it on me here, in front of other people. Maybe he had kept the idea from me so that my surprise would be genuine.

What did I think about more time in the garden, working alongside Zé? For the first time, I went beyond the star seed and thought about possible academic collaborations with local universities. I let forty days open out into a possible future.

'I think it's a very interesting possibility,' I told him, and Clara clapped her hands the way a small child would.

'Do you know what Diderot said?' she asked me. '*It is very important not to mistake hemlock for parsley, but to believe or not believe in God is not important at all.*'

I went home alone that night, courtesy of Fernando's rattling taxi, but when I arrived in the garden the next morning, I could tell that Zé was in a playful mood. He didn't give me a chance to challenge him about last night's ambush. 'I was so inspired by your speech,' he said, 'I have put together something special for you.'

He led me over to a plant with heart-shaped leaves. 'This one is called angelicó, or "a thousand men",' he said. 'I will keep you away from this one – except if the acid in your stomach is very, very bad.' If I had doubts that he was parodying the both of us – my talk of the previous night, and his original garden tour – they were dispelled by the next specimen. It was the most flagrantly sexual plant I have ever seen. The leaves were bigger than my hand, and looked at first like giant dishevelled bats – bats stippled lime white on deep maroon, like a thin slice of marbled Kobe beef. On closer inspection, I realised they didn't so much look like bats, but like giant flapping labia. Which is in fact a term we use to describe flower structures. To be accurate, these were part labiate, part funnel, part flapping elephant ear. A tumescent proboscis thrust out from the funnel base, and, in case there was any confusion as to its intentions, two green fruits hung pendulous and testicular. 'I am not sure why,' he said, 'the *Aristolochia Gigantea brasiliensis* is considered an aphrodisiac and used for magia do amor.'

'That,' I said, 'is the most ridiculous plant I have ever seen!' I started to giggle, and then he joined in, and soon we were in one of those childish laughing fits that feed on their own momentum. My face was streaming with tears, and Zé started choking and coughing, bent over with his hands on this thighs. And then we stopped laughing. I wiped my face. He stood up and looked around at the silent trees. A bird cawed. The forest listened.

'I think I need to sit down,' I said, making a show of fanning myself.

'Actually, there is one more,' Zé said. Reaching behind the log bench, he pulled out some red tapered fronds covered with a fuzzy pubescence. 'Iansã's fire leaf,' he said, handing me the branch, but not letting go. 'I had to go past a garden in Pituba this morning to get this for you.'

It would have been funny if we hadn't let all our laughter run out. But in its wake was another feeling, maybe the one we had been laughing so hard to cover.

'You are a tease,' I told him. He let go of the branch, and stood inches away from me.

'Yes. But I am very serious about it.'

The energy that swirled between us was palpable. But in this garden, it always felt like there was someone, or something, watching over us. Or at least, Zé's belief was strong enough to prevent him acting as if we were alone. For a moment, I thought he might be about to break his taboo. We stared into each other's faces, his river-water eyes with the gold flecks, the crease above his lip. I wanted to take it between my teeth. His breath was coming fast and I could feel it drawing me in, and then the school bell rang. The spell was broken.

'You are very cruel,' I said, standing up and straightening my skirt. 'You know I have a serious meeting now!'

I wasn't wearing my usual cargo pants that day: there would be no lunch with Tia Betinha, as Mãe Gabriella had summoned me.

22
Mother Superior

'Mãe is waiting for you,' Luisa stood up from her desk in the small shop. 'I will tell her you are here.' She oozed disapproval as she brushed past me. For the umpteenth time, I asked myself what on earth I had done to piss her off.

I hadn't been back inside the shop since that first day. This time I saw things very differently. I could pair the beads with their proper deities, for one thing. And I actually knew the authors of some of the books – Clara's collection of columns written for the local newspaper, *A Tarde*, was one of them. Each one recounted a conversation with Mãe Gabriella – her thoughts on the nature of faith, syncretism, the orixás in the body. I opened it at random. 'What we know for sure is that our body is a temple through which we give thanks to our orixás . . .'

I was still holding the book when a small voice from behind me said, 'My aunty wrote that.' It belonged to a little girl, no more than four or five, with shoulder-length braids fastened with yellow beads. Her school uniform was brushed with the dust of the playground. Her knees were scuffed, and on one there was an X where two cartoon Band-Aids intersected. Luisa returned at that moment, and the girl rushed to throw her arms around her legs.

'Liliana,' Luisa said, 'did you say hello to our visitor from Africa? This is Dona Magdalena.'

'Prazer,' the girl mumbled. She was no longer in command of this situation, now the grown-ups had appropriated it.

'My daughter is not usually so shy.'

'You are very pretty,' I told the girl. I recognised her from my talk – she was the one who had been sitting at the mãe-de-santo's feet.

'Mãe Gabriella is ready for you,' Luisa said. She seemed slightly less antagonistic. Perhaps the way to her good favour was through her daughter.

The way the cowries fell was significant. Up or down, open or closed. Towards the centre of the woven circle, or running off to the edges. But the meaning in their code was closed to me.

The mãe-de-santo spent a long time studying them, muttering words and phrases so fast that I could only pick up snatches. There were other things on the floor between us. A grey stone pestle in a wooden mortar worn almost flat from use. A string of beads, alternating red and white, lying slightly separate from a coil of other colours. Herbs floating in water in a ceramic bowl. I tried to work out what they were before they were ground and mixed, but I could only surmise. I detected a whiff of anise somewhere in the mix.

I was so immersed in olfactory guesswork that I missed a question, and had to ask Mãe Gabriella to repeat it.

'Have you found what you need?'

Had I? I had not yet found my *Newbouldia*, that much was certain. But I got the feeling that that probably wasn't what the mãe-de-santo meant.

We'd talked a bit, when I first came in, about my time in the garden. My afternoons with Tia Betinha. 'We get many visitors here,' Mãe Gabriella said. 'A lot of people with a lot of curiosity. Some of those people want to stay on, join our community. But this is not a small decision. The proper initiation is a long one.'

Seven years, in fact. Three years and then another four, if you are iyawo, one chosen to receive the orixás in trance.

'And there are those,' the mãe-de-santo went on, 'who help us to do our work out in the world, through research and education, explaining the ways of Candomblé. A religion of faith. Not a cult. Not a collection of fairy tales. A religion based on love and the pride of our people. I am told you understand this.'

She had picked up the handful of cowries and said, 'Let's see what the búzios say we should do with you.'

When she asked me if I had found what I was looking for, the mãe-de-santo already had an answer to whatever it was she needed to know. She reached into a mound of beads, and pulled out a strand. The beads unfurled, cascading from a loose pile into a long string. Of all the colours I had seen in the rainbow waterfalls of beads, these were the ones I had admired the most. The turquoise beads of Yemanjá.

Mãe Gabriella placed the beads in the bowl of herbs, along with the red and white string. She motioned for me to shift closer, and began to swirl the water, calling on the orixás, speaking words of blessing. When she put the beads around my neck she said, 'Mother of all, queen of queens. Dona protector ...' And more words that I couldn't make out.

So had the Mãe chosen this Yemanjá for me? A mother for this motherless child? Or perhaps it was the deity that did the choosing. While her voice lulled me, I saw mermaids. I saw Aphrodite in the clam shell. I saw the cartoon on the tuna can – 'Chicken of the Sea'. When I was very small, I thought mermaids lived inside that squat can. I remember seeing an empty can on a kitchen counter, a bowl of flaked tuna salad in a clear bowl, bits of onion and red pepper caught up in the flesh and mayonnaise. Screaming and screaming and refusing to eat tuna after that. I still don't. Not even in sushi.

Disney did the mermaid tale an injustice. Hans Christian Andersen's original was a horror story of female self-sacrifice; the mermaid princess gives up speech and dances on the agony of human legs to be close to the man she loves. She doesn't get him, in the end. In the end, she gets martyrdom, and a lifetime – if one can call it that – of insubstantiality. Not even spirit, just foam on the sea.

Mãe Gabriella was telling me about the ritual cleansing I would need to undergo, starting today.

'Ask Luisa to give you some Alfazema oil when you leave. You will need to use it every day.'

I was still in a daze as I paid Luisa for the oil, which she had ready and waiting for me. Had she been listening at the door? Or had this all been decided beforehand? The beads felt clammy against my neck and chest. In time, they would take up the warmth of my body. I reminded myself that I was only playing along because I had to. To get to the seed. I didn't like this lack of control, though. I was starting to wonder who was manipulating who.

Liliana was sitting at the table, nose pressed into a homework book. As I was leaving, she looked up and smiled. She had a charming little crease in her top lip.

If ever there was a sign that I should have interpreted, it was Lili's smile. But I wasn't paying attention.

'Go with God,' Luisa said as I left. It could be taken as an affectionate farewell. I couldn't help feeling it as a threat.

23
Open

I had to face Luisa again, unexpectedly, when Zé and I walked back to the Lua Azul after dinner the next night.

His bike was in the shop, getting a tune-up before our trip to Cachoeria the next week. He had some business there – herbal, I assumed. And there was something there, he said, that he wanted to show me.

I was looking forward to getting out of the city. With him. And I was enjoying this rare, slow walk home through the streets – much as I usually looked forward to riding behind him, feeling the cooling breeze in my hair, slipping my hands underneath his shirt, holding tight over the cobble-wobble.

The night was dark, the gibbous moon curtained by a heavy gathering of cloud. He saw the scrappy crossroad offering before I did, and took my elbow to angle me away across the street. Out of the corner of my eye, I glimpsed candles, red and black, a bottle with some leaves – or were they feathers? – sticking out the top. And what looked like a plate of raw flesh.

'There are some who believe you shouldn't speak with him at all, but I don't fear him. It is just bad when I forget him.' I knew he was talking about Exu. I felt a little shiver as he pressed close and adjusted his step to match my stride. He slipped his hand down to hold mine.

I thanked Exu, silently, for a perfect moment. The feel of Zé's hand, dry and warm despite the clammy heat. The flow of our bodies, in step. I felt buoyed, light. Lighter than air.

Then we rounded the corner, and almost stumbled over Luisa sitting in the doorway of a hole-in-the-wall snack bar. She was with a girlfriend. They sat on stackable plastic chairs, a polystyrene Skol beer cooler box a makeshift table between them.

I took all this in during the moment it took Zé to mutter 'Merda!', drop my hand as if it were white-hot, and in one swift side-step, put an acre of space between us.

Luisa and her friend occupied their sidewalk station as if it were a command post: it gave them a good view of everything going on in the street and the square at its lower end. My guess was that Luisa's friend owned the bar; she had her feet up on the Skol box, and the two of them had the air of regulars, watching the daily drama play out before them in their extended living room.

Liliana was nowhere to be seen, but I heard the little girl's name in the rapid-fire exchange that took place between Zé and Luisa. I couldn't follow all of it, but the tone was heated. I focused my eyes on the deep-fried snacks behind the grimed glass display. Luisa's friend stared at me with frank curiosity, but didn't offer any greeting. Luisa didn't acknowledge my presence at all.

'She doesn't like me,' I said, when we had put enough silent distance between us and the scene. He wasn't holding my hand anymore.

'She just wants to protect me,' Zé said.

'Oh?'

'We've known each other since we were very young. Our families go back.' He rolled his hands in front of him, to indicate a long, long time. 'She is like ... a sister.'

Zé had told me he was a child of the terreiro. His mother had worked as a cleaner in rich people's houses, and died before he reached his teens. He had never known his father. He'd lived at the terreiro, playing in the courtyards and garden, until he was ordained to serve in it. If Luisa had a similar history, she would naturally be protective and suspicious of outsiders. But that wasn't all there was to it.

'Well, it seems your sister is jealous.'

He stopped me then, right there in the middle of the street, pulled me to him, and kissed me long and hard.

'Forgive me,' I heard him murmur into my hair.

But I didn't yet know what for.

That night, for the first time, he came up to my room. We sat on the small balcony overlooking the industrial bay, and took turns drinking from a bottle of cheap 69-brand cachaça. The moon struggled to show itself through the clouds, and lightning played on the water in the far distance.

'All my life I've been waiting for the lightning to take me,' I spoke my thoughts out loud. 'The way it took my mother. Maybe I should have been talking to Xangô.'

'Xangô started as a mortal, like many of the orixás,' said Zé. 'In his earthly life, he was a great magician and warrior. It was only after he committed suicide that he entered Orun, the nine-levelled realm of the orixás.'

Despite the heat of the cachaça in my blood, I started to shiver. Zé pulled me close, and put his hands under my sleeves to rub the gooseflesh from my arms.

The clothes seemed to melt off us. There was no shyness, just our growing familiarity edged with anticipation. I watched him unclasp the woven band from around his waist, roll it up and put it carefully on the small side table. He motioned for me to do the same with my beads. I felt strangely naked without them, but already so right being naked next to him.

Beads and grass. The way they had fallen on the round table, they looked like the two halves of the yin-yang, the seed inside each representing the necessary potentiality of the other.

I had lit candles earlier. Now I could see him, lean and burnished in the moonless dark. His body was so familiar, after weeks of watching and wanting. And also much more than I had imagined. I didn't want to stop looking, but eventually I closed my eyes and gave myself over to the feel of him. Lost myself, finally, in pepper, cardamom and pine.

There are smells that flirt around the nostrils – sharp, astringent smells that hit high on the pituitary gland. Most citruses. The buchus, Cape may. And there are those that you take in deeper, absorb into the back of the throat. Smells that penetrate into your glands and work deep down on your limbic system. Zé's was one of those smells.

Afterwards, we lay spooned together.

'Better now?' His voice vibrated against my back when he spoke. He had one hand buried in my hair, while the other played over my breasts.

'Is there supposed to be a moral in that Xangô story?' I asked.

He brought his fingers up to play against my lips. They brought with them the smell of us both, intermingled. 'Does there have to be?' he said, stroking my hair. 'Some things just are because they are. It is their nature. You cannot change them, you just accept them.'

'Or go mad.'

'Even that,' he said, pulling me closer, 'is an option.'

He didn't ask me why I was crying.

In Transit

Dreams are like memory. Or maybe it's the other way around. Either way, they're the only way you can be two places at the same time.

You have two points of view, split at the place where you see yourself, and are at the same time the one doing the seeing. You are in the scene, watching events from your own perspective. But you're also aware of yourself on the outside, dreaming in.

If you had to draw this, it would look like one of those Boolean diagrams, a math tree branch. Except that Boolean is a binary form of logic – true or false, yes or no, 0 or 1 – whereas dream-scape defies logic. In dreams, all possibilities co-exist simultaneously. Dreams allow infinite possibilities – especially conflicting ones – to feel equally true. Even when you know that at least some of them have to be false.

And then there are lucid dreams. The kind where you know you are dreaming, but still you are asleep.

I'm semi-conscious of the 'real' world outside – the muffled voices, the plastic faux-leather bench-seat sweating under my cheek. The smell of coffee, making me feel queasy. Maybe I've finally had too much of it. Or maybe I really am getting sick. I can't believe I fell asleep again. Must be all those late nights catching up with me after the craziness of the last few days.

This time when his face appears, I can't stop it. Those lips, the thought of what they do to me, makes me ache. I close my eyes and cover him with green. His face becomes a green river.

I'm coursing through the jungle on the river Zé. I'm flying over fields of sugar cane, endless spears of bright green, over carpets of dark coffee leaf dotted with beans, swooping down on fat, flat tongues of tobacco. Now I'm underwater, flying over seabeds. Seaweed swaying in an undersea breeze. I could go for some seaweed right now. I can taste it – salt and brine and iodine. Chlorophyll, flat and green.

I try to tame it into sushi, slice it and wrap it tight around rice and slivers of anything other than tuna. I think of pink pickled ginger as the seaweed unfurls, uncurls, slips away from me, wet and long and waving. Now I'm swimming in a swaying jungle of the stuff.

The sea is the mother of everything. We carry the salty waters within us, just as we carry the stars, elemental in our DNA. In this underwater womb, mermaids are reminders of where we come from. But that's no mermaid, that's Yemanjá, sitting on the seabed, her hair braided and beaded with cowry shells, writhing like Medusa's. She is ordinary and magnificent, flesh and magic. Her iridescent skirts aren't at all out of place here, drifting gently with the currents. I wonder whether there are gills underneath the petticoats? But I dare not ask her, because she's fixed me with her fierce eyes. They are orixá eyes, deep sea-green eyes, piercing. Is that malice or might? Have I done something wrong? The panic flutters deep in my belly, and when I clutch at my money belt, I'm back amid the voices and the vinyl.

I sit up, and the air smells of sulphur and iodine.

And of coffee. I really do think I'm going to be sick.

I go through my things to calm myself. I really should get a new money belt, but this one has been with me for so long. Its faded blue denim is like a talisman. This zip that always catches just there, making me panic that I won't be able to get out what

I need, when I need it. Passport, tickets, money. Check, check, check. Lucky poker chip. Lip-Ice. Emergency tampon.

And there's the secret pocket at the very back, flush against my belly. I planned all along to carry some seeds there, if I found any. In the last known stand of *Newbouldia mundii* in the world.

After all this time, this bag's crescent shape feels like part of my body. Some people call it a fanny pack. I really hate that. I prefer moon bag. It looks like a crescent moon. A blue moon. My blue moon bag.

What were the chances of having a blue moon month while staying at a place called the Lua Azul? Some things you just can't plan. I could try to work out the probabilities, but ... I get lost counting the days. There were two full moons. Filling, full; waning, empty. Then filling again, waxing to perfectly rotund and then – now – emptying again.

Two full moons, with nothing in between.

I see the tampon flashing a signal at me.

Or is it an accusation?

24
Rain

It rained for three days and three nights. It was no time to be in the garden, but we made the most of our time indoors.

Three days, three nights.

During the nights, stories and dreams, past, present and future all tangled up with sheets and sweat and skin.

The days felt interstitial, pauses in what was really important. What was really real.

They were three days suspended. But they were hardly uneventful.

The first day, we hid from the world. On the second, Zé went off to make sure the bike repairs would be done in time for our trip that weekend, and I decided to devote the day to reading and catching up with email.

The pelting rain outside the room was distracting me from *Dona Flor*, as were the sheets, wafting pepper and musk. Zé and I had arranged to meet later at the Beija Flor. 'That place told me to kiss you from the first day, Caçadora,' Zé teased, before he left that morning. I wanted to ask him what had taken him so long, but I knew that everything was playing out exactly right, in its true time.

'If anything ever happens,' he said, suddenly serious, 'if you ever need me, go there and wait. And I will come. Para beijar minha flor.'

I had set a filter so that Nico's emails went into a separate folder. That way, I wouldn't have to look at them unless I really wanted to. I didn't. But my inbox was brimming with messages from Kirk, each more insistent than the next, and those I couldn't ignore. Since our last telephone conversation, I'd been avoiding his calls too. My last message to him was one word long, in caps: 'PAPERWORK?'

His latest salvos were outright emotional blackmail. 'Drug enhances efficacy of chemotherapy', read one subject line, followed by a URL link to a scientific paper. 'We should be leading this charge,' his message said. I didn't click on the link. We were in the business of saving plants, not people. Although the latter would inevitably follow from the former, I didn't feel it was necessary to tell him that.

His most recent mail was more blunt. 'Time's nearly up,' it said. 'What gives?'

I arranged a lunch with Ernesto for the next day. I knew there was nothing much he could do to help me, in the absence of a star seed, but it would at least give Kirk the impression that I was pushing forward, if the two of them were in contact. Plus I was fond of the old man. I knew I was buying time. But time for what? What was I actually doing here now? Apart from avoiding people?

Among the messages I was ignoring were two more from my father. The blue slips were also getting more insistent. 'I know you are there,' said the last one, in Alvaro's apologetic scrawl. 'If you don't answer my calls, I'll have to come and find you.'

The trip to Cachoeira was happening just in time. I decided I wasn't going to tell anyone where I was going. Not even Em.

There was a mail from her too, short and sweet. This time she let Hermann Hesse say it all for her:

'When we are stricken and cannot bear our lives any longer, then a tree has something to say to us: Be still! Be still! Look at me! Life is not easy, life is not difficult. Those are childish thoughts. Home is neither here or there. Home is within you, or home is nowhere at all.'

That was so like her, not wanting to be needy, not asking me to come home – almost reassuring me that I didn't have to – but leaving me with a sense of grasping for it, nonetheless.

Not to mention my tree. The tree. I still hadn't found that, either.

25
Lunch

'I want to know all about how you are getting on, my dear, but wait—' Ernesto reached into a soft leather briefcase and pulled out a feather – deep black, tinged with blue, its quill looking like it had been dipped in blue ink. 'A gift from Lupe. He told me he wanted you to have it.' He delivered the feather into my hand with a wink.

'Thank you.' I wished I could wear it cacique-style, in my hair.

It felt strange to be at the restaurant without Zé. I realised I should have chosen another place when the waiter approached with our beers and menus and a bowl of farofa, and asked, 'Will Senhor Zé be joining you today?' Perhaps he was acting out of loyalty, sending a message to Ernesto – *this one is taken*. Did he have any idea what kind of brew he was stirring? Did I? I stroked the feather. Its determined directionality was comforting.

Ernesto poured a glass for each of us and raised his in salute – 'To African flowers' – before taking a long pull on it. What a charmer. I watched a black and white cat saunter down the sidewalk and slip through the iron bars into the courtyard.

'I sometimes feel something of a charlatan, being welcomed here as an African,' I said, pushing through the foam on the top of my beer as I drank.

'Where do you think you are from, then?'

'I was born here, in the Amazon,' I said. 'My mother was born in Africa, but by way of Scottish Byrne settlers who arrived in the early nineteenth century. God knows what they did to secure the land they lived on.'

'Guilt is the curse of the coloniser, so to say.' His comment carried no blame that I could tell. 'What about your father?'

'My father's people are Italian-American.'

'Ah, a noble Roman line.'

'Not so much – he grew up above the family pizza joint in New Jersey.' In the land of opportunity and immigrants. Cut into patchwork pieces. 'We're all hybrids, aren't we?' I said.

'Mãe Gabriella believes that deep inside, you are an African,' he said. 'That's what she sees in you. Or do you believe traits come only though the bloodline?'

'She said that?'

Ernesto nodded.

'I don't really know. I mean, there's strength in diversity – you only have to look at monoculture in plants to see what it does to the soil, the ecology. We're supposed to mix and merge and share and hybridise . . . it keeps the gene pool strong.'

'And now you are not enough African for us?'

I shrugged. 'I feel more comfortable here than I ever do in Africa.'

'In Brazil, we all speak the same language, which helps. But the Portuguese are still the butt of all our jokes.'

'So we can all love one another, as long as we have an "other" to unite against?'

'Inconsistencies exist only in the minds of non-believers.'

He picked up the feather, ran his fingers along its shaft, smoothing its barbules. 'In the end it is not bloodline or skin colour that counts. Nor is it even intention, so to say. It is action.'

Our food arrived – picanha steak for him, a caldo verde soup for me, with some manioc fries on the side. Comfort food.

'So, how goes it in the garden?'

'I haven't found the plant, let alone any seeds.' Ernesto had known all along that I wasn't just there on some kind of cultural-medicinal exchange, and he'd taken an avid interest in my seed ever since he'd first heard about it.

'If you can look at the seeds of time and tell which grains will grow and which will not . . .'

I looked at him blankly.

'*Macbeth*.'

Of course. Witches and ghosts.

'You might still find it,' he told me. I noted with approval that he was sprinkling farofa liberally over his rice. Would he think me crazy if I put some in my soup?

'Even if I do find it, there will be protocols to follow in terms of transporting the seeds out of here.' I made with the farofa, and he didn't blink an eye. 'But Mãe's permission will be the most important thing.'

He shrugged. 'If you think my word will carry weight with Mãe Gabriella, you are mistaken,' he said. 'And perhaps you should not be so worried about official channels. There are other voices you should listen to.' He looked pointedly at my beads, just visible under the neckline of my T-shirt. 'Also, it seems to me that the seed is not in danger, if it has survived here quietly for a few hundred years, no? It is your mission that is in danger. So to say.'

He had me there. Hypothetically speaking.

'Those trees have survived here because they developed deep roots. It is what allows them to grow tall. And they are protected in a way they wouldn't be anywhere else.'

'You talk as if these trees exist. I haven't found any.'

'You have not finished looking.' He pushed his plate away. 'But should you find any, my hands will be – how do you say? –

tied up.' Ernesto searched the middle distance as the capoeira music started up in the square. 'It's good to know where your roots are, is that not so, Magdalena?'

I couldn't answer that. For the same reason that I can't give a clear answer when people hear my accent and ask where I'm from. 'Transatlantic mish-mash,' I always say. Any other response seems too complicated.

'Our friend Elizabeth Bishop said something very wise,' Ernesto offered. 'It was not in a story or a poem, but in a letter – I can't remember who it was to.'

'Robert Lowell, probably.'

'Very likely,' he nodded. I couldn't help thinking how much he would like my aunt. 'Or perhaps it was something she wrote for herself, in a notebook. But I remember almost the exact words. She said: "Sometimes it seems as though only intelligent people are stupid enough to fall in love, and only stupid people intelligent enough to let themselves be loved."'

The sun was coming under the umbrella from the sides and glancing off the white in the blue-checked tablecloth. It was a relief when a shadow moved in to block the glare. Until I looked up—

'Hello, Maddy.'

—into the face of my father.

26
Farofa

After an awkward introduction, Ernesto excused himself without waiting for coffee. My father pushed aside his empty plate and sat in his place.

'If I was a more sensitive soul, I'd think you were avoiding me.'

His handsome face had softened in the long years since I'd last seen him, but it was still a face that could turn heads. He'd gone a little fleshy around the jaw, his hair had more salt than pepper now, and the swarthy skin was mottled from so much time outdoors. I focused on these details because when I looked at the whole of him, he seemed to have shrunk. It was as if his essence had diminished. It made me feel strangely tender, and sorry for him. And that frightened me.

'Aren't you a little bit glad to see me?' There were grey tufts growing out of his ears. I was sure he never used to have those.

'How did you find me?'

'Pelourinho's not such a big place.' He stopped talking while the waiter cleared the plates. He ordered a coffee. I still had half a beer in front of me, but now I longed for something stronger.

'I knew you were getting my messages. That young porter told me.' (Alvaro, you are toast.) 'When the mountain won't come to Mohammed . . .'

'You know I don't do Biblical.'

There was so much in his smile. So much pain, so much knowing. So much that I knew. So much of *me*. And, it was painful to realise, so much love. 'I hung around outside the Lua Azul until I finally saw you come out alone. That per kilo next door does a good buffet.'

'You've been *stalking* me?'

He shrugged. His coffee arrived, and he added three spoons of sugar to the tiny cup.

I was a little bit flattered in fact, but I wasn't ready to let him off yet. 'That's just too weird, even for you.' I started poking at the farofa that had spilled out of the bowl, pushing it into mounds, then flattening them out.

'"Even for me?" What am I, some kind of pulp-fiction villain?' His eyes creased as he gave me his best Mr Nice Guy smile. It was a smile that said, 'I know where the fun is. Come over to my side, and I'll show you.' Who could resist that? Not many did. People said I had inherited that smile. But I refused to give him the satisfaction of returning it.

Everyone wants to be on the good side, to wear the white hat. *We are not the bad guys*, Kirk said. Now this. Where do they get their sense of certainty? I licked farofa off my finger like a child, and felt him watching me.

'Do you remember that road trip we took to the farm? Just after?' He didn't have to say what *after* referred to. There is one event in our lives that never gets talked about directly, but colours every word that passes between us. We circle it like hungry vultures, but we never land on the carcass.

I remembered the road trip. Black asphalt ribboning through New England autumn colours, and music. Elton John, Jimmy Hendrix, Fleetwood Mac, John, Paul, George and Ringo between oak and elm and ash. The trees had such wonderful names up there. Sassafras and sycamore. Dogwood and horse chestnut. The sweet promise of the sugar maple. I was seized by a physical longing to be standing in crisp, cool sight of them, breathing in the leafy smell of decay as the season turned. The way it would be turning soon.

Talk about saudades.

'I remember you had that golden-oldie radio station on,' I said at last. Blasts from the past, they called it. Every now and again he would tell me, 'This song came out the year you were born', or 'You were just three years old when we went there …' How was it that he managed never to mention my mother in these reminiscences, not once?

I remembered how it felt strange to be sitting up front, rather than in the back with my chin wedged between the seatbacks so I could be part of the conversation. There was no talking, that trip. Too much to say. But it was good to be with him, just the two of us.

And then Melanie went and spoiled it all. '*Look what they've done to my song, Ma …*' When her warbling voice came on, all Edith Piaf in the French parts, my father became unreachably quiet. We were almost at the turn for the homestead, where the charred scaffolding of my mother's studio waited, but when we reached the sign that read 'Fallow Farm', he touched the brakes, slowed, then broke, choked and accelerated away.

I don't remember what song was playing when he finally stopped a few miles later, at a pumpkin and apple cider stand. I concentrated on herding other people's leftover crumbs into the steel siding of the Formica table while my father sipped black coffee and said absolutely nothing. I wanted to ask him why we weren't going to the farm anymore, but I was caught in his spell of no speak. My bag was packed and in the trunk of the car. He'd put it in next to his when we had left Aunt Em's that morning. We were going to catch hold of some memories, he'd said.

He didn't put the radio on again when we got back into the car. We drove in silence all the way back to New York. I woke up to see a bridge of lights over the Hudson, long strings, white on the left, red on the right. Snow White and Rose Red. The swish of tyres through damp streets.

I wasn't going to see the pond. It had tadpoles in summer, and froze solid in winter, so you could walk right over it. I wanted to see it mirror all the autumn colours. It was cider season on Fallow Farm. The first horse I ever sat on was there. I was planning to give him an apple from a barrel.

But there was too much of my mother there.

My father didn't stay at Em's that night. When I woke in the dark, the hot-water bottle Em always tucked in with me was still warm. There was a dent in the bed where my aunt was sitting. She was stroking my foot, and shuddering. I knew that meant she was crying. I could feel the pressure of her hand on top of the covers, pressing and releasing, over and over. I was too scared to move, too scared to open my eyes. I'd heard stories of people being turned into pillars of salt for looking. I feared I would be frozen forever at the sight of so much grief.

'You look more and more like her,' my father said. 'The older you get . . .' The angled sun was bright on the white pants of the capoeiristas gathering in the square. My sunglasses were resting on top of my head, and I pulled them down over my eyes.

'Sarah. She had a name, Dad.'

So did he, and I usually used it. My calling him Dad caught both of us by surprise. He looked at my hand mustering crumbs on the table as if he wanted to take it, but he didn't.

'We never made it to the farm.'

'No.' He was swirling the dregs of coffee in the bottom of his cup as if hoping to divine something in there. 'I couldn't go back,' he said. 'I couldn't face the memories.'

'Maybe *I* needed those memories. Did you ever think of that?' *Maybe I needed to be more than a reminder of a memory.*

'I know. I'm sorry. That's why I'm here.'

'You have a genie bottle full of wishes to make it all different?'

I wanted to take them back. They were vampire words. Making him smaller. Making me meaner.

It occurred to me that there had to be a bigger reason he was here. That this was his way of forcing a life-changing conversation onto me. He looked tired.

'Bill, is there something going on? I mean, are you okay?'

He motioned for the waiter to bring a refill.

'I'm fine,' he said, 'I just wanted to see you.' And then, when his cup was full, 'The longer you live, the more you realise that life is too short.'

'And forgetting is so long.' He looked at me sharply. 'It's a poem.'

He reached into his shirt pocket. 'I wanted to give you this.' He pushed a thick white envelope across the table. My name was written on it in blue ballpoint pen. *Ms Magdalena Bellani.* The way he wrote out my last name – his last name – was in the scrawl of his own signature. So familiar, he couldn't write it any other way. All my life, I had tried to emulate my mother's looping handwriting, but my spiky signature was more like his.

'What is it?' I didn't pick it up. Instead I poured too much sugar into my cup.

'It's not a genie in a bottle. But I thought it might help . . .'

'I thought we were beyond help.' Being too hard was the only way I knew how not to feel too soft.

We watched the capoeiristas for a while. 'You used to have a stuffed orangutan – what was his name?'

'Og.'

'You used to speak through him. You told me he loved chocolate and fairground rides. What ever happened to him?'

He died of loneliness I thought, but didn't say. After a while, he continued, 'You always used to love the fastest rides.'

'You were always too scared to come on them with me.'

'But I always watched from the side, made sure you were all right.' So this was it; he needed to feel like he had been there, some kind of benevolent protector, however distant. That he hadn't ducked out for all those years. That was the truth he needed me to confirm for him, no matter how drastically it differed from my own. He was here to make himself feel better. As if I hadn't known.

The capoeiristas were feinting and ducking. We didn't parry like that, my father and I. We didn't know how to do small talk. We tended to jump right in wherever we had left off, and it tended to end badly. As time went on, we only got from zero to miserable faster. We must have set the land speed record for verbal injury. Sticks and stones … whoever said that words could never hurt you?

He was looking at me now with a kind of hunger, and I knew that meant he would be leaving soon. He saw my beads, and reached out to touch them.

'I thought you didn't do religion—'

I slapped his hand away. The sharp sting of skin on skin was a shock.

'What gives you the right?' The violence of my anger surprised me, and it took all the light out of him. He looked old.

'I have no right, Maddy. I know I did everything wrong. I can only imagine what it's been like for you.'

Imagine away. Because you weren't there.

'Whatever I did wrong, I didn't kill her. I need you to know that.' The farofa was arranged in military lines on the checked cloth, each one the precise length and width of the next one. 'And neither did the lightning.' I corralled the last few grains into submission. 'I know that thinking it did has helped you cope, but that's a child's story. Your mother made her own choices. She made that choice, to go . . .' No, the piles of grain were still wrong. All wrong. 'Try to look at it from my side. Try to imagine what it felt like all those years, to be captive to that kind of madness.' I messed the farofa lines up and prepared to start again. 'It took me a long, long time to forgive her. I don't know whether you ever can. But I think it would do us both a lot of good if you could start by forgiving me.'

I was glad I had my sunglasses on when the tablecloth and the farofa armies and the capoeiristas all started to blur.

'There's a ticket to Manaus in there, open return. Along with something else. Maybe you'll want to talk about it. You know where to find me. When you're ready.'

I closed my eyes. I felt him kiss my cheek, ever so gently. And then it was just the stray cats, the capoeiristas, and me.

In Transit

The airport pharmacy has facing mirrors that double, triple and quadruple my reflection. If I stand exactly here, and look out of the corner of my eye, I can see myself refracting back and back and back, smaller and smaller and smaller.

It seems that a DIY pregnancy test isn't a big sell item in transit. I can't find one on the shelf, and when I ask the assistant, it takes her a while to locate the box behind the counter. Her face is a study in blank as she hands it to me. Results in three minutes, just pee on the stick.

Three minutes. Hell, I've got three hours to kill. I've got the whole of the rest of my life.

I have to get past my father's letter to reach my money and pay for the test.

Don't you think I was devastated too, he had said, *when your mother took her own life?*

I knew it all along. And yet I didn't know. How you can put something away inside yourself, and then forget it's even there?

But now it's as if a big chunk of the story, torn out of the book, has been recovered, the pages put back in their right place. How we all came down the hill, chased by the lightning. Three of us. How we made it home safe, glad of the rubber wheels in the little hire car. How Gran hurried me past the black-eyed-Susans and into a warm bath. Pears soap. She always had Pears soap.

Dizzy. I lean on the farmácia counter, waiting for my change. It's funny – I've been trying so hard not to think about Zé, not to think about my father. I've spent my whole life thinking/not thinking about my mother. And now there's something else to think about. Something I won't be able to pretend away, if it's actually there.

After the close call of that last lightning strike, the one that threw me on the ground, my father ignored my mother's advice not to carry me. He picked me up and started running down the hill. He called her to follow, and he didn't look back. But I did. Over his shoulder, I saw her standing there, receding. Her arms were spread out wide, inviting the lightning. That blue aura was there, all around her. I definitely saw that.

She was always crying, that holiday. 'I'm just blue, baby,' she kept telling me, when I asked her why she didn't stop.

She was quiet in the car on the way home. Maybe she was disappointed to have made it down alive. I was put to bed, and the next morning, my mother was gone.

She left a note. They found the hire car in that same Natal Parks Board parking lot. She had gone back up the same hill. *She's with the dragons now*, my father told me. And then he was gone, too.

The assistant hands me my change, and I put the letter on the countertop while I slip the coins back into my money belt. I still haven't opened it. I'll read it on the plane, when there's no turning back.

There are those who say we have no history left, that the world has become an endless shallow parody of self-reflection. Leaving the pharmacy, I catch sight of myself again, the long refraction. Does anybody ever really break out of this hall of mirrors?

Two more minutes, and I'll have my answer. Two blue lines will change everything. Only one line, and things remain the same.

The cubicle is cramped, but I'm not about to walk around a public toilet waving my white stick in the air. I have no interest in attracting a crowd of strangers to congratulate or commiserate.

I've always been so careful. We were careful, Zé and me. Next to the river. Between our tangled sheets. Surely this is not possible? All those years of reproductive paranoia, years of pills and coils, of rubber rather than risk. After Nico, I wanted to give my body a break. It had been such a relief to ditch the pills, let myself tune into a natural rhythm.

But I hadn't planned on this. How could I possibly be ready for this?

27
The visitor

Zé had to get an early start the next morning. But rain was still keeping us from the garden, so after he left, I turned over, curled up in his space in the warm sheets and slipped into the realm of dreams.

That was when Oni arrived.

I knew it was her. In the way of dreams, I was at both the centre and the periphery of the story. Weaving it and receiving it.

The path was choked with greenery, and the going was slow. I walked some way before I came upon the woman sitting in a dark clearing, on the other side of a small stream. To reach her, I had to cross by way of stepping stones. I looked down at my feet as I went, careful not to slip. At the same time, I could see her watching me intently. Was she willing me to make it across safely – or willing me to fall?

We spoke without words. Oni was a woman of middle years, whose fierceness lent her the vigour of someone much younger. I pleaded with her silently. But she was resolute. When she shook her head, the cowrie shells braided into her hair shook, emphatic. Whatever the question was, her answer, unequivocal, was 'no'.

When I woke up for the second time, the sun was high and the clouds were clearing. I spent some moments allowing my eyes to focus on the here and now, this room. My beads lay coiled on the dresser, next to the unopened envelope from my father.

What was it that I wanted from Oni? Some kind of permission? I couldn't disobey her. That much was absolutely clear. So much so that in the dream, I wasn't even disappointed to give up whatever it was I'd wanted. If anything, I felt relieved; the decision had been taken out of my hands.

I had a shower and three cups of tea – that was the last of my Five Roses teabags – and still I couldn't shake the strange feeling.

I felt as if I was straddling two worlds. Maybe more. Maybe nine. But only Iansã can do that.

Zé had told me the nine levels of the spirit world were arranged like concentric circles around this physical one. The high god, Olórun, resides at the inaccessible outer layer, the realm of infinity. The orixás lived in the realm closest to humans, incarnating through their devotees during trance.

Of all the orixás, only Iansã, the warrior wind goddess, had the ability to traverse all the levels of Orun, from the one closest to humans to the outermost realms. But the dead were scattered among all nine realms. I wondered whether they sometimes broke the rules, and hitched a ride in on our dream time.

My sangoma friends in Cape Town talked about the dream that initiates wait for – usually of an animal totem – so that they can twasa and become fully fledged healers.

I knew that there was some kind of message in this Oni dream. But I didn't want to integrate to this degree. I just wanted my seeds. Mine was a mission of science, not spirituality.

As if you can separate the two. I had a horrible feeling there was going to be some kind of payment to the ferryman to get me to the other side with seeds in hand.

Or perhaps this was a test, handed out by my own unconscious, of how much I wanted to stay.

Mostly, I couldn't shake the worry: Oni had said *no*.

28
Road trip

It felt good to get out of the city, once we were through the worst of the traffic and the fumes. The buses were terrifying. They had right of way in their dedicated lanes, but cared little for cars or taxis – and even less for two people on a motorbike – no matter what lane they happened to be in.

But Zé was as sure on the road as he was with everything else, just the right mix of bravura and care. I closed my eyes and relaxed into the feel of his back, enjoying the wind in my face. When the landscape opened up around us, I sheltered in his slipstream, turned my head and watched the hills roll by; old plantation fields, modern fazendas, crumbling monasteries. Forests of alien bamboo.

Zé encouraged me to call my father to tell him I would be out of town for a few days. 'You should feel lucky you have a father,' he said. So I felt like a rat, and I really had intended to call. But I didn't get around to it. And anyway, if he rang while we were gone, Alvaro would update him. I hadn't told him where I was going, but housekeeping knew when I would be back, more or less.

We left the highway and took the secondary roads, through hillsides infested with bamboo, through small, scrappy industrial towns. We stopped and bought Antarctica Guaraná and bubbly cheese pastéis at a gas-station diner, and ate them sitting on plastic chairs on the forecourt, with the truckers and mechanics.

It was the first chance I'd had to tell him that his great-great-grandmother had appeared to me in my dreams. Not only was he not surprised, he seemed almost to have expected it.

'She seemed kind of fierce,' I told him. 'Angry, even.' He nodded.

'She was like that. Everyone says so.'

I wanted to ask him if he had ever met her, and realised how ridiculous that would sound. Instead, I asked why she had left Salvador and gone to live in Cachoeira after her husband died.

He took a bite of his pastel, and a long string of hot cheese hung suspended until he caught it all up with his tongue. We were in a public place, so I stopped myself from licking the greasy slick left behind on his lips. And then I realised that we were anonymous now, and could be as flagrant as we liked. I had just gathered myself to lean in when he said, 'If her husband Mateo hadn't died in the uprising, Oni would have killed him herself.'

He told me the rest of the story that evening, over cold beers on the banks of the Paraguaçu river, which bisected Cachoeira and São Felix. Cars and donkey carts used the steel bridge that linked the two villages, their lights reflecting in the water as the evening darkened.

Like so many love stories, theirs was a tragic one. Mateo was the love of Oni's life, and he betrayed her.

They met on a slave boat. He had been working with the slavers to secure his freedom, while transporting his fellow Africans into bondage.

'He must have hated himself.'

'I suppose so. Until he fell in love with one of the women he was transporting. Oni was a person of strong morals – she saw things very clearly. What was right was right, what was wrong was wrong.'

'And Mateo did her wrong?'

'But not at first.'

Mateo and Oni set up a life. After her herbs had saved the governor's infant daughter and earned Oni her freedom, Mateo did one last trip, to see out his contract, and to set them up with the goods they needed to start their business, selling healing folios and other comfort items from the homeland. 'I took you near to where their store was,' Zé said, 'at Sete Portas.' Worlds within worlds.

Mateo stopped travelling when their daughter was born – Abeo, the grandmother of Zé's great-grandmother.

Oni's reputation as a healer continued to spread. Their business was successful, and they became active in the civic affairs of Pelhourinho slaves. Oni was a member of Salvador's first terreiro, the Casa Branca at Engenho Velho, set up by three freed African women. She was there when the split happened, which set up the second terreiro, and soon after that, a third. Those original three still exist among the hundreds of terreiros in Salvador today.

The night was warm and there was no breeze, but a coolness rose up from the mud of the river as the tide ran out. Zé ordered more drinks.

Mateo was also politically active, well connected with both his former employers and the men on the street. He could move between both worlds, upstairs and down, between the parlours of the main houses and the slave quarters in the basement.

He was hiding out in one of those basements when the trouble began. 'You know of the uprising of 1835?'

I had heard about it. The revolt led by freed Africans dressed in white – outlawed at the time because it symbolised the proudly organised Muslim slaves or Malês. The men in white rose up in the early hours of one January morning to overthrow their colonial masters and set up their own self-ruled community. 'It was all over in a matter of hours.' Zé stared out over the water, back in time. 'The cavalry scattered the insurgents. They rounded up as many rebels as they could. Some were publicly executed. Some were sent back to Africa. Some faced a life of hard labour.'

'And Mateo?'

'Mateo was asleep in the arms of his lover, a beautiful young slave named Jumoke, when the uprising began. And Oni was at home mixing a poison to kill him.'

Mateo had no intention of taking part in the uprising. But fate had other plans for him. When authorities got wind of the upcoming revolt, the insurgents had to kick-start the action earlier than they'd intended. They ran around in the pre-dawn hours knocking on doors to rouse their compatriots; Mateo was pulled out of Jumoke's bed and into the fray.

'Jumoke ran straight to Oni's house. She was distraught. She swore that they had both thought Mateo would be safer hiding with her than at home with Oni, because he would be looked for there.'

'And that was supposed to comfort Oni?'

'I'm not making excuses for the man.'

Mateo was arrested along with all the others. The overlords decided to make a particular example of him. 'Perhaps because of his relative standing with the commercial class. Or perhaps because Jumoke was the slave and concubine of a prominent government official who didn't appreciate his fruit being sampled by another. In any case, Mateo was sentenced to two thousand lashes at the pelhourinho.'

Two thousand. It was hard to imagine such brutality, sipping drinks in a quaint cobbled riverside square, watching a fat moon rise over a town even more picturesque than the city we had come from. 'How is it possible to bear that many lashes?'

Zé took a while to answer. 'They were very cruel, those governors,' he said, his beautiful mouth stiff with severity. 'But clever. They spread the beating out over many days, so the victim had time to recover his strength in between. So that he would feel the full force of the next beatings. And survive that.'

But they pushed Mateo too hard. He was let down, then strung up the next day, each day, until the gashes stippled his back like tree bark, new wounds opening the old ones. Sepsis set in on day five.

'Between beatings, Oni and Jumoke tended to him together,' Zé went on. 'Instead of poison, Oni prepared salves for his wounds, while Jumoke bathed him and fed him cool water. Together, they watched him suffer.'

Compassion dissolved their enmity and turned it to solidarity.

On the twelfth day, Mateo died.

A part of Oni died, too. As she had known it would.

But Jumoke was carrying new life.

Who knows whether it came from the seed of her lover? The child could as easily have been her master's. Ultimately, the source didn't matter to either woman. They were now bound inextricably together, the powerful herbalist and the beautiful young slave.

29
The river

Zé turned off onto a small untarred road a few kilometres outside of town. There was no road sign marking the spot, just a wire trash bin with a swarm of bees buzzing around the open mouths of soft-drink cans. We followed the two-track road until it narrowed into one, and then Zé pulled over and parked the bike deep inside a clump of bushes. He held apart two stands of wire fence for me to climb though. On the other side, the slope dropped down into a tangle of mangoes and jaca with their enormous oblong fruits, myrtles and jacarandas and stately pau brasil. I felt something shift and settle inside of me. *Finally*. There was no desire greater than the one I felt to be in the forest. Well, maybe one . . . or even two.

This river hike was the reason Zé had brought me along on this trip. Although spending a night in a new place, without prying eyes or a feeling of subterfuge, was gloriously freeing in itself. We were staying in a converted monastery with long corridors and hardwood floors. Its rooms were dormitory-stark, but the spaces high and reverent. The old wooden stairs were bevelled in the middle from centuries of footsteps. The bed was hard, but at least it was king-sized. I'd wanted to lie in, but Zé had me up with the first church bells – Cachoeira was full of them – and out before breakfast. We took fruit and rolls from the buffet. I had my field notebook and a bathing suit in my backpack, and I couldn't wait to get into the green. Real wild Bahian forest. At last.

The sun was already high and hot, the cicadas were in full voice. Zé led the way with a sureness that told me he had been here many times before. I felt my body loosen and relax as we got into our stride.

There were a number of diverging paths, but we kept to the main one until I heard the whisper of water ahead.

Zé paused next to a huge buttressed myrtle, checked to see that I was still behind him, and veered off into the forest.

This path was invisible, unless you knew it was there. Zé began to climb steeply up, away from the water sound, and I followed him, enjoying the way the muscles of his calves pulled and clenched, enjoying the feeling of the hill working my own buttocks and thighs.

We walked long enough that I got lost in a reverie of green. I could feel the sweat under my breasts and at the back of my neck, but I was so energised, I felt I could go on forever. I'd found my rhythm in the steady climb, the occasional diversion around roots or over fallen branches. We passed thickets of bamboo, samambaias spiralling up in the undergrowth – the fern Elizabeth Bishop and Lota Suares named their Petropolis house after – and high epiphytes dangling safely out of reach. Cherry-fruited pitanga grew alongside several species of palm, and in the undergrowth, acerola, cidreira, alfazema, erva doce and viuzinha with its purple underside. The mix of indigenous with useful cultivated plants told me that parts of this forest had once been less wild.

The path began to drop down again, and the water sounded louder as the forest thinned and then opened up onto the river.

Water rushed over stones, then pooled in a deep, wide basin behind them. The far end was curtained by a waterfall; next to it a series of flat, sun-baked rocks.

I kicked off my walking shoes, and stepped into the cool dark water. Zé went one better, taking off each item of clothing with exaggerated care, folding and laying first his shirt, then his shorts, on the flat rock. He stood naked, unselfconscious, magnificent, and began to undo the grass band at his waist.

'What do you call that?' I had never asked.

'Umbigeiro,' he replied, releasing it and coiling it with reverent care into a fold in his shirt. 'It is protection, as your beads are for you.'

'And you don't wear it in the water?' I was looking him in the eye, but taking in every other inch of him with every other sense I had.

'I don't wear it when I'm fucking,' he said, and with a grin, he plunged into the water.

I wasn't far behind.

We were not entirely alone that day. Maybe it was the ragged aftermath of the Oni dream, but I felt the presence of Oxum as we found each other under water. I felt Oxossi's approval as Zé pinned me to the rock face. Iansã's caress was in the breeze that dried us on the flat rock. It was Ossain's laughter that caused the leaves to bend and sway and quiver.

'It feels like we have company,' I told him, as we floated on our backs, little fingers clasped to keep us from drifting apart.

'I think they approve,' he said.

My former self would have called these notions crazy. Romantic. Deluded. Fuck-drunk. But was this any different than naming Gaia the overarching deity for the planet, putting Aphrodite in charge of love, or giving the Bodhisattva command over compassion?

We took a different route back. Zé followed the river downstream, rock-hopping in places, veering into the greenery and out again. I began to see more organised evidence of prior cultivation; a clearing with a strip of bottle gourd grown over, a stand of papaya, mango and avocado trees gone wild. I stopped trying to keep a mental map of our progress, and just enjoyed following him. Enjoyed where he had been in me. We had mapped each other's bodies all day, the hills and valleys of bone and flesh, outcrops and forests and lakes. I had studied his contours like someone who might need to remember them again, if she ever needed to think her way home.

Some way in from the river, on a small rise, was a broken-down old hut. My guess was that it might have been a hideout in the days of the quilombos, when escaped slaves started small settlements hidden in the protective forests.

Zé stopped and sat down on a low, crumbling stone wall. He'd been walking in his purple flip-flops, and scratched absently at the heel of one foot. I could hear the crinkle of condom wrappers in his pocket. Somewhere on his person, he also had a stash of used rubbers, knotted at the necks. I wondered what the bees would think if he left them in the trash bin we'd passed at the turnoff. He had already rinsed them, releasing his spent tadpoles into the water before we left the river. I was touched by the reverence of this offering.

He watched me now, as if he was expecting something.

But I was too sated to feel much curiosity. I grinned at him, stretched my arms up, and arched back to look up into the trees. And there it was. Shadowed with sprays of deep purple flowers. *Newbouldia mundii.*

My shout must have scared away every bird within ten kilometres.

'You knew it was here all along!'

He was grinning, stood up to meet me as I rushed to hug him. Then I pushed him away so I could throw my arms around the trunk of the tree. It was one of a stand of eight, forming a half circle around the house.

I realised I was actually hugging a tree. I didn't care.

I felt like doing a victory dance. Heard him laugh behind me as I began to comb the ground, looking for fallen seeds. I found one, picked it up, held it in the flat of my hand.

'Do you know how rare this is?'

It sat there, the little planet. It was smaller than it had become in my imagination. I'd imagined the Little Prince, microscopic snakes and spiked volcanoes. I gathered a handful before I looked up at the tree itself. There were a few bracts within reach that were just past flower stage, their seeds collectable. I reached up to break them off, already opening the mouth of my string bag, ready to slip them inside.

I felt his hand on my arm.

'Wait.'

30
Urban cowboys

A phrase looped through my head all the way back to Cachoeira. A fragment of Elizabeth Bishop's poem 'The Weed': *(As if a river should carry all the scenes that it had once reflected shut in its waters, and not floating on momentary surfaces.)*

It was in brackets, in the poem, and that's how I saw it in my mind's eye. It was as if the brackets made it round, kicked the end back to the beginning, and started it again, over and over. Turning and returning like the wheels of the motorbike, like time and memory.

It was sunset by the time we arrived. Loving is hungry work, so we decided to stop for a drink and a snack by the river before heading back to the convent. We'd just sat down at an outdoor café when a huge hand laid itself on Zé's shoulder. 'Oi rapaz.' The voice was deep and bold. Zé stood and embraced the man, with a code of beefy back slaps I hadn't seen him use before. Then he introduced us.

Sergio was massive. His muscles bulged out of his yellow string vest, and the way he strutted his machismo set my teeth on edge. We shook hands, and he resisted just long enough when I tried to pull my hand away to suggest he could use force to get his way, if he chose to.

Then he blocked me with his shoulder while he spoke to Zé. I pounded ice and lime with my short straw. Their exchange was so rapid and full of slang I didn't catch all of it, but I saw Zé looking over at me once or twice, uneasy. Sergio was very insistent. Then he turned back to me.

'See you tonight, gatinha,' he said, and strode off. I was repelled by his arrogant certainty, and was about to tell Zé there wasn't a chance in hell I was going to do anything that man wanted. But when Zé sat back down, the look on his face stopped me. He dropped his elbows to the table, his head into his steepled fingers, and stared down at the tabletop through the gap between his hands. He pulled at his eyebrows – those expressive, quirky eyebrows – with his thumbs until they formed a straight line. As if he was trying to force them to behave normally. As if he was clearing something weighty from his mind. When he took his hands away and looked up at me again, he had almost succeeded.

He took a deep breath, and explained that Sergio was from a local terreiro. There was a ceremony that night, and Zé was invited to come along. And to bring me.

I was so intrigued by his strange reaction that I forgot my gut revulsion of the moment before. Someone should have reminded me that curiosity killed the cat.

'Well, why not?' I said.

'It will be a little different from what you are used to,' Zé said. 'This is Candomblé de Jeje, a different nation. It can get a little bit . . . It will be okay, though.' He didn't look totally convinced.

The uneasy feeling persisted on our way back to the convent. I had to remind myself that today was a triumph – I had found my star seed! Or at least, Zé had let me know of its existence. I would never be able to find it again without him. Why would I want to? Surely everything would be okay from here onwards?

We rounded a corner and almost collided with the Stetson. Atticus was striding past the crumbling colonial facades like an extra in a spaghetti western. He actually tipped his hat to us.

'Well hello there! Small world!' He looked me up and down in a way that was most definitely not pious. But at least he didn't call me 'darlin''.

Zé seemed disturbed, rather than surprised, to see the American. He looked off to the side, frowning, while I made small talk.

'Souvenir shopping for the folks back home?' I asked.

We were standing outside a Candomblé curio store, its facade painted deep blue. In the window, I could see a display of powders; to attract money, to repel the evil eye, to bring luck and children, to teach a neighbour a lesson. There was a statue of Exu in there, about the size of a small child. He was midnight-black with two red horns, and the whites of his eyes were painted yellow. Atticus followed the direction of my eye and laughed.

'I ever meet that fella with my guitar at a crossroads, I'll let him know my soul's not for sale,' he said.

'That Robert Johnson story is apocryphal.'

'Depends whether you're into the blues or the Bible.'

I was a little bit impressed. It was almost as if he had shed his missionary mantle now that we weren't in Salvador. But then he slid straight back into gear.

'Just came in on the bus this morning,' he said, looking at Zé. But Zé was still staring down at the street, deep in thought, and didn't answer. If I hadn't known how disturbed he'd been after meeting with Sergio, I would have thought he was being deliberately rude.

'Cattle,' the cowboy said, as if he'd just thought of the word. 'Heard there's a livestock auction over the bridge there tomorrow. Thought I might check it out.'

'Well, I guess you can take the boy away from the farm …' The moment wasn't getting any more comfortable, and I was relieved when Atticus begged an early night and excused himself. The last thing I wanted was him tagging along with us to the ceremony.

Zé stayed quiet the rest of the way back to the convent. We only just had time to change out of our river-damp clothes. It had become second nature for me to have a white blouse and skirt handy, just in case. I was grateful for that. I didn't want to break any taboos in new territory.

'Strange bumping into the cowboy here, don't you think?' I asked him.

'Aonde a galinha tem seus ovos, tem seus olhos.' Zé was pulling a shirt on over his head, so I wasn't sure I'd heard right. It wasn't like him to talk to me in proverbs, but I let it drop. Later I would wonder what he had meant. *The chicken watches where its eggs are.*

When we were about to leave, he pulled me close and stood holding me for a long while. 'Thank you for today,' he said. I leaned back so I could look up at him. I wanted to tell him it was *me* who should be thanking *him*. But there was something of an ending in his eyes, and it shut me up.

Then he pulled a strand of red and white beads from his pocket. The colours of Xangô. 'I want you to wear these tonight. They're from Ilê Axé Bençois.' I wondered whether it was a sign of respect to wear the beads from one's home terreiro, or whether I was in some special need of protection here. I felt a fluttering in my gut.

The terreiro was just outside the town, in the same direction as the river. We drove past the small suburban house, parked at the side of the road, and walked back up to the house.

We heard the drums as soon as Zé cut the bike engine, deep and compelling. People were gathered on the covered balcony of the small house, men and women together, splitting up as they entered the building.

Zé told me this terreiro was headed by a pai-de-santo, rather than a woman. That explained the energy; there was a hard edge to it. Perhaps it was the full moon. Or perhaps it was the warrior goddess making herself felt. Tonight's ceremony was in honour of Iansã, and red was the colour of the mood.

31
Iansã

By the time we stepped past the sacrifice at the threshold, the beat had us in its grip.

I found a space on the women's side between a skinny woman with red toenails, and an immense one whose thigh pressed hotly against me. Zé had been pulled straight into the drummer's circle, where there was more swaggering, backslapping bonhomie. He wasn't playing yet, but by the way he was inspecting their drums, it looked like he soon would be. I looked forward to that. I loved the way he would be there and elsewhere, completely absorbed in what he was doing, but also tuned in to the effect his rhythm was having on the gathering.

The small hall was hardly more than a large living room, with benches lined up two deep against the walls. It was packed, and there was the usual casual coming and going of the early phases of the ceremony. But it felt different. There was a wild edge here. For one thing, the pai-de-santo was wearing jeans and cowboy boots. The way he walked around the circle, greeting his congregants, felt self-consciously showy and combative, very unlike the gentle welcome I was used to. But maybe I was misinterpreting it? I decided to put my prejudices away and concentrate on the ceremony.

The women started circling in their skirts and their beads, greeting each orixá in turn through dance and gesture. It was strange to see new faces, but at least I could recognise the affiliations.

I was starting to get impatient for something to happen when Iansã took the pai-de-santo. He left the hall and returned from the back barefoot, in a dress and a white turban, with a tray of fried acarajé dumplings in a basket balanced on his head. With whoops and howls, he/she began flinging them around the room. I had to duck to protect my white shirt from a missile dripping dendê oil, and the ridiculousness of it made me want to laugh. But the faces around me were serious.

In the corner, Zé and Sergio were having an intense argument. Sergio was wearing cowboy boots and jeans with a big belt buckle. More Brazilian gaucho than cowboy, perhaps, but still oddly out of place. I couldn't get used to the roughness of the energy here. It was so different from the Ilê Axé Bençois, with Mãe Gabriella at the helm. That kind of thing would never happen there, on the roda floor, in the middle of a ceremony. For a moment, it looked as if the two men were going to come to blows. Then my view was obscured by circling women, as the entranced pai-de-santo made his way to the door – he was taking Iansã's whooping out into the street. As he left the hall, firecrackers went off, signalling to the world that an orixá had arrived in the earthly realm. The drums continued their deep, hypnotic pulsing, becoming more and more frenzied. The beat made me feel sleepy, and at the same time, hyperaware.

Zé was not among the drummers. I couldn't see him anywhere now: not in the men's section, not in the bit of the back rooms I could glimpse through the curtained doorway. I looked at some of the other incarnated orixás to see if Zé was among them – I had never seen him change, but maybe this place was different? Ogum was there in his blue robe and silver crown. Omulu, orixá of pox and health, his face hidden by a grass fringe – he looked just like Cousin It from the Addams family, but I could tell by the shape of the feet and the movements that this wasn't Zé, either.

Not having him in sight made me feel slightly panicked. To calm myself, I closed my eyes and willed myself to think of green. Amazon reflective green. It's the place I take myself when I can't sleep. It's as good as meditation. Almost immediately, I started to sense the drums receding. So very quiet, on the black-green river. *As above, so below ...*

And then I was back in the swirl of colour as the procession entered again. The pai/Iansã was circling the room now, hugging everyone in turn, all of them eager to accept his blessing. The hugs were fierce – he seemed to be trying to pull people into his realm. And a crazy number of them were succumbing. They were falling like flies – there were more people on the floor now than the attendants knew what to do with. Typical, I thought. Men are so bloody disorganised.

There was a jostling camaraderie as a group of men tried to decide how best to carry out the prone body of the hefty woman who'd been next to me. They stood around her scratching their heads, and eventually called in reinforcements. Between five of them, they only just managed to pick her up, by the feet, shoulders and elbows. You would have thought they would take her straight out back, but no. They shuffle-carried her to each of the four corners of the room in turn, before disappearing through the curtained doorway. It was like a piece of comic theatre, and I would have laughed at them, if I hadn't been so focused on willing them not to drop the poor woman.

There was still no sign of Zé. People were whirling and dancing around the floor, stepping over and around those who had fallen. Until they could be picked up and carried out, they lay there, covered with white sheets like corpses.

The pai and his procession were approaching my section of the bench. I looked down at the ground, willing him not to embrace me. I did not want his sweat and his dendê oil near me, no matter what blessings went with it. I stared hard at the slim feet and the crimson toes of the woman on my right. In my peripheral vision, I saw his blood-red hemline. I didn't want to look at him, but I felt the thrum rise, beating in my ears, competing with the drums. I sensed, rather than saw, Iansã hold my neighbour tight, then release her. Disappointment mixed with relief as the orixá passed me by. The woman next to me slumped forward, limp as a rag doll.

If I hadn't witnessed what happened next with my own eyes, I would have said it wasn't possible. Up to this point, it was conceivable that everyone who participated in this ceremony, or any of the ones I had witnessed back in Salvador, was playing a carefully choreographed role. But I had no doubt that what I saw was real and impromptu.

First the woman raised her head from her slump, let out a shriek and fell to the ground. But the way that she fell – she seemed to be horizontal before she reached the floor, hovering slightly above it before she began rolling. Rolling in the air, rolling as she hit the floor, she kept on rolling, with frightening speed, from one side of the barracão to the other.

There was no way that motion was humanly possible, not without the aid of other human hands. But there was nobody near her. Quite the opposite – people were jumping out of her way as she rolled towards them. Like a log – stiff, horizontal, eyes lolling back, arms tucked in, legs together – she rolled. Somehow, her body knew when it had reached the end of the hall, slowed, and changed direction. But who was doing the slowing, and the turning?

The men were laughing, scratching their heads. Then Sergio took charge. He timed it perfectly; placing himself directly in the path of her approach, he lifted up one leg and let her roll into the other, then lowered the first back down so that she was caught between his two booted feet. The rolling stopped. He stood there for a moment, hands on hips, looking for all the world like a gladiator astride his conquest. Then someone brought a white sheet and he stepped away. The woman lay, face down, utterly still. I worried that she might suffocate. Surely someone should put her in the recovery position, at least?

It felt like everything had stopped to witness the event, but nothing had stopped. The drums continued and the dancing continued, and there were shouts from outside and more firecrackers, although these ones were so loud, they sounded like gunshots. But nobody took any notice. For the first time, I felt afraid. I knew that there was a great silence, beyond the beating of the drums and my own heart, and on the other side of that silence was George Eliot's terrifying roar, waiting to engulf me. In one moment, the roar and the silence and all the noises everywhere were all inside me. And then the colours swirled together and disappeared.

'What is she doing here?' The man's voice was gruff and unfriendly.

'She is a sister,' came the reply, gentle but defiant. 'We are taking care of her.'

I opened my eyes and looked into a face that was kind, but completely unfamiliar. No, not completely – I recognised the broad cheeks, the wide eyes. The skirt, patterned with flowers and leaves under a white blouse. Green strands in her rainbow of beads. I had seen this woman circling during the earlier parts of the ceremony. It came back to me in a rush – the strange terreiro. This must be the back room. It was dingy, and mosquito-damp.

The woman handed me a glass of water. 'Sou Imalia,' she said. 'What is your name, querida?'

I told the woman my name in between long gulps of water. Such a thirst!

'Don't worry,' Imalia soothed. 'I've been with you the whole time.'

'Did I . . .'

'You passed out.'

'I wasn't . . . taken?'

Imalia shook her head. 'I'm sorry.'

I wasn't. The drums were still insistent. Where was Zé? Why wasn't he here? There was no way of telling how much time had passed. I sat up. The mattress I'd been lying on was so thin, it was sagging into the bed springs. Through the open doorway, I could see a woman costumed, yellow satin skirt, the headdress with the curtain of beads hanging down in front of her face. A mirror in her hand. Hello, Oxum. There was another woman fussing and settling her skirts – another attendant, like the one seeing to me now.

What just happened?

I stood up shakily, while Imalia hovered, ready to catch me. I asked to use the bathroom, and was led to a cement ablution alcove with a seatless toilet. There was a midge-filled bucket next to it, and a showerhead hanging over the middle of the room. I tried the tap – there was no water. I didn't really need the toilet. I just needed a moment alone. The place was creeping me out.

When I emerged, the corridor was even more crowded with people in trance and their attendant minders. I felt a rising claustrophobia. I needed to get out.

There was a back door to a garden. I slipped out into the fresh air and took deep breaths. Imalia appeared in the doorway, and I signalled to her: *I'm okay*. She went back inside.

The garden was more like a scrapyard, and there was a path around the side of the building to the road in front. I could see Zé's bike parked down the street. That meant he was still here, at least.

The procession came down the road, led by the pai-de-santo/ Iansã, who was still whooping and flinging dumplings. I heard Patsy Cline singing *Wayward Wind*. I was imagining it, of course. Inserting the queen of country into cowboy territory. I felt dizzy again, and sat down on the kerb. Light spilled through the terreiro windows onto the front terrace. I had no desire to go back inside.

There was a series of loud bangs. This time, the sound of gunshots was unmistakeable.

And suddenly, Zé was beside me, breathing hard. He grabbed my hand.

'Let's get out of here.'

I was so relieved to see him, to press against the back of him on the bike and hear the noise of the drums recede beneath the roar of our engine, I almost forgot to be angry with him for deserting me. And I was afraid to ask him whether the dark patch on his white shirt was oil from acarajé, or blood.

Oni's interlude

When I say the words over your grave, I will tell that you saved me, even while you sold yourself.

When they talk about you in the town, they will say that I saved you, even as I tied you to my bed.

Only we can know the covenant we had, how we needed each other. What we overcame to be here.

My name means 'born in a holy place'. But I was taken from there in a way most unholy, and cast into the bowels of hell – not a hell of fire, but of water.

Some of us survived the endless, icy passage, the foul stench, the shivering disease. You were there. You saw to it.

I will tell how we found each other on a voyage not of our choosing. Stolen, we did what we had to do to survive.

We made a new life in a new world.

I will tell that you tried to do right, even while working on their ships. Even when you gave up your many gods, and took their one.

You allowed yourself to be shackled, but not with chains.

You did what you had to do to survive.

Even so, you questioned your new god endlessly.

I will tell how you saw us suffering in that floating coffin – although it was I who touched you most.

I will tell how you could stand to witness it no more. How you brought out the plants you had stowed away to sell on the other side.

You cured me simply by having the right herbs. You did not know how to use them. I did.

I cured you of a loveless heart. I released you from the bondage of that punishing sea. Doing penance to a god that was not your original god, for a sin that was not your original sin.

It was I who freed you from the guilt of plying your own people.

It was I who led you back to the land and to the light.

It was I who took you to an earthly paradise, night after night after night.

I helped you redeem yourself. Because I believed that you never meant to cause pain.

Until now.

This time, there will be no redemption. It is too late for you. Although you are not yet dead.

We built a life together.

I was the curandeira. You the curator. You procured the herbs, I put them to good use. Mostly to good use. When the situation demands, the herbs can be turned to darker magic.

You brought me the seeds, the roots, the stems, the leaves. I knew how to grind them, and when, with what, and how much.

I know the secret purpose of the vine whose flowers funnel into a deep black heart.

I have many uses for the purple berries that come from the buttressed tree.

I feel the seeping sorrow of the milky shrub with the silent, tongue-shaped leaves.

Still, it is true, you are not yet dead.

I will tell how we made new life, in this new place. How we grew the bush and the vine that came from the old lands. How we found new ones here, and planted them in fields.

You planted a seed in me, and when she was born we called her Abeo, because she brought us so much joy.

I will teach her what I know. But I will not teach her this.

I will not teach her how to mix a powder so potent that a smudge of it from under a fingernail can extinguish a fire forever.

This will be your last lesson.

We were strong, you and I. Our people looked to us for comfort and for cures. We helped them. We helped each other. Together, we became powerful.

That power has gone to your head. And you allowed your head to be turned.

I have seen the way you look at her. You will look no more.

I have borne many things. I will not bear this.

Your position, your status, the respect you command, is because of what I know how to do.

How could you forget what I know how to do?

Tonight you will drink this draught. And then I will incant other words over a stone to mark your decomposing body.

I will celebrate your strength.

I will mourn your weakness.

I will tell of many things. But I will keep this secret.

We do what we must do to survive.

32
Knots

I sat up with the feeling that all the breath had been sucked out of me. The small, dark room, the woman pounding herbs with a stone mortar and pestle, speaking her betrayal to her absent husband: they were gone.

I was in the convent bedroom, with its high ceilings. The white sheets were crumpled at the bottom of the enormous too-hard bed. Zé was not in it with me. He was sitting on the wide windowsill across the room. The shutters were open, and he was silhouetted in the light from the yellow street lamp. He was bare-chested, and the light hazed the edges of his white capoeira pants. The fireworks were still crackling in the hills. As the saints came marching in.

'Who is SeedCorp?' His voice was rough.

'I don't know, exactly . . .'

'Sergio introduced me to a man from SeedCorp tonight. He said you would know why he was here.'

'I've heard of them. But I've never had any dealings with them . . .' It was almost true.

'He offered Sergio a lot of money.'

Newbouldia.

'Does Sergio know where the trees are?'

Zé snorted his derision.

'So he needs you to get what he wants?' His nod was almost imperceptible. I had to make him understand that I'd had nothing to do with this. 'Look, I've never spoken to anybody from SeedCorp. I promise.' Not directly, anyway.

'It's okay. I defended you.'

I don't think I have ever felt so ashamed.

Zé put me on a bus back to Salvador after breakfast. He had some things to take care of, he said. I knew better than to ask him what. But I felt like a banished child. And like a child, guilty for all the things it doesn't know it has done wrong. And for all it knows, deep in its heart, that it has.

I wasn't sorry to leave, but I was sorry to leave him. And sorry to leave the place where my star seed was, so tantalisingly close. I held his face when we said goodbye. There were circles like bruises under his eyes.

The bus station was near the bridge. It was full of men on foot leading animals or driving donkey carts piled high with fruits. Farmers, many of them in wide-brimmed gaucho hats. As the bus drove off, I looked hard, but I didn't see Atticus's Stetson floating in the crowd. I pulled out my iPod. I had a sudden urge to hear R.E.M.'s 'Losing My Religion'.

I hadn't expected to be spending any time alone, so the only thing I had to read was my tiny copy of *The Seven Signposts*, which now lived permanently in my backpack side pocket. I opened it randomly. 'If the beast knows what herbs of the forest are his friends,' I read, 'what plea shall man make that boasts superior knowledge, yet knows no empathy with moisture of the air he breathes, the juice of leaves, the sap in his roots to earth, or the waters that nourish his being?'

The light streaming through the bus window fell on the book in my hand. My thumb and forefinger were still yellow with dendê oil. I'd scrubbed and scrubbed at it this morning, but I didn't think I would ever be able to get the stain out.

33
Double-bind

The conversation I had with Kirk didn't make me want to rush back to Cape Town.

'What the hell was SeedCorp doing in Cachoeira?' Even as I said it, I knew I wasn't going to get a straight answer. I had let too many things slide in my eagerness to get away. I'd let Kirk take care of the details, knowing the kind of pressure he was under.

'I guess they wanted to keep an eye on how things were going.'

'So they've been watching me all along? Jesus, Kirk – and don't you dare tell me I'm being paranoid this time. They threatened a friend of mine.' Indirectly. But half-truths were my new currency.

Actually, I didn't know exactly what had happened in Cachoeira. Zé wasn't back yet. But my mind hadn't stopped racing. Who else knew where we were going? And who could be speaking to SeedCorp? Surely not someone from the terreiro? And then the light bulb went on over the obvious. The big hat, the cornfield childhood, the vague 'mission'. There had been something bogus about Atticus all along. I had to hand it to him, though; he'd perfected the art of hiding in plain sight.

'SeedCorp isn't the only one interested in *Newbouldia*, Maddy. It's a race now. Winner gets the spoils. And if it's not us, it will be the other guy.'

My mental light bulb flickered. Maybe Atticus P. Jones had nothing to do with SeedCorp. He could be working for anyone.

'You really aren't in your right mind, Kirk. You know what this will do to your reputation? You're gambling with your entire career here.'

'No one needs to know.'

'Oh, and how do we manage that? I get back from Brazil and before too long SeedCorp releases new findings on the efficacy of *Newbouldia*'s miracle peptide . . .' Light bulbs were pinging on all over the place now. 'It's me. I'm the one who'll take the rap for this!'

'I could plead total ignorance, it's true,' he said, as if he were thinking it for the first time. 'Tell them you put in for leave and went off on your own. Or . . .'

'Or?'

'None of this has gone through official channels.'

'The papers . . .'

'Were never going to come.'

A great big rubber-band ball of guilt and betrayal tangled up my gut.

'I'm sorry I had to put you in this position. But I had no other choice.'

'Oh really?'

'Don't be a child about it.'

How dare he? '*I'm* being a child? You're throwing everything away on a fantasy cure? A long shot that will probably come too late to help Gwen anyway?'

'It's not just about Gwen. It's about our kids. The medical bills are crippling us, and they're both headed for university.'

'And I'm the price you're prepared to pay? Nice.'

'Well, of course I'm hoping it isn't going to come to that. You'll be richly rewarded for your part, and no one need be any the wiser.'

'I'll know.'

'Get off your high horse, Maddy. We all know how corrupt this game is. The rules are bent all the time. It's not as if we're wiping out a species here – quite the opposite. Once the benefits of the *Newbouldia* compound are proven, the tree will become famous. It will be saved. Reintroduced to Africa. Propagated far and wide.'

I thought of a small stand of trees near a riverbank, an old, broken-down hut. A flat river stone, sun-baked, warm as skin. *All the scenes that it had once reflected shut in its waters.*

'And even if I had any seeds – which I don't – just how do you propose I get them back without papers?'

'In your suitcase. Or even better, carry them on your person.'

'Like a drug mule?'

'Don't be a drama queen. Wrap them up with bags of coffee and other duty-free stuff. Say they're peppercorns, whatever. You'll think of something.'

'Kirk, it's the principle. You can't have one set of rules for yourself, and another for everyone else. This is thin edge of the wedge stuff, you know that.'

'Nobody loses anything, Maddy. But if you leave the seeds there, things stay the same. Nobody gets a cancer cure. Nothing happens.'

But things were already happening. There was a SeedCorp guy in Cachoeira. Maybe some other pharma company sniffer hounds. How long would it take them to find the trees? And who would be there to protect them when they did? Is that why Zé stayed behind?

'How do you know somebody else isn't close to finding them?'

'That's why you need to be the one to get there first. Get your hands on a decent amount of seed. Then we can start the proper process to protect them. Best of all possible worlds, Maddy.'

What did he know of possible worlds?

34
Teosinte

'I feel sorry for your seeds, in that cold, cold place.' Zé was sweating. He'd been swinging his machete for what felt like hours without saying anything. Now this. 'They belong out here in the sunshine.'

I wondered if he was talking about the seeds that were already in storage in Cape Town, or the *Newbouldia* seeds that soon would be. Or so I hoped. This was the first time we'd seen each other since his return to Salvador, and we were both circling the subject. There was a new awkwardness between us, but I told myself that could happen when lovers have been apart. Cachoeira seemed very far away.

'You can keep seeds for five hundred years in the big vaults. But you also need to keep growing samples out in real time so they can adapt to changing conditions. Those ones definitely see sunshine.'

'Lucky for them.' His eyebrow lift did little to soften the cynical bite. This was a new side of Zé. I watched a beija-flor, his wings whirring invisible, probe its beak deep into the orange throat of a flower. 'Seeds are social,' I said. 'They need to have conversations to survive.'

'Like between the corn?'

'Exactly.' When Vavilov travelled to the Sierra Madre, he noticed that corn grew better and stronger in those fields where its ancient ancestor teosinte grew on the verges. The conversation between the cultivated crop and its wild cousin had been going on for millennia, like good neighbours who didn't feud, but shared what they had in times of need, helping each other out with vigorous new genes so that both became stronger. With development had come more airstrips, fewer verges. Less conversation.

I had to find a way to weave this conversation back to *Newbouldia* without giving Zé another excuse for telling me the seeds were safer where they were, far from the polluting influence of monoculture.

'The plants that grow here,' Zé interrupted my thoughts, 'will not be the same as the ones in Africa – not the same as their parents or grandparents.'

He sat down next to me on the fallen log, and pushed his machete tip into the ground. There was a web, still dewy, on the underside of the log. No sign of its spider. And no fire ants today. Even with him so close to me, I hated this new space between us. I feared I was losing him. Losing us.

'There are certain places – sacred places – where plants grow special qualities,' he went on. 'Your estrelinhas could be very different here than they are back in Africa.'

'There aren't any left back in Africa,' I reminded him.

'Theoretically speaking,' he insisted.

I shrugged. There is a beautiful, intelligent symmetry to the way plants adapt and survive and mutate to their own benefit. It is only when we start playing god, believing we can use science to isolate a gene, put it in a pill, patent it and sell it, and expect the same happy result, that we go wrong. On this score, Zé and I were in complete agreement.

'Tia Betinha told me there is not one illness that doesn't have a plant cure,' I said. 'It's just that we don't have the knowledge of it yet. Or we once had it, and lost it. Doesn't it excite you at all that there might be that potential here?' I watched his jaw clench. I wished he would look at me. 'Don't you want to be the person to facilitate finding out, rather than leaving it to some SeedCorp cowboy?' I hadn't had a chance to voice my suspicions about Atticus. Maybe this was the time.

'You sound a lot like a biotech person right now, and not so much like a botanist. Caçadora.' He got up and started pacing around the glade, leaving the machete to mark his place next to me. His nickname for me usually had a tone of playful affection; now it sounded like an accusation. I desperately wanted to restore the trust between us. But to do that I would have to be completely honest, wouldn't I?

'Look,' I said. 'I don't know what gives a plant its healing power. Whether it's in the genetic coding of the plant, or the condition of the soil, or the wordless conversations they have with other plants in their area. We are not yet, perhaps never will be, the alchemists we long to be. Not with the Petri dish and lab coat. Not with pure science alone.' Not without some kind of magic, I should have added. 'But if we don't save the plant, we'll never know.'

I was trying so hard to tell him that we were on the same side. But the more I said, the more I felt like we were talking at cross-purposes. He came back to the log and took up the machete.

'That gringo wasn't a missionary, you are right,' he said. 'But he wasn't with SeedCorp, either.' So much for Atticus the Pious.

'Where was he from?'

'Another company.'

'And where is he now?'

Zé didn't answer. He just wiped the flat of the blade along his thigh, cleaning one side and then the other, like a knife sharpener against a strop.

'Where?'

'He's gone.' He held my eyes with his for a long time. I shivered.

Zé walked back to the edge of the glade and started hacking again, punctuating his words. 'Things.' Thwack. 'Could.' Thwack. 'Be.' Thwack. 'Different.' He paused his chopping for a moment. 'They could be different,' he repeated.

'What? What things?'

Now he was beating the blade on the ground, softly, like a drum stick. As if the rhythm would call forth clarity.

'What if I don't want you to take those estrelinhas?' he said eventually. 'What if I were to ask you to stay here, and work with the plants we have here. Could you do that?'

He wasn't trying to end it. He was offering a compromise. Relief ran like warm blood through cold veins. The chasm was gone. I wanted to be somewhere else, with him. Somewhere I could breathe in his smell, inhabit him and be inhabited. In that moment, it was all I really cared about. The seed could stay where it was.

'I think, maybe. Yes.'

Do seeds change? Do people? Evolution happens over generations, through trial and error and luck and circumstance. Through many misses and near misses.

I had missed my father. When I got back from Cachoeira, he had gone. *You know where to find me*, the note said, in his own handwriting on Luna Azul stationery. I still hadn't opened his envelope. But I already knew there was a ticket to Manaus in there.

'Maybe I should go see my father, and think about what I should do next,' I said now. 'I mean, I only have a few more days at the pousada, and then I'd have to find another place to stay.' If I stayed.

Emotions shadowed Zé's face.

All the shining seeds take root, conspiring root, and what curious flower or fruit will grow from that conspiring root?

Ah, Elizabeth. What indeed?

35
Coffee

I had to pass the canteen to get from the garden to Tia Betinha's. Ernesto was sitting on the balcony alone, nursing a small cafezinho. He was wearing a white fedora with a black band, even though he was under the shelter of the porch roof. Men in hats.

'Join me for a coffee?'

I hesitated. I was already late for Tia's. But he read me like a book.

'I've just come from Tia Betinha. She says to tell you that Mãe wants to see you today. But you have some time yet.'

He stood up and pulled out a chair for me. Then he took a clean cup from the ones lined up on the tray and held it under the thermos spout. Steam hissed out as he pressed the top down, followed by a strong coffee smell. The terreiro coffee was already sweetened, so he didn't need to add sugar. He set the cup before me.

'Obrigada.'

He resumed his place and we sat in silence for a long while, sipping.

'It is difficult to imagine Brazil without coffee,' he said eventually. 'But our very first coffee seeds were obtained by lust and subterfuge.'

Interesting opener. I knew by now that more was coming, so I waited.

'Francisco de Mello Palheta was his name. He was the envoy

the King of Portugal sent to French Guiana to negotiate for some coffee beans. But the French governor refused to share his precious nuggets.'

Both our cups were empty by now. I stood and refilled them from the flask. It was nearly empty, and I had to push hard. It made a rasping gurgle, but there was enough for two more small servings.

'Obrigado.' He took a sip and continued. 'However, the governor had a beautiful wife. A wife who was perhaps a little bit bored by the tropics.'

I looked out over the tops of the tall ficus trees in their white cummerbunds and imagined the woman, sweating underneath her layers of skirts. Eating pastries and talking to birds in cages.

'She was beautiful, the envoy was charming. It's an old story. He convinced her to give him some beans.'

'What did he give her in return?'

'Ah, things happen between two people that only they know of. That secret went with them to their graves. But her parting gift to him was a bouquet of flowers. Right under her husband's nose, she gave them to him – coffee shoots and beans tucked in with the tropical blooms. It was enough to start the Brazilian coffee industry. Enough to change the course of history.' He drained his cup and smacked his lips. 'But I have had too many of these already today. Too much of a good thing, so to say, is often not good at all. And I think you have an appointment now.'

His beard tickled me as he planted a warm kiss on each of my cheeks.

I had the distinct feeling Ernesto hadn't been talking about coffee at all.

36
Conchas

Mãe Gabriella looked down at the spiny spheres I held out in my hand. The few *Newbouldia mundii* seeds Zé had allowed me to collect from the ground – after offering blessings to Iroko, Xangô and Ossain – so that I could show them to the mãe-de-santo and ask her permission to collect a proper sample for the seed bank.

Later – much later – I would realise that, once again, we forgot to ask permission of Exu. Zé was always forgetting Exu. Funny, because he was also always the first to point out that that was a really bad idea.

All I could do was hope against hope that I would be able to convince Mãe Gabriella of the noble nature of my mission. Because my mission *was* noble. Or at least, I had a plan to make it so. Kirk was not going to get his hands on these seeds. And even if SeedCorp, or any other company, found another way to get them, I would do my best to make sure Kew had a sample first. With the terriero's permission, and the terreiro's right to use and grow them protected by law.

The old woman held the seeds in the palm of a wrinkled hand. 'These are completely gone now, in Africa?'

I nodded. She said nothing for a very long while, simply rolled the seeds around the ends of her fingers with her thumb, as if testing for an essence, or an answer. It's the same gesture people make to signal money. As if you can only touch true value with the very tips of your fingers.

'From Cachoeira.'

I nodded again. I tried not to let my mind return to the river. Just in case Mãe really could read thoughts. 'And you went to a terreiro of Candomblé de Jeje?'

I nodded yes.

'How was it?'

'A little wild.'

Mãe smiled, motioned for me to shift closer. 'Each has their own journey through Candomblé,' she said. 'Zé tells me there was someone there to help you, from the Irmanidade.' I longed to ask her about Oni and the sisterhood, about the crumbling cottage by the river, and the stand of *Newbouldia* trees. But now was not the time. It would have to wait.

Mãe cupped the seeds in both hands now, and began moving them over the small table between us. There were a few things laid out on it, one of them a bowl of herbs, floating in water. I held my breath as the mãe-de-santo held out her hands over it – surely she wasn't going to drop my precious seeds into the brew? She dropped them instead into a wooden mortar bowl, scored from countless years of grinding. The pestle was lying next to it, and again I prayed that Mãe Gabriella would not take it up to crush my estrelinhas.

But the mãe-de-santo gestured to the beads I was wearing around my neck – the ones Zé gave me in Cachoeira. I took them off and handed them over. These she placed in the herb water and began to swish them around. 'This is your terreiro now,' she said. 'You should wear these along with the contas of Yemanjá.' Then she called on the orixás to bless and protect me in all my endeavours, to keep me safe, and to keep me close. It felt good to be so held.

'Ask Luisa to give you some folios to cleanse with,' she said.

The audience was over. The five seeds were still huddled in the bottom of the mortar bowl.

'What about the seeds ...'

'A fruta só dá no seu tempo. One thing at a time, child.'

Things ripen in their own time, Mãe had said. Still, when I left her room, I felt like I was abandoning five small children.

Luisa had the herbs waiting for me as I exited. How was it that the woman always seemed to be one step ahead of me?

I'd never before returned to the garden after the bell signalled midday. But I wanted to see Zé one more time, to tell him I had Mãe Gabriella's blessing. I needed to ask about what had really happened in Cachoeira. And there was something else I needed to know.

The sun was blazing hot, but the welcome cool embraced me as I descended into the garden forest. Zé was still sitting on the log where I'd left him. As if he'd been waiting.

'Mãe blessed my beads.'

He smiled. 'And the estrelinhas?'

'She kept them. She says to wait.'

He nodded.

'Oni planted those trees, the eight, didn't she?'

'Yes.'

'I dreamed about her in Cachoeira.' One day I would tell him about Oni's incantation over poison intended for Mateu. Before she tried to save him, together with his mistress. 'You never told me what happened to Jumoke's child.'

'Jumoke and her daughter,' he said, 'stayed here, in Salvador, at this terreiro, when Oni and Abeo left for Cachoeira. But the families were always connected. We stayed close.'

The garden itself seemed to be listening. And then a small voice piped up, 'That was my bisavó, não é Papa?'

'Sim, minha filha,' Zé replied.

I usually left the garden before the school bell. That was our agreement. Now here was Liliana, in her uniform, with her scuffed knees and the Band-Aid that matched the one that had long ago fallen off of Zé's toe. I hadn't seen her squatting behind the log, poking at the column of fire ants.

It was not unusual for men to use the terms 'my child' for a young boy or girl. But Liliana had said 'My grandmother'. Did she mean Jumoke's child? Was she, was Luisa, a daughter of a daughter of Jumoke's daughter? The generations reflected back, multiple mirrors in my mind.

She had called him Papa.

I looked from the man to the child. Lili had her mother's unruly hair, but she had Zé's green eyes. And that crinkle on the lip when she smiled.

So many things understood now. Luisa's hatred of me.

Why hadn't he told me?

I excused myself, politely, for the little girl's sake. But I couldn't get away from the garden fast enough.

If I had known I would never be coming back, I would have paused for a moment to say goodbye.

37
Blood

'You have a visitor, Senhorita Magdalena.'

It was the first time Alvaro had ever called up to my room. His voice had none of that suggestiveness he never quite managed to lose when it came to Zé. So I knew before I looked down over the balustrade at the lobby that it wasn't going to be him.

But I didn't expect to see Luisa standing there.

It was hard to tell which of us was more uneasy. 'May I?' Luisa indicated upstairs. She obviously wanted some privacy, but I didn't want to bring her up to the place Zé and I had carved out for ourselves. Where my sheets still smelled of pepper and musk. Where I had been waiting for my lover to come and explain himself.

'We can talk here.' I led her to an alcove off the reception area, with uncomfortable square sofa benches built into the walls, and a low wooden table. Luisa perched on the edge of the bench like a bird who couldn't wait to fly away, and put a plastic shopping bag on the table.

In another life, we might have become friends. Right now the last thing I wanted was to be talking to this woman. I thought I might as well front-foot it. 'I saw Zé with Lili in the garden. I hadn't realised . . .'

'Ours is an old story,' Luisa shifted in her seat. 'It is not perfect, but it is what I have, and I will do anything to protect it. Even this.'

She pushed the packet towards me. Even before I picked it up, before I felt the heft and shift of a small galaxy, I knew what it was.

'I saw you coming,' Luisa said. 'Now I want to see you go.'

'But this?' I still hadn't looked inside the packet.

'Whatever it takes to make this problem go away.' It threw me to hear myself described as a 'problem'.

'What about Mãe Gabriella? Does she know about this?'

'I will face those consequences.'

The irony was not lost on me. Luisa was giving me what I came for – she was betraying her terreiro to protect her relationship with Zé. A man who did not love her, although he would always do right by his child. I knew that much.

I also understood that if I accepted the seeds, I would be making a choice. Zé had made it clear in the garden that morning that he didn't want me to take them away from here. If I accepted them, I would be betraying him, which was worse than my disloyalty to Mãe Gabriella, the terreiro, and everyone in it. I would also be declining his offer to stay. Did Luisa know about that, too?

I muttered a quick thank you to Exu. Zé would approve of that, at least. Then I pushed the bag back towards Luisa. Surprise was an expression I hadn't yet seen on her freckled face.

'Don't you care about him at all?'

It was my turn to be surprised. 'I care about him very much. This isn't just about the seeds. Not anymore.'

For the second time since we'd met, we shared something like a moment of solidarity.

'Then you will leave to protect him. After what happened in Cachoeira.'

'What happened in Cachoeira?'

Luisa's look was pitying. 'There is blood on those seeds. Blood shed to protect you. And if you stay, Zé will pay the price. Again.'

I looked down at the packet. Blood? It was just an innocent-looking yellow plastic bag, with the name of a supermercado printed on it in red. I wanted to hold it again. I picked up the packet and rubbed at the writing, as if to show that the marks were only ink, not actual blood. I knew Luisa didn't mean it literally. Still, I *had* heard shots. And there were gaps, even now, in what I could remember about that night.

The seeds shifted and rattled inside the plastic. I had to look. There they were. Hundreds of little stars, unmistakably *Newbouldia mundii*. There were enough seeds to make two healthy sample sizes – one for the Institute, and one for Kew. But not this way. Not now. I needed to find out what had happened in Cachoeira first.

But when I looked up again, Luisa was gone.

38
Beads

I watched the cats from our table in the Beja Flor. Through the bars of the wrought-iron gate, they gathered around the separate bowls of fishy leftovers and milk. I wondered again who put the food out every day. I imagined an old nun, bent into her habit. But I'd never seen any human there. Only the cats. Fat and free.

Our favourite was there. Her peculiar markings suggested a white inkblot on a black page. When she sat up straight with her front legs together, one half of the white circle was on one side, the other perfectly mirrored on the other. It wasn't as noticeable when she moved around. But she spent a lot of time sitting upright, watching the other cats. Queen of the free feast. Zé had named her 'Manchinha' – little smudge. But Zé wasn't here now.

After so many nights of passion, so many days of waiting ellipsis-like in between, I watched the sun suck its last sweetness from the honey-coated buildings, and realised that Zé wasn't coming.

So many things seem filled with the intent to be lost that their loss is no disaster . . .

But it is, Elizabeth. As you well knew. It *is* a disaster. *Even losing you (the joking voice, a gesture I love)*. I should have been more careful, singling this out as my favourite poem. Things have a way of self-fulfilling.

I will always come, he said. But five hours and as many caipirinhas later, I began to make my way back to my pousada – alone. He knew where to find me, if he wanted to.

The cobbled streets that seemed so appealing when I first came here, the stones so full of history and stories, snapped at my feet now, jagged and treacherous as I stumbled the familiar narrow roads towards my empty bed. Every time I heard an engine, I hoped it might be his motorbike. But it wasn't.

Loneliness is not a factor of being alone, but of being without someone you've allowed yourself to become accustomed to. That is all. It didn't help to tell myself that. Or to remind myself that when I first came here, I was hell-bent on being a lone ranger. Which is always a lot easier, in transit. Even the incident with the capoeira boys on the Passo steps hadn't unnerved me. *But that time*, I reminded myself, *Zé was watching your back.*

I knew with sad certainty that he wasn't watching me now.

I turned up the Rua da Igreja, where the tops of the tall buildings lean together conspiratorially before pulling apart at the cathedral steps. How many nights had I sat on these steps while steely timbaus beat the questions that guitars and voices answered, enjoying the heat and camaraderie of the crowds? Tonight was not a party night; there were no bright lights or celebrants here. Their absence was palpable, the very dark itself a different kind of presence.

I had only climbed three steps when I sensed them.

'Oi gatinha, cadé o seu namorado agora?'

Where was my boyfriend, indeed? Good question.

The leader's inflection conveyed no obvious malice, but the studied sensuality with which he eased himself off the steps made the hairs on the back of my neck rise. What I felt was not déjà vu, but a sick sense that to escape once was lucky, to escape twice, unlikely. I knew better than to show weakness. Two more shapes coalesced out of the gloom. I kept my eyes down, avoiding direct acknowledgement, and at the same time sharpening my night-time peripheral vision.

Breathe, I reminded myself.

A corner of my brain registered the puffed-up, neon-green trainers. He was the one with the bravado. The third man was nervous, unpredictable. Their leader was the sensuous one. The dangerous one. The one with the too-tight black bicycle shorts that made his bulge conspicuous, the one with the shoulder roll, who continuously clenched and flexed arms ringed with red-black-green-yellow Olodum bangles. The one sliding closer while the others fell in behind.

Adrenalin cut through my caipirinha fog as I weighed the options. Run? Not a chance. It was half a kilometre at least to the Lua Azul. Play coy? That'd play right into their hands. Pretend I was meeting Zé at the top of the stairs? For all I knew, they already knew that he wasn't coming, and why. News travels fast in a small place. And after all, what did *I* really know about Zé?

In that small moment, my disappointment congealed into anger, and anger brought clarity. I turned to face the man-boy, reaching without thinking for the beads around my neck, the turquoise and the red-and-white, together.

I said nothing, simply stared my defiance. He eyeballed me back, arcing his body back, then forward, heel to toe, a pendulum swagger with his lycra'd pride as its fulcrum, a pretend laziness that contained within it the tight-sprung potential of attack.

Still I said nothing. I dug my toes into a crack between the cobbles, drew strength from the stones, with their memories of grief and blood and joy and pain, and I knew that my moment was a mere speck in the firmament of all that, and yet a legitimate part of it. It was the only part I had. I shucked my chin at my challenger, a short, sharp defiant gesture that defined the spirit of this place. I felt the strength in doing it, felt *myself, here.*

The man-boy returned the gesture, chin up-down, let his eyes slide to the bead necklace, then up to my face.

'Garota não deve andar sozinha a noite. Tem perigo.'

Yes, there is danger for a woman walking alone at night. But there was also a lisping sibilance in the way he said the word 'alone' – sozinha – that made his warning seem petulant.

So childlike, in fact, that I suddenly wanted to laugh. My lungs filled with air again, like an inflating parachute, and something tight inside me unfurled. I shrugged one shoulder and looked around me, affecting nonchalance. The space seemed lighter. Even the dark shadowed corners breathed benevolence.

'Não sou sozinha.'

I didn't wonder what I meant as I turned to walk up the stairs again, leaving the men with their deflated bravura. I just wondered how I could have said it with such total certainty.

I am not alone.

39
Folios

I shouldn't have acted on a hangover. But to resist the mania I felt would defy the definition of the condition. Plus I was so tired of waiting. And in the moment, it felt like I didn't have anything to lose.

'Kirk.'

'Maddy?' In his voice, relief mingled with anxiety. No captain gags this time. 'You're leaving tonight?'

'I am.'

'And you have our little star ships, safe and sound?'

I lifted a section of the candlewick bedspread so that the seeds rolled around in the flat spaces between the bobble pattern. They were like little organic pinballs, or those tiny steel marbles you'd find inside Christmas-cracker games, plastic-encased miniature maze traps. You could spend hours trying to get all the balls into the holes, but there was always one that eluded you, and when you pushed geometric limits to catch it, all the rest came tumbling out of their holes, and you had to start all over again.

'I could just send them direct to Kew.'

Telling him about the seeds had been a mistake. The pause was so long now, and so quiet, so devoid of transatlantic crackle, I wondered if he was still there. Then I heard his forced exhalation.

'Risk the future of the species to the Brazilian postal system? You wouldn't do it. Not even you.'

That last comment snagged. But the small spiked balls, themselves snagging on the cotton of the bedspread, focused me. I felt a rush of maternal protectiveness for the little plants in potentia. He had no idea what I had risked to get them. What Zé had risked. But then again, neither did I. Only Zé could tell me. And Zé still wasn't here.

I had told enough people that I was leaving that he would surely have got the message by now. I'd gone to Os Agogos first. Roberto gave me a miniature cuíca to take home. He showed me how to rub the little stick inside the drum, to make its loopy sound. The movement was too sexual. 'In Africa, they used this to call lions. They said it made the sound of a female lion calling to her mate,' he told me. So much for deranged toucans.

After that, I had written a note for Ernesto. I was going to ask Fernando to deliver it for me after he dropped me at the airport. I couldn't go back to the terreiro, couldn't face anyone there. I didn't want to think about how they would feel – Mãe, Tia Betinha – knowing I had left without saying goodbye. I wondered what spin Luisa would give the story.

'I'm surprised SeedCorp hasn't sent somebody to get them.' I was fishing. I hadn't seen Atticus around lately. If he wasn't their guy, was there another one? Unless there had been more than one Cachoeira casualty.

I still could have turned everything around. It wasn't too late to change my plans. I don't know why all I could think of doing was running. Actually, I do know. It was stupid pride. What if I had been wrong about Zé? I was scared of feeling foolish. So I told myself that what I was doing was the best thing for the seeds. For the future of *Newboldia mundii*. But I wasn't even sure about that.

'Yes well, it seems the SeedCorp man has gone AWOL,' Kirk said. Bingo. 'Distracted by Brazilian delights, no doubt.' I hadn't told Kirk my suspicions about Cachoeira.

'Even if I bring them back with me, I'm not handing them over to SeedCorp to patent. I'm not handing them over to you. They're going to Kew, via the Institute, with proper protection. And the rights of the Candomblé terreiro to propagate and use them will remain intact. Those are my conditions.' Mistake number two.

'Conditions?' Kirk snorted. 'I think you underestimate the gravity of what you are doing, Magdalene.' When had he last called me that? Had he ever? 'Let me remind you that there are papers and protocols, protections that you don't have. Officially.'

I fingered the seeds, relishing the spikiness of their armour, willing the physical sensation to chase out an image of the unfortunate Canadian scientist convicted of bio-piracy we'd all heard about. I saw him now, stuck in a Brazilian prison, talking to his pet yard-weed.

'Look, right now, SeedCorp will look out for you if anything should go wrong.' Kirk's tone turned disarmingly gentle. 'They know where you are, and they'll do anything to protect their interests. So just come on home, and we'll sort it all out when you get here, okay?'

I was so tired. All I wanted to do was lie back on the bedspread, close my eyes and sleep. Get lost in a dream that Zé might come and wake me from. Succumb to something that felt like madness. For once in my life, to just give up, give in. Then what?

I cradled the phone on my shoulder, pulled a needle from my travel sewing kit, and fed a strand of black thread into it.

'You're not going to change my mind on this.' One by one, I picked up the seeds and slipped them into the small incision I'd made in the inner lining of my moon bag. Right at the back, where they would nestle next to my belly.

'All I ask is that we talk about it before you do anything rash.'

I said nothing, pulling the lips of the incision together, folding the edges inward to make a neat seam.

'So you'll bring the seeds back yourself? You'll keep them on your person?'

I began to sew, closing up to the denim edge with small, neat stitches. Undetectable, I hoped. 'They'll be on me.'

'Bon voyage, then.' All at once, he was in a rush to go. 'See you on the other side.'

I knew I shouldn't have called in the middle of a hangover. I was wrung out, so tired I didn't even pause to wonder: *on the other side of what?*

When I'd finished sewing, I took a shower with the fresh folios, crushing them into a ball and rubbing them over my skin, rubbing at the guilt and the shame and the hurt and the missing-missing-missing Zé. The hot water was comforting, but the herbs didn't make me feel any better.

They fell apart in my hands and clumped together in the shower drain, blocking the flow of water so that it rose in a soapy pool around my feet. If nothing else, it was a cleaner way of drowning one's sorrows.

In Transit

Stuck in the small bathroom cubicle, counting minutes, counting days, I finally understand what *not alone* really means.

I got so caught up in the seductive spell of it all, I forgot to do some simple maths: forgot to divide the twenty-eight days between the two full moons and realise that somewhere between them, my body should have bled.

One line or two? If this isn't a crossroads, I don't know what is. *Exu*, I say (superstition be damned), *come what may, I need your blessing now.*

Two full blue moons. And now there are two blue lines.

So I'm taking back more than stolen seeds. I'm carrying something else that's only partly mine. I guess Luisa and I share something else now. Something in common with Oni and Jumoke.

> *I lost two cities, lovely ones. And, vaster,*
> *some realms I owned, two rivers, a continent.*
> *I miss them, but it wasn't a disaster.*

I push the stick evidence into my backpack and stumble out of the bathroom. The concourse is too glaring. The lights in the CD store are a little dimmer, so I retreat to where I can pretend to be engrossed in the items in the fifty per cent-off bargain bin in case I give in to the urge to cry. Of course, what should be playing as I come in but Salvador's song: 'É d'Oxum.' Synchronicity, serendipity. I'm not surprised. If the gods want to have some fun at my expense, if a parallel universe wants to dip in and say 'Hello, I've been here all the time,' that's fine with me. I surrender.

Goodbye, Zé.

In this city we are all of Oxum, man, boy, woman and girl ... It's going to take a while for me to register that there is an actual little boy or girl child, forming inside me. Will he or she be of Oxum?

'Can I be of assistance?'

The woman behind the counter has bleached white hair and caramel skin, horn-rimmed glasses and a spotted scarf around her neck. She wasn't born when Tom Jobim first sang about his Girl from Ipanema, but she's nailed her retro bossa nova chic.

I thrust the copy of Gal Costas' greatest hits at her, and hum along while she secures it in a duty-free package.

The entire city radiates magic ... Gal dogs me through the duty-free concourse. *It's there in the sweet water, it's there in the salty, and the entire city shines.*

If it's a myth, this idea of harmony, it's a living one. *The orixás make no distinction between sexes, or colours, or race*, Tia Betinha told me. How did I repay her for her kindness, her many lunchtime hospitalities? I didn't even say goodbye.

When would they notice the missing seeds? Is there a designated seed counter? Or some divination technique for knowing when they are on the move?

Maybe I'll never belong anywhere. But then, I thought I'd never belong to anyone, either. Or that anyone would belong to me. And now I'm growing my own little star seed. *Hey there ...*

No more coffee for me. I buy a bottle of water and find a quiet corner looking out onto the runway. Which of those waiting planes is taking me away from here? And back to what, exactly? I can't conjure up any enthusiasm for Cape Town. I suppose it will come in time. Springtime is almost over. I've missed most of the daisies, but the watsonias and the pelargoniums will still be in bloom. And Vavi will be waiting.

So will Kirk. And Nico. I don't want to think about how he'll take the news. *Surprise!*

I perform my umpteenth OCD money-ticket-passport check – everything seems in order. I zip up my moon bag and slip my hand underneath it, against my belly. Imagine I can feel a swelling there. *I'm going to take you home*, I tell this new thing, *I just don't know where that is exactly. Not yet.*

I have an urge to mail Em, but this is something I should really tell her face-to-face.

I check the flight board. Everything on time. Two hours until take-off.

There's a flight to New York on the board, two flights beneath mine. I could switch flights.

Crossroads.

Hello, Exu?

There's that airport official with the sniffer dog over in the corner. I've got Brazilian coffee in my suitcase. Not too much, but enough to declare at customs. Just to put them off the scent. Not that sniffer dogs are trained to pick up star seeds . . .

The dog handler is in a huddle of five policemen – well, four plus one woman, police*persons*? – blue-grey fatigues tucked into their boots. Two of them are leaning against the cafezinho stand. Now there's an airport official in a brown suit. Brown. Why does anyone wear a brown suit, ever?

They are all looking over at me. WTF? *They'll do anything to protect their interests.* I bend over and scrabble inside my backpack for the water bottle. Keep busy, avoid eye contact. *Whatever it takes to make this problem go away*. I'm rearranging my books, my inflatable travel cushion, the fleece I haven't worn once in the last five weeks, but which I will definitely need at altitude. *And you'll keep them on your person?* Now there are shoes – men's shoes, office shoes, brown shoes, polished to a high sheen. The shoes of a fastidious person. And they're pointing right at me.

I look up into the face of the airport official who looks too young for this suit, even if he's determined to fill it well. There are beads of sweat on his upper lip, which is stubbled with five-o'-clock shadow. Even as I wonder what he wants, I'm amazed at the acuity of my perceptions. Is this a side-effect of my new condition? Or just the heightened awareness of a guilty conscience?

The official looks over his shoulder at the police group at the cafezinho stand for reassurance. They are all looking my way. *What makes you think you can just walk in there and ask them to hand it over?*

'Com licença, Senorita Bellani? Magdalena Bellani?'

'Sim?' My mouth is dry, but when I try to bring the water bottle to my lips, it weighs a ton.

'Would you come with me, please?'

Epilogue

Surrounded on all four sides by glass.

Green, outside and in.

The trees outside are early-summer green.

Inside, my reflection pale on the glass, washed in echoing green.

Institution green. Still, if I half-close my eyes, I can imagine trees.

Newbouldias *are suited to temperate climes. But they might suit a more deciduous place.* A not-so-Fallow Farm.

There is a flash of russet as a sort of sheepdog chases an imaginary squirrel across the lawn and up the stairs of the clapboard cottage. The porch is new. It contrasts with the rest of the house, which has weathered over three decades of summer scorch, alternating with frozen winters.

Em reads a book in a deckchair, wearing a wide-brimmed hat and a pair of oversized shades, with something green – mint, no doubt – sticking up out of a tall glass. She holds a cigarette in a long holder between two fingers while she turns the book pages with her thumb. How many times will I have to ask her not to smoke around the baby?

Em will argue that they are outdoors, that the wind is blowing away from the pram – she refuses to call it a stroller. The wind will curl the smoke up over the railing and off into the oaks and the maples beyond. She'll jiggle the stroller back and forth absent-mindedly with her foot while she reads, and the tinkling from the chain tied to its hood will reach me over the green lawn, and through the glass.

The baby-sized balangandan *would be a gift from Edge and Alé. I imagine it hung with charms – a silver* figa *fist, Xangô's double axe,*

Oxossi's bow, Oxum's mirror. Each one sent by someone from the terreiro: Clara, Ernesto, Mãe, Tia Betinha. The rabbit's foot would be Em's addition – from an old key ring she pulled out of a forgotten drawer. Her version of a good-luck charm, until I can take her to Brazil to experience the spirit of the orixás for herself. I'll add my lucky poker chip, the red one with the hole in the middle, made for hanging. There'll be a patterned silver ball locket with soil in it, a gift from Ernesto. Soil from the terreiro garden. I'll wonder whether Zé gathered it himself, weaving word spells for a child he has not yet seen. How long will it take him to forgive me? Surely he will forgive me?

His baby will sleep and feed and watch the world with curious eyes. Eyes a particular shade of green. And a smile that folds the top lip into a little horizontal crease.

I'll come back to Brazil. When the smoke clears. When the paperwork is done. There'll be lots to do once I get to New York. I've missed my Cape Town flight, but that's okay. I wanted to change it anyway. I guess Exu was listening after all.

Is Exu the orixá of paperwork? The unopened envelope from my father, the one I was so wary of. Em would call it a Freudian slip, a parapraxis of forgetfulness, that I left it behind, on the counter of the farmacia where I bought the pregnancy test. I hadn't noticed it was missing. But for the diligence of that store assistant, I wouldn't know that I had. If she hadn't gone out of her way to track me down … but she did. I guess you remember a person at a crossroads.

My name was on the envelope. Someone fed it into a system, leading to a flight and a gate and a time.

Except that I didn't get on that flight. Not after I was reunited with my envelope. While they keep me waiting – for reasons they still haven't fully explained – I decided it was finally time to open it. It contained the title deeds to Fallow Farm. In my name. I changed my future, right there and then.

I've had a lot of time to read the document. I've had time to dream the farm alive. I can't wait to get started on it. If they'll just let me out of this place they keep calling an 'office' …

It feels more like a holding pen. But they have no real reason to keep me here. I don't have any seeds on me, other than the few sewn into my money belt, and those were just for luck – and so that I wasn't entirely lying to Kirk when I told him I would have them on me. I can only assume that's what they were looking for, after they gave me back my letter, and started searching through my hand luggage. They were very apologetic about having to call my suitcase off the flight. I told them I was fine with that, because I wanted to change my destination anyway. My poker savings will get me to JFK. Then I can tell Em the news face-to-face.

I need to arrive there before the parcel of 'Brazilian peppercorns'. Or at least tell her not to put them in her grinder! The Newbouldia *sample I airmailed to her is small enough to pass under the official radar, but large enough to ascertain whether this is, in fact, the rare subspecies extinct in its original Africa. I sent one of a similar size straight to Kew. With a plea to Exu to take care of the Brazilian postal service.*

I'm sorry I'm going to miss the look on Kirk's face when his parcel of coffee arrives in Cape Town. I even attached a little gift card: Hope this doesn't keep you awake at night.

While I'm visualising my future, I imagine him a lucrative position at a biotech company. He won't be able to stay on at the Institute, not now. He'll miss all the fun. There'll be people on the case soon enough, working to make the sample I sent them retroactively legal. There'll be lawyers in Bahia and Brasilia drawing up contracts, ethnobotanists tracking Newbouldia mundii's *journey from the Ivory Coast to the coffeelands, from Guinea to Cachoeira. There'll be scientists testing the chemicals contained in the little star ship, looking for any miracle cures coded in its blueprint for root and bark and leaf.*

But they won't be able to find the stand of trees next to a rocky river near Cachoeira. Not without the help of the Candomblé community. Not without Zé.

As for me, I'll germinate my seeds in a glasshouse upstate. I know just the place to build it; over the charcoaled remains of an artist's studio. I'll grow row upon row of sapling Newbouldia mundii. *I can see Vavi waiting for me outside the greenhouse, ready to escort me to the little prince – or princess? No, I think it's a prince – living in the new cottage. I'll take my child to Cape Town one day, to meet his godmother Marilese, and Vavi's hairy cousins. I'll teach him to look closely at the tiniest fynbos flowers, watch his eyes open wide as he feels the shock of the icy sea for the first time.*

But Brazil first. He has family there. A father and a grandfather.

I imagine introducing him to Zé. In a garden of green. And many other colours.

As soon as they let me out of here, I'll say a proper thanks to Exu, and ask him for a safe journey.

A note on pronunciation

- Double r, as in 'terreiro', is pronounced as an 'h', thus: te-hay-row
- X, as in '*Orixá*' is pronounced 'sh', thus: or-ish-ah
- An acute accent over a vowel denotes an emphasis on that vowel/syllable. In the example above, the emphasis is on the last syllable: or-ish-*aah*
- The cedilha is used to denote a soft c, as in 'cachaça', thus: ca-sha-sa.

Glossary

a fruta só dá no seu tempo	fruits ripen in their own time
a semente estrelinha	little star seed
acarajé	savoury fried dumplings
akokô	type of tree
angelicó	type of plant
aonde a galinha tem seus ovos, tem seus olhos	The chicken watches where its eggs are
avô	grandmother or grandfather (see also *bisavô*)
Bahiana	citizen of Bahia
bairro	neighbourhood
balangandan	charm belt/bracelet first worn by slaves
barracão	hall
basso profondo	deep bass voice (in singing)
bateleur	species of eagle
beija-flor	sunbird (literally 'kiss the flower')
beijinhos	kisses on both cheeks, traditional Brazilian greeting
bisavô	great-grandparent (or ancestor)
boto	river dolphin

buchu	strong-smelling herb indigenous to the Cape fynbos floral kingdom
búzios	shells
cachaça	strong Brazilian alcoholic drink
cacique	chief
café com leite	coffee with milk
cafezinho	small coffee
caipirinha	cocktail of cachaça, lime, sugar and ice
caju	cashew
caldo verde	green/vegetable soup
Candomblé	Afro-Brazilian spiritual tradition
Candomblé de Jeje	sub-sect of Candomblé
capoeiristas, capoeira	Brazilian fight-dance developed by slaves
chá com leite	tea with milk
choro	jazz music
com licença	with your permission/ excuse me
contas	beads
cuíca	little drum
curandeira	healer
dendê oil	palm oil
desculpes	apologies
dona	lady
E toda cidade é d'Oxum	the entire city is Oxum's
estrelinhas	star seeds
falou	I hear you

farmácia	pharmacy
farofa	toasted manioc
fazendas	farms
feijoada	black-bean stew
figa	small fist totem, believed to ward off the evil eye
fitas	ribbons
folios	leaves
fruta de mar	seafood
fynbos	indigenous plant kingdom found only in the Western Cape, South Africa (literally 'fine bush')
garota	girlie, chick
Garota nao deve andar sozinha a noite. Tem perigo.	Girlie, you shouldn't walk alone at night. It's dangerous.
gatinha	little cat (slang)
gaucho	cowhand
guaraná	soft drink
havaianas	flip-flop sandals
hi-hat	type of cymbal
iyawo	someone chosen to receive the orixás in trance
macaco	monkey
mãe-de-santo	high priestess and head of the terreiro (see also pai-de-santo)
magia do amor	love spells
Malês	organised Muslim slaves

mão-de-ofá	one responsible for tending the herbs and plants of the terreiro
maracuja	granadilla vine
merda	shit
moqueca	fish stew
não sou sozinha	I am not alone
obrigada/obrigado	thank you (feminine and masculine)
Oi gatina, cadé o seu namorado agora?	Hey, kitten, where's your boyfriend?
Oi rapaz	Hey, guy (slangy greeting between men)
orixá/s	gods and goddesses
Orun	the nine-levelled realm of the orixás
ostinato	in music, a repeated phrase
pai-de-santo	male priest of the terreiro
para beijar minha flor	to kiss my flower
paradiddle	in music, a series of rapid drumbeats
pastéis	fried savoury pastries (pastel is singular)
pelhourinho	whipping post
peregun	herb sacred to Oxossi and also Ossain
picanha	type of steak
pousada	guesthouse
prazer	a pleasure (a response to 'thank you')
pudim	crème caramel
Que maravilhosa	How marvellous
querida, querido	dear or darling (feminine/masculine)
quilombos	communities of escaped slaves
quinta feira	Thursday

rapido	quick
reias	Brazilian currency
roda	makeshift circle or arena for ritual
saudades	missing or yearning for something
saúde	salute (‘cheers’)
sewejaartjies	everlasting flowers (literally ‘little seven years’)
sim, minha filha	yes, my daughter
supermercado	supermarket
telenovela	soap opera
terreiro	place of gathering for worship in the Candomblé religion
timbaus	steel drum
tranquilo	be calm; don’t worry
umbigeiro	grass rope worn around the waist for protection
umfincafincane	wild dagga

Acknowledgements

Apart from well-known artists, poets, authors, musicians, scientists and historical figures, all characters and events in this story are fictional. I am passionate about fynbos, but I am not a botanist, so any plant-related errors or taxonomical flights of whimsy are entirely my own.

I am indebted to ideas, information and inspiration from: Michael Pollan, *The Botany of Desire – A Plant's-Eye View of the World* (Bloomsbury, 2002); Gary Paul Nabhan, *Where Our Food Comes From: Retracing Nikolay Vavilov's Quest to End Famine* (Island Press, 2009); Jeffrey S. Rosenthal, *Struck by Lightning – The Curious World of Probabilities* (Granta, 2005); Gilberto Freyre, *The Masters and the Slaves – A Study in the Development of Brazilian Civilization* (University of California Press, 1986); Cléo Martins, *Lineamentos da Religião dos Orixás: Memórias de Ternura* (Alaiandê Xirê, 2004); Robert A. Voeks, *Sacred Leaves of Candomblé – African Magic, Medicine and Religion in Brazil* (University of Texas Press, 1997); Pierre Fatumbi Verger, *Legendas Africanas dos Orixás* (Corrupio, 1997).

I have quoted or paraphrased from *Elizabeth Bishop, One Art – The Selected Letters*, edited by Robert Giroux (Chatto & Windus, 1994); Brett C. Millier, *Elizabeth Bishop: Life and the Memory of It* (University of California Press, 1993); *Words in Air – The Complete Correspondence between Elizabeth Bishop and Robert Lowell*, edited by Thomas Travisano (Farrar, Straus and Giroux, 2008); Simon Winchester, *Krakatoa – The Day the World Exploded* (Penguin, 2004); Anaïs Nin and Henry Miller, *A Literate Passion: Letters of Anaïs Nin & Henry Miller, 1932–1953*, edited by Gunther Stuhlmann (Harvest, 1989); A. S. Eddington, *The Nature of the Physical World – The Gifford Lectures 1927* (The Macmillan Company, 1928); Oliver Sacks, *Musicophilia* (Picador, 2007); Rachel Carson, *The Sense of Wonder* (Harper Collins, 1965); Steve Biko, *I Write What I Like* (Picador Africa, 2004); Mãe Stella de Oxóssi, *Provérbios* (Brasil, Bahia, 2007); Wole Soyinka, *The Seven Signposts of Existence: Knowledge, Honour, Justice and Other Virtues* (Pocket Gifts, Ibadan, 1999); Hermann Hesse, *Bäume Betrachtungen und Gedichte* [*Trees: Reflections and Poems*] (Insel Frankfurt, 1984).

My grateful thanks to Alfred Publishing for permission to use the lines from John Prine's 'Angel from Montgomery', and to The Random House Group Limited for permission to quote from Elizabeth Bishop's poems 'The Weed', 'Santarém', 'One Art', 'The Waiting Room', 'Crusoe in England', 'Songs for a Colored Singer, IV', 'Exchanging Hats' and 'Brazil, January 1, 1502', all from *Poems* by Elizabeth Bishop, published by Chatto & Windus. Lines from 'Tonight I Can Write' by Pablo Neruda, translated by W. S. Merwin, in *Twenty Love Poems and a Song of Despair*, published by Jonathan Cape, are also reproduced here by kind permission of The Random House Group Limited.

Many people sustained this story's journey. In Salvador, Bahia, my thanks to Tia Detinha at the Ilê Axé Opô Afonjá, and Dona Ceci at the Pierre Verger Foundation Cultural Centre, for their time and stories. To Gabriel Tavares for turning Salvador and Cachoeira inside out, and to Ildasio Tavares for planting the first seed; I am deeply sorry that he was not able to see it take root. My thanks for all time to Rodrigo dos Santos, who first introduced me to the saints.

Carly Cowell of SANParks (previously of the Botanical Institute at Kirstenbosch) and Rosemary Newton at Kew's Millennium Seed Bank both shared their time, knowledge and seed lore, as did the Kirstenbosch Botanical Society seed-banking volunteers who were there when I first saw the magnified possibilities in a tiny pelargonium seed.

My thanks to the Cape Town bruxas, especially Hannah Young for her patient readings (and wine!), Lee Jones for guiding me through fynbos so many years ago, and Stephen Watson for bringing me to Elizabeth Bishop.

To Helen Moffett, editor extraordinaire: working with you on the manuscript was a total joy and pleasure. Thank you.

To my publisher Umuzi, and in particular Fourie Botha and Beth Lindop, for believing in the story and working so hard to bring it to fruition, my deepest gratitude.

Last, but definitely not least, to my partner David and my son Ruben – without your patience and support, this wouldn't be here.